VENGEANCE IN THE MIND

DOCTOR WISE BOOK 8

ARJAY LEWIS

MIND
BENDER
PRESS

Vengeance In The Mind: Doctor Wise Book 8
Copyright ©2019, Updated 2026

Cover Design: Marianne Nowicki, https://www.premadeebookcovershop.com/
Editing: Libby Broadbent; https://libbybroadbentauthor.com/

ISBN-13: 978-1732659384
ISBN-10: 1732659389

Published by:
Mindbender Press
474 South Main Street
Phillipsburg NJ 08865
www.mindbenderpress.com

DEDICATION

To my faithful Beta-Readers
And reviewers.
You help me strive to improve.

"And now…farewell to kindness, humanity and gratitude. I have substituted myself for Providence in rewarding the good; may the God of vengeance now yield me His place to punish the wicked." — *Alexandre Dumas, The Count of Monte Cristo*

"Vengeance is not the point; change is. But the trouble is that in most people's minds the thought of victory and the thought of punishing the enemy coincide." — *Barbara Deming*

PROLOGUE

The pre-dawn chill of September bit through Margaret Jamison's thin pink scrubs. She hated this drive — the transition from the quiet safety of Choctaw Lake to the sterile intensity of the hospital.

Usually, the rhythmic humming of her tires on Route 40 was a meditation, a way to mentally "put on" her nurse's persona before the 7:00 a.m. shift began.

She checked the rearview mirror. She had sprayed her hair into its usual, rigid updo. Frank called it her "battle crown." It made her look capable, formidable. At nearly forty, with a mortgage and two kids, "formidable" was the only thing keeping her together.

She'd skipped the hash browns at the West Jefferson McDonald's, the bitter black coffee sitting heavy in her stomach. *Ten pounds by the wedding,* she promised herself.

She could almost feel her relatives' judging eyes already. She'd starve herself for a month if it meant her cousin's wedding felt like a victory instead of a family reunion.

She looked forward to the wedding in October. The kids would stay with Frank's mom, so the pair of them could dance and stay in a hotel. Frank always got frisky at a hotel. In fact, he might be frisky several times over that weekend, and Margaret was looking forward to that as well. Careers and kids, mortgages and money concerns had interfered with the romance in their lives.

The Ohio landscape blurred past — skeletal corn stalks and trees bleeding autumn reds. People raved about New England, but Margaret found the local transition more honest. It was beautiful, sure, but it felt like a warning.

Winter was coming.

She was approaching the turnoff for the hospital complex when she looked for the landmark, a beacon that signaled she was three minutes from her shift.

It was a massive billboard, a local fixture that usually screamed into the darkness: **YOU MUST GET RIGHT WITH GOD.** The five-foot letters stood beside a life-sized cross made of weathered fiberglass.

Usually, the sign was flooded with industrial lights. Today, the sign was dark.

Margaret slowed. The rising sun caught the top of the cross, casting a long, distorted shadow across the road. There was something... extra. A shape perched atop the horizontal beam that hadn't been there yesterday.

"Disgusting," she muttered. Some overzealous deacon must have added a plastic Christ for the "shock value." It was heavy-handed, even for a believer like her. As she drew closer, she saw the dark streaks — fake blood painted to drip down the fiberglass.

Then her foot hit the brake, hard.

The figure wasn't wearing a robe. It was wearing a tracksuit.

And it had breasts.

Heart hammering against her ribs, Margaret pulled onto the shoulder and swung her compact car around. She parked directly beneath the towering sign, the engine ticking in the sudden silence. She grabbed the heavy flashlight from her trunk, her breath blooming in the cold air.

She walked a hundred feet back, her sensible nursing shoes crunching on the gravel. She needed a better angle. The sun was behind the sign now, turning the billboard into a black monolith.

"It's a mannequin," she whispered, her voice cracking. "Just a sick prank."

She clicked on the high-powered lantern. The beam cut through the shadows, climbing the wooden structure until it hit the figure.

Margaret's knees went water-thin. The flashlight slipped from her numb fingers, shattering on the concrete. Darkness rushed back in, yet the image had already seared itself onto her retinas.

She fumbled for her phone, her hands shaking so violently that she nearly dropped it.

"911, what is your emergency?"

"I... I'm on Route 40," Margaret gasped. She collapsed onto the cold sidewalk, the nurse in her fighting the civilian who wanted to scream.

I handle car wrecks, she told herself, the mantra a desperate rhythm in her head. *I handle amputations. I handle death.*

"Ma'am? I need your location."

Margaret forced her "head nurse" voice to the surface. It was cold, sharp, and detached. "I am west of OhioHealth Doctors' Hospital, across from the Advance Auto. Send everyone: police, medics. Now."

"What are we looking at, ma'am?"

Margaret looked up at the silhouette against the orange sky. The girl's blonde hair caught the morning breeze, swaying gently. Heavy railroad spikes driven through her wrists pinned her to the fiberglass. The blood wasn't paint. It was dark, tacky, and very real.

"There's a woman on the billboard," Margaret said, her voice dropping to a horrified whisper. "She's been crucified."

1. RETRIBUTION

I was driving to Mindy's Diner on an early September morning to meet Jyanette Emery. It seemed like that was the only place my ex-girlfriend would meet with me anymore — some public place, where I had to keep my voice down.

I didn't blame her. At least for that.

Our last meeting at her apartment ended in a shouting match, where she told me to leave or — and I quote — she would "kick my lily-white ass out the door."

I knew she could do it.

Although I've studied Aikido and had vastly improved my fighting skills, I doubted I would be the victor in a conflict with a six-foot-tall, African-American Assistant District Attorney, who was also extremely hormonal from the early stages of pregnancy.

What had I done to cause this shouting match?

I'd asked her to marry me.

Again.

A guy really understands rejection after three recent attempts to get the woman he loves to say, "Yes."

We had broken up in June after confronting a demon that attempted to set up residence inside Jyanette's head.

That had been the same night that we had a rather amazing physical encounter hidden in the shadows of a building at the university where I teach, only a few hundred yards from a party where I was to give a speech a half-hour later.

That encounter was spontaneous and exciting. We didn't consider birth control, leading to the pregnancy I learned about when I returned from assisting at a haunted house in August.

Yes, a haunted house.

That's what I do.

I have a PhD in parapsychology and am blessed — or cursed — with actual psychic abilities. I investigate haunted houses, strange phenomena, and even cases for the local police where my abilities give them the edge to make a difference.

Most days, I teach Parapsychology in college classes at Garden State University in Mountainview, New Jersey. This morning, my teaching assistant was covering my classes so I could meet with my recalcitrant lover.

Pulling my specially designed minivan into the lot for Mindy's Diner, I found an empty accessible parking space, making sure my blue disability placard was hanging from my rearview mirror. I shut the car off and took a deep breath, calming myself, knowing I needed to be centered if I was going to talk with Jyanette.

I opened the door, grabbed my cane, turned my handicap-enabled swivel seat to face out, as it lowered me to the ground. Because of a car accident years ago, doctors fused my right leg permanently straight, and I no longer have a knee joint. With the use of my cane to help my balance, I stood, shut the door, and headed up the ramp to the front of the diner, clicking the fob to retract the seat and lock the van.

I stepped inside to come face-to-face with Carl Sokolov, the owner of the diner, who apparently had seen me park and wanted to catch me at the door.

"Hi, Carl."

"Len, your lady friend does not look happy," he said in his thick Ukrainian accent.

I exhaled heavily. "Not with me, anyway. How is Anna?"

Anna was his daughter, whom I had helped rescue from a kidnapping just a year earlier. She had certain mental abilities that had helped me find her, and I wanted to know how they were developing.

"She gets headaches lately. Migraines."

I frowned. "What does the doctor say?"

"Not much. He says I should just make sure she doesn't have a lot of tension." He shrugged, almost comically. "How do I do that? She has no mother, and I work all the time."

I slipped one of my cards out of my wallet. "Have her call me if she needs someone to talk to, okay?"

The smile on his face was wonderful to behold. "That's so nice of you, Doctor Len. You are my wonder man!"

"Well, I don't have a lot of experience with teenagers, but I'd be glad to help if I can." I glanced into the restaurant. "I'd better not keep Jyanette waiting."

"Your lady friend is in the back section. I got you away from the other customers."

"Thanks, Carl."

I moved deeper into the restaurant, which was broken into sections to allow people some privacy. I would have to avoid any yelling this time.

If I had any brains, I wouldn't have shouted the last time.

The problem was that Jyanette treated me with — I wasn't sure — anger, contempt? It wasn't like I planned to make her pregnant. Each of our limited interactions since I returned from California had a sharp edge, as if I'd done something malicious.

As I turned a corner, there she was. It took my breath away to see her. They say pregnant women have a glow, and Jyanette's was palpable.

She is statuesque, even while sitting. She has ebony skin, like her mother, who had emigrated from Africa. Her mother was the daughter of a Nganga, an African healer, which some might call a "witch doctor" in a less enlightened time.

She did her hair in a beautiful up sweep, adding to her beauty by framing her face.

"Can you ever get anywhere on time?" she chided, her lips a tight line.

I glanced at my watch. I was five minutes late.

"Sorry," I muttered.

She wore her usual courtroom attire: a pantsuit with a white top that hung loosely over the pants. I knew her body so well that I could see the slight baby bump that the clothes barely hid.

I so wished I could touch it.

There had been no touching or any other affection since our last interaction — resulting in her current condition.

She held out a thin folder. "I have paperwork I am going to need you to fill out." She was all business. "I want to make sure that everything is in place when the baby is born."

I opened the folder. The first form bore the title "Child Support Case Information" and asked everything from my marital status to my driver's license number. Another was a "Non-Divorce Application for Child Support." There were other forms, which were just as depressing.

I nodded sadly.

"Don't give me the puppy dog eyes," she warned. "I need you to act like a grown, responsible man and not a petulant child."

I wanted to snap at her, to tell her she was the one being petulant, but I knew this would not help my case or make the problem go away. Instead, I asked, "How are you feeling?"

She relaxed a little. "Still puking at inopportune moments, so if I get up and leave for a few minutes, it isn't you."

"It's nice to know something isn't me," I grumbled.

Her back stiffened again. "What is that supposed to mean? You're mad because I won't play the game and become good little wifey?"

"No. Instead, you come at me like a district attorney after a criminal," I fumed.

"I want things handled legally, in advance." Her voice was quiet, but filled with anger. "I don't believe in 'winging it' or expect some 'psychic buzz' to take care of my problems."

I sighed and focused on calming down. It happened again. I let my temper get the best of me. Looking at her, I decided I needed to back off and give her space.

"I'm trying to think of what I've done to make you hate me so much," I attempted, trying to let my softer emotions take over.

This was the woman I loved, that I'd slept with and laughed with and talked with about dreams and plans — having her despise me was more than I could bear.

"You—" she began, then stopped. She considered it for a moment.

"I know that night in the asylum was terrible and frightening. I can even understand you not wanting to be close to me because I am ground zero for weird creatures on the hunt. But I cannot understand why you act like you hate me."

She stared at me, and I could feel her reservations give way. "I don't hate you."

I moved closer and even dared to take her hand. She allowed the contact.

"Then what is it? What can I do to change? I mean, even if you aren't with me, we have to raise this child together."

She turned her head, and tears fell.

"What can I do, how can I help?" I asked. "You don't have to do anything in return. I just want you to be happy."

"How can I be happy?" she sobbed.

I grabbed a napkin and handed it to her. She pressed it to her mouth.

"I'm angry at myself," she confessed in a hoarse whisper.

I drew close. "The pregnancy is because of both of us. I mean, I was an active participant."

"It's not that," she went on, unable to look at me.

"What is it then?"

"What if… what if you're not the father?" she whispered.

I sat back in the chair, stunned, unable to think or even breathe.

"What — what do you mean?" I stammered, my voice low.

She glanced around the diner to make sure no one was near. "That night… that awful night in the asylum. When I woke up, tied to the chair where that man… that thing… took me, I was sore."

I turned to her and the fear must have shown in my eyes, because I saw her move back from me.

I tried to find words. "When we… I mean… our lovemaking had been pretty intense…"

"Len, I've made love with you intensely in the past and I only ended up sore when we went at it twice in one day."

"So you think—"

Her tears did not stop. "What if, while I was unconscious, that monster raped me — assaulted me? What if the baby is his?"

The enemy that almost took our lives had possessed the body of a man, but it was actually an ancient demon within him. The entity had been looking to gain a new host, and at first had wanted me, but in the end had taken control of Jyanette.

I had exorcised the monster or thought I did. What if it had left a way to return? What if it had left a flesh avatar to be raised at the bosom of the people that it had wanted to possess?

All this ran through my head as Jyanette crushed the napkin to her mouth and suddenly stood.

"Excuse me," she croaked and ran off toward the ladies' room, the napkin in front of her mouth.

I remained sitting, too stunned to move.

The thought was terrible, but possible. After all, the demon possessed a body that, at one time, had been just a man. The creature, with its appetite for blood and torture, had enabled that man's resentments and anger to take control more and more, until he'd destroyed the original human mind and only the diabolical persona remained.

But he had been a man, a human man with desires twisted by a monster. He could mate with a woman as easily as I did. I had never even considered that such a situation could have occurred. And what could I do about it now?

My cell phone rang, and I stood to pull it from my pocket with a glance toward the ladies' room.

"Wise."

"Len, have you seen the news?" a voice boomed in my ear.

It was my police liaison, Lieutenant Bill McGee, his hefty baritone as loud as any stage actor. Actually, Bill is more than merely a police officer; he's also my Alcoholics Anonymous sponsor, my biggest supporter, and a friend.

"No, I'm meeting with Jyanette."

"Oh?" he queried. He was aware of the ongoing battle between Jyanette becoming a mother and my desire to make her my bride. He carried on with the situation at hand. "It's all over the television. They crucified a woman on a billboard in Ohio."

"Crucified?" I couldn't keep the shock out of my voice.

"Yes, and they just released her name to the public. Len — it's Aubrey Andrews."

I could no longer stand, and I leaned against the nearby table to support myself as I collapsed into the diner chair.

Aubrey Andrews had been my student. She was interested in becoming my teaching assistant.

A year ago, I'd gone up against a mind-controlling madwoman who presented herself as a therapist named Anika Vanya. Instead of treatment, she used a combination of unique drugs and hypnosis to program ordinary people into doing anything she commanded. She caused several of her patients to commit suicide, after leaving large sums of money and property to her.

Aubrey had investigated the woman and ended up getting programmed herself. They sent her to my office, where she attempted a clumsy seduction that I refused. She began to systematically tear at her own clothes and bruise her own skin with a terrifying, mechanical intensity. By the time security burst through the doors, she was a convincing picture of a victim, and I was the monster who had supposedly tried to rape her.

We had deprogrammed Aubrey, which is the only thing that kept me out of jail and my career from being destroyed. With Aubrey's help, we stopped Vanya, with the evil doctor being shot. From what I knew, she died before the medics could save her.

But even as the case went cold, a single thought kept me up at night: Vanya was a mastermind, but she wasn't a god. She hadn't built that empire of shadows alone.

"Emma Truesdale," I blurted. "Is she still in prison?"

"I checked on that this morning. Len, they've released her."

"How... how could that happen?" I stammered. "She was an accomplice, killed people, for God's sake. She was part of an assault on a police station."

Vanya's ultimate move had been to manipulate a police officer, who she'd treated for PTSD, to set a bomb in the Mountainview Police Station. Bill and I stopped him, but we barely survived. Another officer had shot me, with only the police vest they had ordered me to wear saving me.

"Her lawyers went with an insanity defense. Truesdale claimed Vanya had hypnotized her, and she did what the good doctor told her under duress. They committed her to Ancora Psychiatric

Hospital in South Jersey. I have a call in down there to find out what happened."

I glanced again at the ladies' room. "Do you need me?"

"Do you have classes today?"

"No, it's a first-year class. My TA, Teddy Santos, is covering it for me so I could meet with Jyanette."

"Then I would appreciate your insight."

"I'll be there soon," I responded, and ended the call.

As I sat in stunned silence, I tried to get my mind around this shocking news.

Jyanette, looking like she had touched up her makeup, returned to the table, her stern lawyer face in place.

She sat down and wouldn't meet my eyes. "If you want a paternity test, I will cooperate."

I took her hand. She resisted, and I almost stopped in the attempt, but finally she allowed me to hold her fingers lightly.

"No, I don't need that, but I'll tell you what I want."

Her mouth was a tight line. "Please don't ask me to marry you again," she implored with a hitch in her throat. "I don't think I could take that right now."

"No, I won't. But I want to be there, in our child's life. I don't care how this baby was created or by whom. I will love our child and make sure he or she will be safe."

A sob escaped her throat before she could fight it back.

"I need something from you," I told her.

She eyed me with suspicion.

"I just found out that Emma Truesdale is out of prison."

"What? That crazy bitch who used me as her puppet!" she growled.

It was nice to see Jyanette angry at someone other than me.

.

"It's worse than that," I clarified quietly. "Aubrey Andrews is dead."

"Dead?" she gasped. Then she swallowed several times, as if to prevent herself from throwing up again.

"They murdered her very publicly," I explained.

"Ohmigod, ohmigod," she repeated.

"I'm worried that she might come after the people that stopped her and Vanya."

"Len, you know Vanya programmed me, right? I still have whatever she did stuck in my head."

"I just want you to be careful. One of Vanya's techniques was to send texts with activation codes. Have your office manager or the people you work with read them for you."

"Right, right."

"It also might be a good time to visit your parents in Virginia," I suggested. "That way, you could be out of the way and safe."

"Len, I have a heavy caseload right now," she argued. "Plus, I take maternity leave in about six months. I can't lose more days."

"Do what you can. I have to go to McGee and find out how I can assist."

She nodded, her face serious.

"You should eat," I suggested.

She shook her head. "I feel like that's all I do, eat like a horse. I'm hungry, and then I'm puking. It isn't much fun."

"You look great," I assured her, and for a second, the tension in her shoulders mirrored my own.

She hesitated, then nodded. "I think I'll eat. I have time."

I tapped the edge of the folder against my palm. "Do you think we actually settled anything?"

"I told you my fears, Len. That's a start. If the child is his—"

"Then we deal with it," I interrupted, stepping closer. "Together. I'm in this for the long haul, every step of the way."

"Thank you," she whispered.

I gave her a final, lingering nod and turned toward the door. The domestic drama was heavy, but a darker cloud was waiting for me. It was time to find out exactly what had happened to Aubrey Andrews.

2. RECRIMINATIONS

It took about ten minutes for me to drive to the Mountainview Police Department, in the Public Safety Building shared with the Fire Department. It is in the middle of the town of Mountainview, past the stores and small businesses that line Bloomdale Avenue, right up the hill from the NJ Transit Train Station.

Since Mountainview is a college town, the university takes up over 300 acres of prime real estate, just minutes from Manhattan. In response, builders filled the rest of the town with mansions of various sizes that are clustered as tightly as they can be, preferably with an acre of land and a view of the Manhattan skyline.

Mountainview was built on a mountain, so getting multiple viewpoints is easy. This makes real estate on the expensive side, and I couldn't afford to live here unless I rented the "mother" section of a mother-daughter house from a remarkable lady.

I pulled into the police lot and locked up my car as I limped along with my cobra-headed cane. The metal handle fits my right hand well, and since the cane contains a twenty-four-inch blade, it has come in handy in emergencies.

I felt as if I was in one now.

Anika Vanya had been a busy and highly regarded therapist when she was alive, but very few people had known of her clandestine activities. Word on the street was that at one time she had worked in some shadowy governmental covert operation where she had perfected a cocktail of mind-controlling drugs.

A couple whose daughter had been lost to Vanya's manipulations had given me that information. They told me of a black-suited thug who had shown up at their house and threatened them. He had been a professional assassin, and they believed he had been unleashed by the same quasi-governmental group that Vanya had worked with.

Yet it was far more insidious than that. Using her hypnotic "keys" to access a person's subconscious instantly, she could then use a person's "lock" to create elaborate and intricate mental programs that would make her victim feel justified in doing whatever terrible thing Anika had needed them to do.

People will not do things under hypnosis that they would not do in their regular lives. You can't order someone to take a gun and shoot someone in the head for no reason. The internal conflict with the person's moral code will get in the way. Instead, create a scenario where the target is a threat and trying to kill you. Then the hypnotized patient feels vindicated in killing to save their own life.

With the correct set of commands, the patient won't even remember they did it. Or they would remember a story that Vanya had concocted, word for word.

She was a monster.

And now her second-in-command, devoted servant, and former lover was out of prison, and I was sure she wanted to seek revenge on the people who had taken down her mistress. That was what she had threatened to do at our very last meeting. Was this her opportunity to make good on her threats?

I walked into the lobby of the MPD. After going through the double doors, I was in a small waiting room with several chairs, currently empty. A face appeared at the bulletproof glass window on the left wall. She was a blonde woman in uniform, about thirty-five, handsome, though not pretty. She smiled as she saw me.

It was Carrie Carter, who everyone called CeeCee.

She hit a button on the ledge in front of her, and her voice came through a tinny speaker on the wall.

"As I live and breathe, Doc Wise."

"Hi, CeeCee," I said jovially. She was an amazing woman who ran the Police Dispatcher Unit. She kept a cool head in rough situations, and from what I heard, could take down a suspect with the best of them.

She smiled, and it was amazing how her face changed from the stern look she needed for the job to someone who was beautiful in her own way.

"I heard you're single again, Doc."

I sighed. "Afraid so, CeeCee."

"I'm still available, you know? I could show you a good time."

I laughed, glad for the release. "Thank you for the offer, CeeCee, but you would snap me like a toothpick."

"I'd be gentle… the first time."

"You're too much woman for me, CeeCee."

"For most guys, that's my problem. You need me to buzz you in, Doc?"

I pulled my magnetic ID from my pocket and held it aloft. "Thanks, CeeCee, but I'm good. See you around."

"Let me know if you change your mind. Don't leave a girl hanging."

I scanned my card, and the door clicked as the lock opened. I stepped in and turned to my left to head toward the command offices.

CeeCee was all bluster, but I had to admit, I was missing female companionship.

Okay, I was missing sex.

In our eight months together, Jyanette and I had a very steady, and sometimes quite busy, sex life, until she broke up with me.

Then, last month while working on the haunted house in California, I had reunited with a former student who still had a crush on me. She was in her twenties and all but threw herself into my bed, which led to several amazing nights. Now, a month later, I was missing the dependability of a steady partner.

Pretty odd, since while working on my PhD, I had basically been celibate for two years.

I turned the corner and knocked on the door marked "Lieutenant William McGee".

Bill sat at his large horseshoe desk, file folders stacked in some incomprehensible order. On the wall was a monitor where a cable news channel played with the sound off.

The grainy image on the screen suggested a telephoto lens. It was a billboard, with the catwalk holding a crew of police and men and women in scrubs. They were carefully removing a body from a small outcropping on the sign in the shape of a cross.

Even in the fuzzy video, I recognized Aubrey's blonde hair, and for a moment, I was almost overwhelmed with grief.

My sadness quickly turned to fury.

"How could this happen?" I snapped. "How did Emma Truesdale get released? How did she track Aubrey down in Ohio?"

Bill glanced angrily up at the screen. "A doctor, Harold Veller, signed off on her release."

"Is that important?" I grumbled, my eyes still on the video, as one police officer used a crowbar to pull loose one of the large nails from Aubrey's wrist. How could they even show this on television? Had they no decency?

"It is. I Googled him. Turns out that Doctor Veller interned at none other than Unique Therapies, LLC."

My eyes moved away from the screen to focus on Bill. "That was Vanya's clinic. That's where she programmed people."

"Yes, but this was about five years ago, when Doctor Marcus Houser was in charge."

"Did Veller have contact with Vanya?"

"They were both there at the same time. Then Vanya took over the place two years later."

"After Doctor Houser killed himself, no doubt because of Vanya's ministrations." I stared down at the desk. "You're thinking she got to Veller as well and programmed him for future use?"

McGee frowned. "Seems like a logical deduction."

I nodded. "Truesdale must have been able to discover Veller's key and lock."

"If that's the case, why didn't she activate him to release her sooner?" Bill pointed out as he rose and dropped a folder on the desk. It made a loud noise as it struck. "I mean, if somebody can write you a get-out-of-jail-free card anytime, why wait a year before you use it?"

"I don't know," I reasoned. "Perhaps she needed a place to plan and prepare. She might have needed to find out things. The most obvious one is finding out where Aubrey lived."

"Yeah, I got a copy of the missing person report from the Ohio State Police. She was living with her parents in a town called Plain City. Aubrey went out jogging two days ago, never came back. The police had search parties out on the jogging trail she used."

"When did Truesdale get released?" I asked.

"Four days ago," Bill stated solemnly.

I took a deep breath. The timing was obvious. "She had a plan, and it was time to put it into action."

We both stood silently. I glanced up at the screen to see the team of police and emergency medical technicians lower Aubrey's body to the catwalk with care.

"None of us are safe," I murmured.

"I called the State Police to check on Truesdale."

"And?"

He shrugged. "They'll get back to me. She's out, but it was a conditional release. If she went to Ohio, then she went out of state and they can pick her up for violation of the release order."

I shook my head. "She couldn't have done this alone, Bill. She needed transportation and a weapon. We had deprogrammed Aubrey. Truesdale couldn't just phone her up and order her to do what she wanted." I then made a hard realization. "Bill, I didn't undergo deprogramming."

"What?"

"Remember last spring when Kate Yearling hypnotized me? She used Vanya's programming to put me into an altered state."

Bill rose from his desk. "What the Hell? Does that mean this woman can walk in and take over your mind?"

I shrugged. "I think it's a possibility."

"What can we do?"

"I need to get deprogrammed. But we need a therapist with training in hypnosis."

Bill returned to his seat, a thoughtful look on his face. "How about Kate Yearling?"

The name hung in the air, cold and unexpected. I stared at Bill, waiting for the punchline that wasn't coming. "Kate? Bill, the woman was barely alive three months ago. After what she went through, it's a miracle she's even drawing breath."

Bill's expression flattened into something grim and professional. "You mean after your serial killer surgically removed her scalp? I agree, by all rights, she should have died."

"Exactly," I snapped, the clinical horror flashing behind my eyes. "If the trauma didn't kill her, the strokes, the infections, or the permanent brain damage should have. I'm surprised she isn't staring at a wall in a long-term care facility."

"She isn't." Bill leaned back, his chair creaking. "The surgeons worked wonders with the skin grafts — repaired the damage as best they could. I drop in when the paperwork lets up, and Stan Frazier's been visiting her almost every day."

I blinked, momentarily derailed. "Stan? I thought he finally hung up the badge."

"He did. Retirement didn't take, so he's made Kate his full-time project. She's been back in her own place for two weeks now. She can manage the day-to-day, but from what Stan tells me, she's bored out of her mind."

A dry chuckle escaped me as the image of Kate Yearling took shape — not the victim, but the firebrand. I could see her pacing a living room like a caged leopard, teeth bared at the quiet. She was one of the most brilliant profilers I'd ever worked with, a woman who lived for the hunt. The idea of her being sidelined was probably more painful than the scalpels had been.

It was nothing short of a miracle.

"She was never good at sitting still," I admitted, a sliver of hope cutting through the grim morning. "Where is she living now?"

When I first met Kate, she'd come up from Baltimore. Before her injury, she'd been profiling for the FBI New Jersey Task Force, working out of an office in Morris Plains.

Another person I had failed to save from the demon in human form. I had stopped a serial killer, but I had lost my relationship with Jyanette. Kate, whom I considered a friend, almost died, as well as the injuries I suffered.

That monster might have sired the baby Jyanette carried. I still couldn't get my head around that concept.

Welcome to the Leonard Wise guilt parade. I failed to protect my friend, my lover, and even my unborn child.

"She has an apartment in Morris Plains. She wanted to stay close to the doctors that treated her," McGee disclosed, pulling me out of my self-loathing. "If I call Gabe Petrie, he could probably arrange it."

"Petrie is not my biggest fan."

"He still thinks you didn't tell him everything from that night in the asylum," McGee pointed out. "To be honest, I don't think you told me everything."

"There are some things that happened that even I have trouble accepting. Jyanette and I got out alive, Kate, too. That's all that mattered."

"Let me make some phone calls, see if Kate is up to it," McGee decided, then gazed at me worriedly. "You don't look good, Len."

I inclined my head toward the screen, still showing the team moving Aubrey's body. "It seems like I let down another person."

"You can't blame yourself for that, Len."

"Can't I? Christ, I want a drink."

Since McGee was my AA sponsor and an alcoholic himself, he understood how stress makes the craving for alcohol worse.

"Good idea," he smirked. "Go drink some coffee while I phone people."

I nodded grimly, heading out the door and up the corridor to the canteen.

Sitting at the table in plain clothes, which in this case comprised a drab brown sports coat, was Sergeant of Detectives Joseph Tice. He was an older man; his thinning hair was gray, and his hawkish features turned away from me.

I almost didn't go in, as I was not in the mood for the usual jibes that Tice offered, calling me everything from a "voodoo priest" to a "half-ass sorcerer."

I resented that. I am at least a full-ass sorcerer.

He merely nodded and returned his eyes to the television screen on the wall, which was turned to the same channel McGee had been watching.

As I got coffee from the huge urn, I noted the volume was low, but a female reporter was speaking.

"This crime has Columbus officials shocked, and they immediately called an FBI team to the scene..."

She went on, but I tuned her out and sat across from Tice, who continued to watch.

"Congratulations on your promotion," I told him. He'd been a police sergeant and a detective, but when McGee moved to lieutenant the previous November, that left Tice in limbo. In August, they finally put him in McGee's old position, where he ran the detectives so McGee could focus on paperwork.

I knew that this meant he probably got a pay bump, and he would end up with a larger pension. Tice deserved both; he was a hard worker and a good cop.

He just didn't like me.

"Thanks," he said. It surprised me he didn't throw in some crack about, "Didn't need a psychic to do it," or "I didn't have to cast a spell," or some other nonsense. Instead, he kept his eyes on the screen as I sipped my coffee.

Finally, he cleared his throat. "That girl. She was the one who accused you, right? She was hypnotized or something."

"Yeah," I sighed.

"Got anything to do with what happened to you?"

I had no reason not to share data with Tice. "Yes, it's directly related. Emma Truesdale, Vanya's right-hand woman, got out of confinement four days ago."

He turned to look at me. "You okay?"

Just this bit of compassion from someone who'd hassled and berated me for so long almost made my reserves break down. "Not really," I gasped.

"You can't blame yourself."

Anger suddenly filled me. "Can't I?"

He turned to me, eyes aflame. "No, you can't. You know why? 'Cause one day you arrest some creep for smacking his girlfriend around, and the next day some lame-ass judge lets him go. Then, he goes back to her and slices her up."

His vehemence took me aback.

"Look, Doc. You're playing in the big leagues. If you want to agonize over every loss, I understand. You wanna go hide under your bed, you go do it. But you are working with cops, and we don't have time to beat ourselves up over every loss, when there was nothing we coulda done about it." He pointed his finger in my face. "You got that?"

This stunned me. This was actually Tice's attempt at a pep talk.

"I... uh... got that."

"And you and McGee share every scrap of information you get with me and the detectives. No holding back, you got that, too?"

"Seems like a good idea."

"Yeah, now I'm gonna go arrange uniforms to do a drive-by on the Stoller house. This Truesdale broad used to work for them, and she might wanna blame them for getting you involved."

I nodded. That was a good precaution.

"We'll get this lady in a cage. *Then* you can have your frickin' pity party."

He stood and threw his empty Styrofoam cup into the nearby open trash bin.

"Thanks, Tice," I murmured.

He didn't say a thing, but made a small nod as he exited the room.

As I finished my coffee, McGee came in with a sheet of paper.

"Kate wants to do it. She'll meet you at the FBI offices. Here, I printed up the address for you."

He slipped that page in front of me.

"I remember how to get there," I told him, but I folded up the paper and slipped it into my pocket anyway.

"She expects to see you in an hour," McGee said. "Go get those commands taken out of your head."

3. MALEVOLENCE

The drive to Morris Plains was beautiful on this sunny fall day. It should have been cloudy to match my mood and the oppressive feeling that weighed heavily on my heart.

I should have visited Kate during her convalescence, but I knew why I hadn't. I felt guilty for what had happened to her, that I hadn't been smart enough or quick enough to save her.

Now I was up against someone worse than a demon.

I recalled the last time I had spoken to Emma Truesdale. She was locked up in the holding cells at the Mountainview Police Department. The power was still out after the place was shot up and almost blown up by one of Vanya's programmed drones.

At first, Emma claimed innocence, stating that she had also been under Vanya's control. When I made direct eye contact, I could reach into a person's mind and read their thoughts and memories. Sometimes, in a dire emergency, I could force my will on them.

It isn't a talent I employ very often, as I feel it is an invasion, perhaps even an assault on a person's secret self.

But with Truesdale, I reached right in.

When I did, I saw scenes of her with Vanya: laughing, drinking, making love. I went in deeper, back to the beginning of their relationship, to find a time when Vanya had actually hypnotized her.

I received memories of Vanya explaining what she did as she brought Emma into her world. Rather than resisting her, Emma delighted in sharing Vanya's control of others. As they got to know each other, Emma offered to help with the process. It was thrilling for her to have such pure, unfettered power.

After my reading, which Emma experienced along with me, she dropped all pretense, as she knew I was aware of the truth. Before I left, she cursed me.

"She was magnificent, and you took her from me. Somehow, some way, I'll get out of here, Doctor. And when I do, I will be the harpy from Hell that takes everything you hold dear away from you."

I envisioned Emma as that mythological creature with bird's wings on her back, claws on her feet, and a human head with Emma's vicious glare of hate in her eyes.

Her laughter rang in my ears as I walked away.

Now she was back.

How did she track down Aubrey or get to Ohio? I assumed that somehow she had access to some kind of hidden records of Vanya's minions. If she knew who the people were and had the codes that she needed to activate them, they would do anything she demanded. It was the only thing that made sense. She would need help, and she would only need a few choice words to make the programmed people follow her orders without question.

That meant that anyone could attack the people I cared about, from a stranger on the street to a dear friend.

It had been one of my friends, Officer Tylissa Booker, who shot me. Vanya had programmed her and then made her forget they had even met. The day Bill and I saved the Public Safety Building from being blown up, he stepped outside to announce, "The shooter is down." This phrase activated a prearranged response in Tylissa, impelling her to pull her gun and shoot me. Fortunately, she only hit the Kevlar vest I was wearing.

We arranged for Kate Yearling, who had a background in hypnotherapy, to deprogram Tylissa once we discovered she was compromised.

I hoped she could do so with me as well. I would be a lot less nervous if I knew I wasn't a threat to myself and others.

I found a spot at a meter on Speedwell Avenue, right in front of a row of weathered brick buildings that anchored the heart of Morris Plains. Directly across the street, the train station stood as a silent witness to the morning commute, but my focus was on the structure in front of me.

It was perfectly, almost suspiciously, innocuous. The street level was a forgettable blend of local commerce — a retail drugstore with sun-bleached displays and a dry cleaner that smelled faintly of starch and chemical solvents.

I stepped out of the van; the city sounds faded as I approached the entrance. Upstairs, the second-floor windows told a different story. Heavy, light-blocking drapes sealed the windows tight, creating a deliberate shroud that hid the inhabitants — and their business — from the prying eyes of the street.

I walked up the stairs slowly, as my crippled leg required me to take the stairs one at a time.

At the landing at the top, there was only one door, opening into an unusual space. A sealed room stood directly ahead behind a large pane of glass, where a man and a woman in white lab coats and surgical masks worked at machines analyzing data and checking evidence from crime scenes.

Even from my limited knowledge, I recognized a spectrometer, an electron microscope, and a chromatograph. The other machines were foreign to me. The two people glanced up to note that I had come in, then lowered their heads to focus on what they were doing.

I turned left and headed for Kate's office, which faced the street at the front of the building. I knocked on the door, and Kate opened it.

I sucked in a breath and tried to put on my best poker face.

She was far too thin and looked small and brittle. Her bones jutted from her flesh. She had been of above-average height when I last worked with her, but she looked smaller. She had been a flaming redhead before the demon removed her scalp with her hair, and she still had eyebrows of fine red hairs. But on her head, she wore a cloth turban, and the emerald eyes that looked up at me were still clear and bright.

"Don't fight it, Len," she acknowledged me with a sigh. "I have no illusions about how I look."

I tried to recover, but seeing the vibrant woman I'd known reduced so much struck me hard.

"I'm sorry I didn't visit…" I muttered.

She waved her hand as if to push away my concerns. "I was busy. It's difficult to come back from the dead, you know." She paused for a moment. "Then again, maybe you would. Come on in."

I stepped into her private office. It looked much the same as it had last spring, with a large desk and a red leather "psychiatrist" divan like you see in the movies. Next to the divan was an overstuffed, padded green chair.

Natural light poured in from the pair of windows on the right wall, which looked down on the street and the train station. The carpeting was an ugly brown, but a fake Oriental rug was now under the legs of the desk.

The new thing was the layer of dust on the nearby bookshelves because of Kate's long absence.

"How are you feeling?" I asked.

"I'm better," she told me, and plodded to the overstuffed chair. "But my head and my ass still hurt. They took the skin grafts from my butt... a tough way to get a smaller ass."

She smiled at her own joke, and I couldn't help but smile myself.

She sat gingerly in the chair and held out her hand to indicate the divan.

"You want me there?" I said and drew closer.

"I think it would be easier than hanging from the ceiling like a bat," she quipped.

I sat down. "I never had a chance to tell you how much you helped Jyanette that night."

She looked down at the floor. "I got what I deserved."

"Don't say that!"

"I went into a dangerous situation without backup. Just charged in there and almost ended up dead. This is my penance. That and moving to New Jersey."

"You live in Baltimore, don't you?"

"No, I *lived* in Baltimore. They have reassigned me to the New Jersey Task Force, which is a demotion from the fast track I was on, but at least I'm not in a pine box."

"I would prefer you didn't joke about it," I told her.

She leaned forward and patted my hand. "Len, you are the only person I can joke about it with. Look, doctors, nurses, caregivers, and well-meaning people have surrounded me, tip-toeing for months. Thank you for giving me a reason to get back to work."

"Do you think you can deprogram me?"

"I had success with Tylissa Booker. Heard she got reinstated."

"She did. She's back on the force."

"Good. I also heard some rumors about you."

I exhaled loudly. "I'm sure you did."

"I heard you and Jyanette broke up. Is that true?"

I nodded. "The confrontation at the asylum scared her badly."

Kate shrugged her shrunken shoulders. "Didn't do much for me either."

"Can you cut out the dark humor?" I grimaced. "I feel bad that I let you down."

"There's nothing you could have done, Len," she said and sat back. "I heard other rumors about Ms. Emery."

"Might as well get it all out there."

"I heard she's expecting."

I nodded.

"And she doesn't want to be with you despite the 'blessed event'?"

"No, and I've asked her to marry me five times at last count."

She considered this. "I'm sorry, Len. Really."

"And now all this with Aubrey and Emma Truesdale…" I gestured helplessly, hoping to direct the conversation away from my ruined romantic life.

"Bill sent me the file. Do they know how she got out?"

"A doctor at the facility was an intern at Vanya's Unique Therapies, LLC. He's the one that signed the release statement."

"You believe Vanya programmed him and put him in place?"

"That's our supposition. I'd have to read the guy to find out."

"Pretty crazy stuff."

"And now Aubrey's dead. I should have done something."

"What? Leap tall buildings in a single bound? Bend steel with your bare hands?" she badgered. "Look, Len, you have some remarkable abilities, that weird precognition thing — what do you call it again?"

"A buzz," I replied.

"Right, a buzz. That and the fact that you can get readings off objects and from other people's minds, it's pretty amazing. But you are only human."

"Kate, as a profiler, what's your read on the way Emma killed Aubrey? I mean, crucified on a billboard with a religious message? To me, that's just sick."

"Truesdale wanted to make a very public announcement that she is out there and about to take revenge on the people she feels wronged her."

"Wronged *her*?" I gulped.

"Of course," Kate explained. "In her world, everyone is cattle, prodded and eaten, except for herself and her mistress. She cannot conceive that any of the herd may fight back." She shifted in her seat uncomfortably. "Next time, I bring my donut."

"Your what?"

"I have an inflatable donut I sit on while the skin on my ass regrows. But, back to the case. I have to tell you, this was obviously a message, and I have no doubt she directed it at you and Bill."

"Great," I moaned.

"Well, it gives us some insight. She's very organized, because she took almost a year to plan this out. She knows that there is sure to be an APB put out on her, so I'm sure she is planning to hit her next target hard, fast, and soon."

"How does that help me?"

"It means she has to act. If she delays, the police have time to find her before she can complete her revenge scenario."

I considered this. "You think she has an entire plan ready to put into action?"

"Yes. If what the file told me about Vanya's ability to control people is true, I would surmise she has people in place to carry it out."

I shook my head. "I don't see how she could do all this while incarcerated."

Kate didn't even have to consider it. "If she had control of a doctor, she probably arranged private sessions. During those sessions, she could put the doctor into a trance state and Truesdale would have the use of his computer or phone."

The depth of the situation struck me at that moment. "Wow."

"Big wow. Now let's get you deprogrammed."

I placed my cane on the floor. "Hard for me to relax now," I told her as I lay back.

"Oh really? Raymond Shaw."

"And coming up… feeling good… and you're back!" Kate announced.

I was lying on the couch in Kate's office, suddenly cold. I turned my legs to the side and sat up. In whatever time had passed, Kate had placed a cushion on her chair to allow her to sit more comfortably. "How long was I out?"

Kate glanced at her watch. "About an hour."

"Did you get it?" I asked, feeling drained.

"Let's find out. Raymond Shaw."

I felt nothing. "I guess that's it?"

"It would appear so," Kate told me with a smile.

"I feel tired."

"It was a tough session. She programmed you quickly, but deeply. She had commands that had you respond to texts and catchphrases, as well as the key and lock."

I shook my head. "Why don't I remember anything? When I cleared Aubrey, she could recall everything that Vanya told her and all of her commands."

"Len, I am a trained hypnotherapist. You told me you deprogrammed Aubrey, is that correct?"

"Yes."

"Well, it's lucky you didn't totally mess with her mind. There were layers to your programming, like an onion, and I had to strip them away carefully."

I sighed. "I guess you know what you're doing."

"Yes, I do. You'll be able to face Emma Truesdale without her being able to order you to do anything." She gazed at me wearily.

"You look tired."

"I am," she exhaled. "I'm still weak. But I'm doing physical therapy, and we hit the gym tomorrow. I'll fight my way back from this."

"I have no doubt, Kate. Do you need a lift?"

"No, Gabe will drive me back to my place. It's not far," she said. "Keep me in the loop, will you?"

"I will, Kate," I told her, and headed down the stairs. I wondered where Agent Gabe Petrie was during my session. He was an active FBI field agent, so he was probably out saving the country.

Descending the stairs as slowly as I'd gone up, I tapped my way with my cane to my van. I was about to start the engine when my phone rang. I pulled it from my pocket to see the call was from Jyanette.

"Hello?" I said, my throat tight. "Jyanette, are you all right?"

"Fine, really fine," she replied brightly.

This was a big change from the morning. I cleared my throat. "What's up?"

"I've done a lot of thinking since I saw you this morning, which made court interesting."

"I didn't mean to distract."

She grew serious. "Did you mean what you said? I mean, about not caring if you're the father or not?"

I exhaled. This sounded like progress. "I did. My only concern is you. I want this child." I wanted to add, "I love you," but that might not have been the right tack.

"Okay, if that is really how you feel—"

"It is—"

"Then, yes."

"Yes?" I echoed, unsure.

"Yes, I will marry you."

I sat there in stunned silence for a moment. This certainly was a day filled with surprises.

"That's… good!" I exclaimed.

"You worried me with that long pause. I was afraid you might've changed your mind."

"Me, no, no! I'm just… surprised. Happy, but surprised. What caused this decision?"

"I realized that the best thing for the baby was to have two parents. And once I got over my anger and guilt, I realized — I still love you."

I sighed as I felt a wall to my feelings come down. "I love you, too, Jyanette. So very much."

"Why don't I come to your place for dinner? We can celebrate, make plans, and get reacquainted."

Thoughts of connubial bliss traveled lustily through my brain and all but short-circuited it.

"That would be lovely," I gushed.

"I have to get back to court. See you tonight." She ended the call.

I stared at the phone in my hand. Dinner with Jyanette! This wasn't just lucky; it was a miracle.

I pinched myself to make sure I was actually awake.

I started the car, pulled into traffic, and used the hands-free Bluetooth built into the vehicle to call Mrs. Higgins. She was more than just my landlady and the person with whom I shared her amazing house; she was a close friend.

"Halloo!" came her voice over the phone, her Irish lilt making me smile.

"Mrs. Higgins, it's Leonard."

"Oh, Doctor, what a day ye moost be having. I saw that news about that poor girl."

That was a slap of cold reality, but I was in too good a mood to be brought down.

"Mrs. Higgins, I wanted to let you know we are having company for dinner," I bubbled.

There was a pause on her end of the phone. "Oh, Doctor, if ye're dating, I think it's a mite too soon."

"No, Mrs. Higgins, I'm not dating." I chuckled. "I'm getting married. Jyanette said yes!"

She squealed like a fourteen-year-old girl at her favorite boy band concert. "Oh, what glorious news on such a hard day," she crowed.

"I've got to get to the market. Jyanette is coming to dinner."

"No, no, Doctor. Ye let me take care of everything. Oh, me prayers have been answered. Jyanette has come to her senses!"

"Mrs. Higgins, I can't ask you to make dinner—"

"I'll do it, my treat! Oh, to think Jyanette will be a bride! Her mother will be so pleased."

"Okay, do you need me to pick up anything?" I asked loudly to be heard over her monologue.

"No, no, just be home by 5:30! I'll want ye cleaned up and in a good suit for dinner."

Then, without further ado, she ended the call, still regaling herself with her own excitement.

I grinned and drove toward my office at Garden State University. I hadn't intended to get Mrs. Higgins to make dinner, but I had to admit, I was not a chef anywhere near the quality of her skills from her years of cooking for the well-to-do.

I needed to do something, though, so I made it a point to pull into a small strip mall where I knew there was a good florist. I sauntered into the shop, feeling light and free.

I ordered a dozen red roses and was all but floored when the lovely lady behind the counter told me the price. I decided it would be a gracious gesture and a good place to show my darling how much she meant to me.

She quickly brought out a flower box and placed it on the counter in front of me. She then moved to a refrigerated cabinet with a glass case to get the roses.

The box seemed to draw my attention.

Danger…

A warning flashed through my mind as I looked at the simple flower box, and it puzzled me. I could see that it was empty. The box wasn't dangerous, except for the possibility of a paper cut.

The woman laid out the roses on the counter, lined the box with tissue paper, and put them carefully in, adding a few sprays of baby's breath as a compliment. Each of the roses had an individual plastic bottle of water at the stem, and she included a small envelope labeled "flower preservative."

I paid the lady with my overtaxed credit card, and with the box under my left arm, I made my way back to the van. Once on the road again, I phoned Bill.

"McGee."

"According to Kate, I am now control-free."

"You sound pretty upbeat," Bill noted.

"On this awful day, I got some good news," I confessed. "Jyanette has agreed to marry me!"

"That's great!" Bill boomed as delight entered his voice. "I know how much you wanted this. What changed her mind?"

"I'm not sure," I replied. "I guess I said the right thing at breakfast this morning."

"I guess so!"

"I'm taking the night off and having dinner with my fiancée," I gushed.

"You do that. I'll keep working the case. Can you meet with me tomorrow before your 1:00 p.m. class?"

"Sure thing, Bill. I'll see you then."

"Got it. I'm happy for you, Len."

He ended the call as I pulled into the handicapped space in front of College Hall. As I stepped out of the van, I glanced over at Alumni Green, where students were milling about and enjoying the fall weather. I opened the side door to get to the box of roses, to pull one from the box and give it to Trisha Heywood.

Trisha is the executive assistant to the associate dean, who is also my best friend, Jon Baines. She is the one who actually runs the place, while Jon presses the flesh and raises money, his actual function.

I reached for the box.

Danger...

This time the buzz was so powerful that I stopped and fell back. As I had explained to Kate, a "buzz" is my code word for a flash of precognition, which often comes as a warning. My teaching assistant, Teddy Santos, calls it my "spidey sense".

I glanced around to see if there was a threat or someone watching me. It seemed safe, unless someone was using binoculars or the scope of a sniper rifle.

I reached toward the box—

DANGER...

Once again, I held back. It was definite. There was something about that box that was giving me a warning.

Often, I get a word or a mental impression when I get a buzz that clues me in, but one problem I had fighting Anika Vanya and Emma Truesdale before was that I couldn't get readings from their programmed people. My best explanation was that since they were not operating under the control of their own minds, my abilities couldn't tap into their intentions.

I carefully gave the lid a quick flip and cowered back in case the box should explode or something.

Nothing happened. It was a box filled with red, long-stemmed roses, each with a small plastic vial of water.

The feeling was gone.

I had to assume it was a psychic false alarm, but this concerned me. To get a warning three times in quick succession was disturbing. I grabbed a single rose and returned the lid to the box. I shut the door carefully and backed away from the van.

Since there were no explosions or gunfire, I turned and walked into College Hall through the impressive oak door.

The marble floors beneath my feet, which reflected the dim glow of the overhead sconces, were polished to a mirror finish. College Hall wasn't just a building; it was the original heartbeat of the sprawling Shadowvale estate. The first version, a Victorian fever dream built in 1885 for town founder Quentin Monclair, burned to ashes during the Great Fire of 1920.

A man named Monroe Templeton took over the scorched remains; he didn't just rebuild — he aimed for immortality. He commissioned Julian Tutelage, the trailblazing African-American architect, to craft a masterpiece of stone and shadow.

Tutelage's genius was evident in the fine wood paneling that felt like velvet to the touch and the hand-hewn stonework salvaged from Monclair's ruins.

But the architect never saw his vision realized; he vanished just weeks before the scaffolding came down. They renamed a second, smaller structure on the grounds in his honor — originally an overlarge stable, now a theater.

Walking through the lobby, the weight of history was palpable, but so were the scars of "progress." A few years back, some well-meaning board of directors had slapped a three-story glass atrium onto the side facing the quad. It was a transparent wound on the historic stone, designed to showcase the masterful marble stairwell that spiraled toward the ceiling.

The addition was an architectural middle finger, a sterile cage of steel and glass that refused to speak the same language as the dark, intricate wood of the original hall.

Local legend says Tutelage's spirit still wanders these corridors, checking the joinery and smoothing the panels. If his ghost is here, I couldn't blame him for being a little vengeful watching that glass monstrosity reflect the New Jersey sun.

I entered Jon Baines' office with my hand behind my back. Trisha raised her head and smiled.

I drew close to her desk and held out the rose, then gasped in shock.

The rose was dripping a thick red liquid that had slipped down the outside of the flower and onto my hand. It was thick and viscous and appeared to be blood. I looked back along my path through the room to see drops of blood staining the carpet where I had stepped.

"Len?" Trisha said.

I turned to face her with the rose in my hand. It was restored to a beautiful flower, and my hand was clean.

"What's this?" she asked, indicating the rose I held out.

"I... um... brought this for you," I stuttered as I attempted to recover from the odd vision I'd just experienced.

"What's the occasion?" she wondered.

"I'm getting married," I replied, and stuck on a smile, still troubled by the momentary hallucination.

Her delight was genuine. "Jyanette said yes!"

"Finally," I sighed.

"Oh, Len, I'm so happy for you."

"I have to see Jon. I'm going to need a best man."

She nodded and hit a button on her desk, which made a buzzer go off behind the closed door of Jon's office.

"Yes," he grumbled.

"Doctor Leonard Wise to see you, Dean Baines."

"I was expecting this," he replied glumly. "Send him in."

"Maybe you can help his mood," she suggested.

"It's been a trying day," I replied, and walked to the door and into Jon's office.

It wasn't a large room, but with the fine wood paneling from floor to ceiling, the built-in bookcases, and Jon's large and impressive wood desk, it shouted "importance".

"When did you get the news?" Jon asked.

"News? You mean about Aubrey?"

"Aubrey? What happened to Aubrey?"

I grew solemn. "She's been murdered. We think by Emma Truesdale."

"What? Truesdale? I thought she was in prison—"

"They released her. Somehow, she tracked Aubrey down."

He looked at his hands. "Christ."

"You'll see it all over the news tonight. She wanted to let us know she was out there. Did it publicly."

"Well, that explains what I was hit with today," Jon countered. "The university — and you — are being sued."

"What? By whom?"

"Lawrence and Elana Prentiss. They filed a ten-million-dollar lawsuit against the university — and you personally — for wrongful death."

4. MALICE

My mouth fell open. "Who did we kill?"

He pulled out a legal-size document from the top drawer of his desk and handed it to me. There was a lot of legalese, but the lawsuit named Amanda Prentiss as the "decedent."

I frowned. "Amanda Prentiss? I don't even know who this is."

"Neither did I, but I did some research. She was a student here at GSU, got her Bachelor of Science in Family and Marriage Counseling, then three years ago, she spent a summer internship at—"

"Unique Therapies, LLC," I interrupted as the realization hit me. "She was the woman who was Vanya's secretary."

Jon nodded. "That's right."

"But the police shot her after she pulled a gun on them and fired on officers. How on earth is GSU to blame?"

"The lawsuit states that GSU should have made sure the internship was with a legitimate therapist. It blames our screening procedures for her being exposed to Vanya at all. They feature you in the suit because, and I quote, 'Doctor Wise had specific information about the dangers Amanda faced, yet did nothing to warn Amanda, the plaintiffs, or the police of the possibility of a fatal outcome,' end quote."

"That's crazy! First, I wasn't teaching here three years ago. Second, this woman was never a student of mine, and third, I had no way of knowing that she was one of Vanya's drones."

"That's not what the lawsuit suggests. I spoke with Irving Shapiro, the university's lawyer. He says the parents might pull this off if they get it in front of the right judge."

I shook my head. "This can't be a coincidence. The timing is just too close."

Jon looked panicked. "You think this Truesdale woman is behind it?"

"Could be. If Vanya got to the parents and programmed them, they'll do whatever they're told."

He ran his hands through his unruly hair.

"I have some good news."

"I could use it," he grimaced.

"I'm getting married."

His entire face lit up. "Jyanette said yes?"

I nodded, a smile on my face.

"Len, that's great news! Where, when?"

"I don't know. We're going to talk about it tonight. Mrs. Higgins insisted on making a special dinner."

"That should be great," he sighed, familiar with Mrs. Higgins' culinary talents.

"As far as when? Probably soon, something local and quick. It depends on when we can get her parents to town."

"Well, lawsuits be damned. I'm so happy for you."

"I wanted to ask if you would be my best man."

Jon looked at me seriously. "It would be an honor."

I exhaled with relief. "Okay. I'm going to talk to Teddy and catch up on anything I missed today, then I'll have dinner with my lady."

He stood, held out his hand, and when I shook it, he pulled me into a bear hug. "We'll get through this lawsuit, wait and see, Len."

"I hope so. Also, keep your guard up. Truesdale might know that we're friends."

"I'll keep an eye out, and on Jenny as well."

"Tell her the good news."

He smiled. "I will. It devastated my wife when you two broke up."

"I was pretty upset too."

With that, I headed for the door.

Trisha waved as I left.

A lawsuit from the parents of the woman Vanya used as her puppet. Had Vanya gotten to them as well, or had Truesdale sent a lawyer to persuade them to file? It seemed like Emma was piling on as much as she could. It went back to what Kate said about her having to attack and attack fast. Every new thing she put on my shoulders would affect my concentration and focus, the things that made my abilities work best.

I stopped by the computer room two doors down from my office to see my teaching assistant, Téodore Santos. He wore thick glasses, had shoulder-length straight hair, and the olive tint to his skin belied his Hispanic heritage. He came from a family of eight kids and grew up in Dover, New Jersey, in a rambling Victorian his father was perpetually renovating.

"Hey, Teddy," I said, not too loudly, because when he gets involved in his computer work, he shuts out the world and can startle easily.

He looked up and smiled. "Hey, Doc!"

"How did the class go?"

"Very well. I'm really getting the hang of it," he said with a relaxed wave of the hand. "How did the meeting go with Ms. Emery?"

"Better than I hoped. Teddy, we're getting married!"

"Really? That's awesome!" he roared as he rose and grabbed my hand to shake it. "When?"

"I'm having dinner with Jyanette to figure it out."

"Great!"

"I also have a mission for you, if you don't mind."

"Really? Is it this thing about Aubrey Andrews?"

I hissed my breath out. "You've heard?"

"Everyone has been talking about it all day. That footage is pretty disturbing."

"I know," I grumbled. "I think there might be a way to stop the person who did this."

Teddy returned to his chair. "And I can help?"

I nodded. "I think there might be an online database that Anika Vanya put together when she was alive."

"Database?" he repeated.

"Yes, with all the codes needed to activate every one of her minions."

Teddy considered this. "I can see that. Having it online would be the smartest way to go. That way she could access it from any computer, anywhere."

"Is there a way you can track that down?"

Teddy was quiet for a moment. "Most times, no, because it could be in so many places, from a Dropbox account to hiding in a website we don't even know exists."

"You sound like you might have an idea," I guessed.

Teddy paused again, as if to consider how much he wanted to tell me. "Well, you know my major is computer sciences. I've been... uh... getting pointers from Ben Galland."

"Officer Galland?" I inquired. "McGee's aide-de-camp?"

"Yeah," Teddy said. "He was a big-time hacker until he became a cop—"

"I'm familiar with his computer skills. He's good. Do you think he can help?"

"Well, the FBI made copies of the hard drives from Vanya's computers. MPD has one of those clones, and Galland's worked on them a little. He put them aside when Vanya died, and they locked up Truesdale. But he has access to the drives."

"With the hard drive, would it be difficult to track down this database, if it even exists?"

"It might be easy, except Galland never got past the double and triple security. But, together, we might crack it and track down this database."

I frowned. "So Galland just told you about all of this?"

He looked down at his hands. "We're... uh... kinda... seeing each other."

I blinked at this. "You're dating Galland?"

"Yeah, and he's teaching me a lot about hacking."

I felt confused. "Didn't you say you found Kate Yearling attractive last spring?"

He brightened at this. "Oh, I was. She was hot." He sensed my uncertainty. "I kinda like women... and men."

"So you're bi?"

He shrugged. "I don't like labels. I like to think I'm attracted to beauty. And you have to admit, Galland is really good-looking."

I couldn't argue with that. "Teddy, I didn't mean to intrude. Who you want to be with is your business."

His brows knitted. "I wanted to tell you. Makes it less awkward if you run into me on a date." He then checked the door to make sure we were alone. "But say nothing in front of my family. My mom'd freak."

"No problem. If you could talk to Galland, let him know what we are looking for, I would appreciate it."

"You got it, Doc."

I limped out and headed for my office. This was quite a revelation from Teddy, and I had to think about it for a moment. I am pretty vanilla in what I like sexually. My biggest adventure had been a one-time event with two women while in California. It had been a very interesting experience, but not really the sort of thing I would seek as an ongoing situation.

Teddy was looking at other paths, and he would have to discover the things he enjoyed, as well as the people he wanted to be with. On the one hand, it was nice that he had a variety of choices. On the other hand, I could see how it could be confusing.

It was easy for me. I wanted Jyanette. I wanted a family and a simple life. And it looked like my dream was going to come true.

I unlocked the door and stepped into the room, flicking on the light as I entered. My office is not large, but the oversized desk makes it look even smaller. With my bad leg, the large kneehole in the desk makes sitting for hours easier. My laptop was on my desk where I had left it, and I booted it up so I could check my email.

It's amazing how much spam finds its way to my simple email account, and the filters to send them to a "junk" folder only relieve me of a small portion.

I reviewed the latest missives, and the ones that were not offers for "fabulous cannabis oil" or "the best drone ever" were pretty mundane: university activities and department meetings. I paused at a message from Kate Yearling:

Len;

Something is wrong,

But I can't tell you

K

I looked at the email, puzzled. It certainly was cryptic. I pulled my phone from my pocket to call Kate, then hesitated. I needed the night off to talk to my lady and focus on our plans.

I put the phone away, closed up my laptop, slipped it into my leather messenger bag, and with my cane in hand, headed for my van.

One night away from all the insanity wouldn't hurt.

The drive home was a gentle hum through Mountainview's quiet backstreets, the air carrying a faint scent of pine. My destination:

a modest two-story stone house, small compared to its affluent neighbors.

A recent, dark-beige addition with wide, gleaming windows had been added onto the first level. This newer section, a stark contrast to the stone, housed my bedroom and the sunlit sitting room I'd claimed as my office.

There were two entrances: the original front door and an entry just for the addition, with a gravel, circular driveway that served both. The house is in a slight depression in the land, lower than the nearby street.

As I pulled off the street and down into our driveway, I saw Mrs. Higgins' little car pulled into the small gravel outcropping. She doesn't go on long trips like I do, but limits her driving to shopping and her Tuesday-night quilting group.

I pulled into my usual parking spot, pulling over as Jyanette would bring her car and I wanted to make space for her to get by me.

Would she spend the night? I fervently hoped so. After all, we were celebrating our engagement, and the last time we'd made love was months ago.

However, I didn't want her to feel pressured.

I tried to focus. I had to let go of any expectations. Jyanette had gone through a lot of emotional upheaval because of our situation. Add to that, she was pregnant, and although my darling was a strong and smart lady, hormones can do strange things to your brain. I would do as she wanted.

I went in the front door, through the small vestibule, and into the long hallway that linked all the rooms on the first floor and led to my end of the house. I yelled out, "Mrs. Higgins, I'm here!"

Mrs. Higgins popped her head out of the swinging kitchen door. "You're early! 'Tis a miracle."

Feeling nervous about the upcoming evening, I simply said, "I should get… uh… showered."

"That you should, Doctor. Don't worry, I have it all in hand," she assured me, then disappeared back into the kitchen.

I had been so lucky that Mrs. Higgins asked me to rent the two rooms in her house. The monthly fee she asked for was well below market value, and she was a great asset, not just for her cooking and other skills, but because of her innate psychic ability that she referred to as her "wooman's intooition."

I reached the far end of the hall and stepped through the door to my sitting room, turned the corner and headed into my bedroom. There, I pulled off my suit jacket and hung it in the closet.

I paused for a moment to get a small jewelry box off the shelf. I took it down and folded back the hinged lid. Within it was a gold ring with a tiny diamond that sparkled in the fading light coming through the window.

It was Jyanette's size, and although the jewel was tiny, it was pretty much all I could afford. I had bought it in August, after Jyanette had revealed she was pregnant.

I had so hoped and prayed that I would get to give it to her.

Who says that sometimes I don't win one?

Bill and I would meet tomorrow, and with Galland and Teddy's help, maybe we could locate the place where Vanya hid her codes, if it existed at all. With their commands, it would give us the ability to stop anyone she might send after us.

I left the jewelry box out, undressed, and jumped into the shower in my private bathroom. After washing, I shaved for a second time that day, and even put on a little of the cologne I knew Jyanette liked.

Once cleansed and stubble-free, with my hair combed and styled, I pulled a white shirt from my closet. I dressed in my dark-blue pinstripe suit, with a red tie that had a subtle heart design. I looked at myself in the mirror.

Gone was the college professor, replaced with a very dapper gentleman who might even win the heart of his lady love.

I pocketed the small jewelry box and my phone, took a deep breath, and headed down the hall and the main part of the house.

Reaching the swinging door to the kitchen, I pushed my way in. "How do I look?" I asked.

Mrs. Higgins looked up, oven gloves on her hands. She used her forearm to push back a lock of her hair and observed me. She nodded her head slowly and said, "Noice, Doctor."

"Can I help at all?"

"Nay, I'm joost finishing up. I've got everything keeping warm. But I'd best go upstairs and make meself presentable."

She pulled off the oven mitts, took off the apron she'd been wearing, and hung it on a nearby hook on the wall. "There's a surprise in the icebox."

I was standing next to the large refrigerator, so I pulled open the door. On the top shelf, looking very much like champagne, was a bottle of non-alcoholic sparkling cider.

"Cider," I praised her. "Good choice!"

She looked at the bottle, which I now held. "I figured with you not drinkin' and Jyanette bein' in 'the family way,' it t'were the best choice."

"You think of everything, Mrs. Higgins."

"If only I had time to get flowers," she sighed.

This sparked my memory. "I stopped and got roses. They're in my van."

I returned the bottle to the icebox and headed down the hall toward the front door. I had thrown my car keys into a nearby candy dish on a small table in the hall. Mrs. Higgins and I both used the dish for key chain storage when we were home, making it easy to move each other's cars if needed.

I went outside, and as I opened the side door of the van, I again felt nervous about the box. As I reached out for it, no warnings or alarms filled my mind, and I relaxed. I gathered it under my left arm, and using my cane with the right, returned to the house and into the formal dining room.

The room has a view of the deck behind the house, where Mrs. Higgins and I would sometimes linger on summer nights.

Tonight there was a cream-colored tablecloth on the table, and she had put out the sparkling white china in three place settings on the near end. The curtains at the far end of the room moved lazily in the light breeze from the open window.

Mrs. Higgins was in the dining room, where she had set out two candle holders with tall white tapers. She was lighting them with a long-nosed butane lighter as I stepped in. She had also left out a matching vase for the flowers, and it stood on the table.

"Put those in the kitchen, Doctor. I'll take care of it," Mrs. Higgins said as she lit the second candle.

"No, you go up and get ready," I said as I leaned my cane against the head of the table and grabbed the vase. "I can do this much."

She glanced at her watch. "True, Doctor." She moved past me to the open doorway.

"Mrs. Higgins," I called, and she turned to glance at me. "Thank you so much."

That made her smile. "It's me pleasure. Now take care of those flowers. Yer lady will be here any minute!" She exited the room and headed up the stairs.

I limped into the kitchen, the vase in one hand and the flower box in the other. Opening the box, I extracted the foil envelope of preservative, which I poured into the vase, followed by water from the spigot. I grabbed a pair of kitchen shears and snipped off the ends of the flowers with the little containers of water, being as artful as possible.

I cleaned up and limped back to the dining room with the vase in both hands to place the flowers in the center of the table — just in time for the doorbell to ring.

I stood still for a moment, closed my eyes, and focused on letting go of the stress of the day. For one night, I pushed aside the thoughts of Emma Truesdale and her crime spree, grabbed my cane from the table, and headed for the door.

I reached the front door just as the bell rang a second time, and pulled open the heavy oak door to reveal Jyanette.

She looked amazing.

She wore a black velvet dress with a black satin jacket with silver sequins woven in a floral design, and heels that brought her six-foot-tall frame eye level with my six-four. She carried a purse in one arm and a flower box in the other.

I think my mouth fell open, and I quickly shut it.

"You may gawk, if you wish," she teased.

I could finally form words. "You… you changed!"

"Court let out early, so I thought I'd get dressed up for you," she said and walked in the door.

She put the flower box on the floor and leaned it up against the small table with the candy dish where I put my keys. She moved past me and glanced into the dining room. "My, you went all out. Or is all this Mrs. Higgins?"

"Mostly her," I confessed, and I moved to hug her.

She leaned forward and gave me a quick hug without pressing her body against mine. Then she moved back before I could kiss her and added, "We have all night for that. I don't want to embarrass Margery."

"Mrs. Higgins is thrilled you're here. We could be naked in the hall and she'd be fine with it."

Jyanette smiled. "Maybe later. I think we should eat first."

"Jyanette!" Mrs. Higgins crowed as she came downstairs, her arms open. She had changed into a simple green outfit that looked dressy but still relaxed. That was good. I wanted my landlady to enjoy herself.

When she reached Jyanette, my girlfriend pulled the same trick with Mrs. Higgins as she had with me, leaning forward to make it an upper-body hug only. She then pushed herself back to arm's length to stare down at the matronly woman. "Margery, so good to see you."

Jyanette turned and held Mrs. Higgins to one side, and then took my arm to lead us to the dining room. "So just the three of us, then?"

"That's all," I said.

"Good." She smiled. "What's on the menu, Margery?"

Jyanette was not her normal, relaxed self. It must have been a day with a lot of tension for her. We'd argued in the morning, and she'd made a decision that was completely different by the afternoon. She probably felt bad after a month of saying no to me.

Mrs. Higgins saw the flower box leaning against the table and said, "Oh, I'll get that."

But Jyanette laughed and held onto Margery. "Don't worry, I brought that for later. I don't want to ruin the surprise."

I looked at the box.

DANGER…

There it was again, a loud buzz of warning. I could only guess that there must be something about flower boxes to which I should pay heed.

That is the one downside to having a precognitive ability. I get these flashes of insight, but often the reason to be aware does not become clear until I'm actually in the situation it warned me about.

A memory of the vision of the bloody rose appeared in my mind.

We stepped into the dining room and separated to go to our traditional seats: me, on the left near the door to the kitchen, Mrs. Higgins at the head of the table, and Jyanette across from me.

As Mrs. Higgins went through the swinging door to the kitchen, Jyanette and I sat. I moved the napkin from the center of my plate to my lap. Jyanette took hers from her plate and left it on the table, and then moved her clutch handbag to her lap as she looked at the roses and the candles.

"This is certainly beautiful," she sighed.

I reached out my hand. "Not as beautiful as you."

She smiled and took my hand across the table. I pulled out the box and, with only one hand, flipped it open to expose the ring. I placed it within her reach and met her eyes.

Her eyes...

There was something wrong with her eyes.

Suddenly, alarm bells I had ignored started going off in the back of my brain. I met her eyes and, on a hunch, attempted to reach in...

I couldn't.

I've looked death in the eye before. I've been pinned to the dirt with a blade biting into the skin of my chest, and I've felt the icy, metallic stare of a service weapon leveled at my forehead. In those moments, adrenaline is a cold comfort; you fight because you have to.

But this was different. This was the first time I felt the hollow, paralyzing weight of true terror.

I reached out, trying to bridge the gap to her consciousness, but I hit a slab of pure, reinforced silence. It was a mental fortress — the same impenetrable wall I'd encountered when trying to crack Vanya's drones while they were deep in their hypnotic trance. My gift didn't just fail; it recoiled.

Sweating, I gently let go of her hand and straightened up, my eyes fixed on her every move, as I sought to pick up on any subtle clues I had missed on a psychic level.

Jyanette tilted her head in curiosity. "What's wrong, Len?"

As slowly as possible, I slid my chair back. "Did you let your associates answer your phone today?"

She frowned at that. "Why would I do that?"

I slid back a little more. "Because I warned you about Emma Truesdale."

Her expression hardened. "Oh, you mean that bullshit you told me, so I wouldn't see what was really going on?"

My heart was crashing in my chest as I felt the full impact of the fight-or-flight response. Adrenaline coursed hotly through my body, so much I trembled.

I held my open palms up in front of me. "What do you think is going on?"

She gave a hollow laugh. "You think I don't know that you and the old lady are trying to steal my baby?"

My mouth didn't seem to work as I watched anger burning in her eyes, sheer hatred that frightened me with its intensity.

Calmly, with my hands still out in front of me, I spoke. "No one is trying to do that."

"Liar!" she roared, rising to her feet. The small gun she carried for protection was in her hand, apparently pulled from the purse in her lap. It was about five and a half inches long, a Smith & Wesson Bodyguard that shot a .380 caliber bullet.

She shrieked in rage, "You will never have my baby! Never!"

I dove under the heavy oaken table as a shot rang out, and chunks of wood flew into the air like confetti. In the enclosed space, it sounded like a two-by-four block of wood smashed against a wall. I heard a scream of surprise from Mrs. Higgins in the kitchen.

I was under the table, and from my angle, I had a view of the swinging door. It flew open and Mrs. Higgins stood there, terrified.

I heard Jyanette yell, "I know you're helping him!"

Mrs. Higgins dove out of sight as a second shot rang out. As the door swung closed, a corner of it exploded and a chunk of wood disappeared.

Truesdale had gotten to Jyanette, and I did not know what she had programmed her to do, or what false narrative was active in her mind that had turned my darling into my assassin.

Nor did I have any time to consider it. She had a gun, and I only had a cane.

And a dining room table.

Time was of the essence. I placed my back on the floor, took my one good leg and my arms, and with all the strength I had, pushed up on the heavy table.

"Come out, you coward!" Jyanette screamed.

There was a groan of wood, and the table shifted toward where Jyanette had been standing. The angles must have been right, and leverage was on my side, because my side of the table rose into the air. The heavy tabletop slammed Jyanette against the china cabinet.

I heard glass break and glanced back to see Jyanette bodily go through the glass front of the cabinet.

I crawled to the doorway and slipped through it just as Jyanette screamed and another shot rang out.

Wood flew off in a spray on the doorjamb inches from my head. All of it magnified my feelings of vulnerability. I stayed low and rushed down the hall to pull open the kitchen door.

Mrs. Higgins was cowering on the floor, and I held out my hand and gasped, "We have to run."

She nodded, rose into a crouch, and we exited the kitchen and headed down the hall toward my end of the house. I didn't want to hurt the woman I loved, but we needed to get away.

There was a cry of anger and the sound of tinkling glass as Jyanette pried herself loose from her temporary prison.

Mrs. Higgins and I were more than halfway down the hall when I glanced back to see Jyanette come out of the dining room. There was blood on her face, and I guessed, going into the cabinet, she'd gotten cut.

Instead of pursuing, she moved away from us down the hall in the opposite direction, put the small pistol on the table with the candy dish and car keys, then picked up the flower box.

She pulled open the lid to extract a pump-action shotgun.

I hate it when I ignore a buzz, especially a loud one.

"Run, run, run," I gasped, my lungs burning as we stumbled through the heavy oak door into my sitting room as Mrs. Higgins and I plunged inside.

Behind us, Jyanette's weapon clicked with a sharp, metallic snick, a surprisingly loud sound that echoed down the hall. I slammed the door shut, the solid thud vibrating through the floorboards, and pulled Mrs. Higgins down beside me.

A deafening roar erupted, like thunder directly overhead, and the door to my sitting room buckled inward, exploding with a violent crack. A jagged hole ripped through its center, and the entire structure flew inward on its hinges.

The air filled instantly with a choking cloud of fine dust, acrid smoke, and the sharp, splintered scent of shattered wood. Mrs. Higgins let out a piercing shriek of pure terror.

This wasn't the usual buckshot used in the weapon. There were shotgun bullets that ran up to fifty caliber. Judging by the destructive power of the shot, this might be what she was using.

I struggled to the exterior door, which was my separate entrance, yanked it open, and gestured to Mrs. Higgins.

"Go, get help!" I yelled.

She stayed low, headed out the door and toward the back brick wall that surrounded our house.

I only had moments before Jyanette came into my room with her enormous gun, and I couldn't think what to do. My mental abilities wouldn't work on her. She had the same barrier I had faced with other Vanya minions, and I couldn't get past it.

I had misplaced my cane, which was an effective weapon, but I had no intention of using it against the woman I loved and the mother of my child.

Teddy Santos had abducted me under Vanya's orders when I last fought her. I had knocked him unconscious, and that had broken the control. When he woke up, he was himself again.

I didn't think Jyanette would let me get close enough to punch her. I needed to stop her, or at least shock her.

And then it occurred to me: an electric shock.

In my last Vanya encounter, I'd confronted a crazed bomber at the Mountainview Police Station. While searching for him, I got into the police armory. There, I had located a Taser electric defense pistol that had darts that plunged into the skin and wires that reached several feet. The pistol sent out an electric current that temporarily incapacitated the man.

After that incident, I got one of these devices for home defense. I am not comfortable with a traditional firearm, as I have had no training and prefer a non-lethal confrontation when possible.

I had invested in a small device called a Taser Bolt. Unlike the one I used at the police station, it did not resemble a traditional pistol. Instead, it looked like nothing more than a top-of-the-line flashlight, but it could fire darts and convey a shock equal to the one I had used.

Staying low, I yanked open the top drawer of my desk. The compact unit was halfway back, and I grabbed it and headed for the door to my bedroom. I reached the doorway just as I heard the familiar click-clack of the shotgun being racked again.

I dove through the door as a second explosion occurred, this one deafening in the tight space. The woodwork over my door exploded in a shower of plaster dust and wood shards as I crawled behind my bed.

Jyanette was shouting as she came toward me, but I couldn't understand a word she said because of the ringing in my ears from the detonation of her rifle.

I used the bed to pull myself upright and lifted the Bolt, gripping it. I slid back the panel to the activation button. In only a second, the button lit up, and a laser flashed from the front of the weapon to make a tiny red dot on my open door.

Jyanette stepped into the room, the menacing rifle in her hand. She had removed the sequined jacket, and now came at me in just the sleeveless black velvet dress. There were cuts on her arms and face with red lines of blood on her dark skin.

I moved the red dot to point it below her chest just as she racked the shotgun. With the whoosh of compressed air, the darts flashed through the air and struck Jyanette just below her ribcage. She looked surprised for a moment, and then the voltage hit her.

The rifle fell from her hands. Her body convulsed, and she fell to the floor with a scream of agony.

Leaving the weapon, I dashed around the bed and grabbed the shotgun. I ejected the remaining cartridges; the shells were very large projectiles in a shotgun cartridge. I tossed the weapon over the bed and into the corner.

I knelt at my lover's side and pulled the two darts out of her. With my frozen leg straight out and my other leg bent under me, I lifted Jyanette's head into my lap and checked her pulse. Her heartbeat was fast but slowing down.

I went for my phone in my pocket, only to hear police sirens in the distance. Either Mrs. Higgins had contacted the police or a neighbor had heard the gunfire.

"Len," Jyanette moaned.

I looked down at my lady. "Jyanette. Are you yourself again?"

"How did I get here?" she asked weakly.

"Truesdale got to you, or one of her drones."

"I'm hurt," she groaned.

"Glass cut you. We'll get you an ambulance."

"No, Len, I hurt inside," she said, and her eyes filled with panic.

The lower part of her dress was a slightly darker shade than the area around her chest. She touched beneath the small mound of her belly, and when she turned her hands over, blood covered them.

"Oh God, Len," she blubbered. "The baby."

The sirens pulled into our driveway as I sat on the floor, helpless and filled with dread.

5. REPRISAL

The sterile air of the hospital waiting room offered little comfort as I sat with Mrs. Higgins. Plaster dust covered my suit, and Mrs. Higgins' hair was a wild tangle.

Bill McGee strode in like a hurricane. One look at Mrs. Higgins and me, and his jaw tightened. He spoke in a low voice. "What did the doctors say?"

"Not much so far," I answered, torn between rage and terror.

"The EMTs said she lost a lot of blood, poor dear," Mrs. Higgins told him.

Bill shook his head. "Let me see if what I was told is right. She shot at you?"

"Yes," I confirmed. "With the little gun she carries for defense, and then a shotgun loaded with large-caliber shells."

His eyes widened. "A shotgun? Where did she get that?"

I shrugged. "No idea."

He considered this. "I saw the house, went there before I came here. There are still uniforms watching the place. Do you think Truesdale got to her?"

"It's the only explanation." I frowned. "I tried to peek into her mind, but it was sealed away from me—"

"Just like one of Vanya's people," Bill finished.

"But it's worse than that, McGee," Mrs. Higgins said. "She did something to herself."

Bill frowned. "What do you mean?"

"Something to hurt the baby," Mrs. Higgins explained, as tears appeared in her eyes.

"What?" Bill's face went slack with shock.

"It's the only thing that explains all the blood," I added bleakly. "We still don't know the extent of the damage."

He looked at me, stunned. "Could she die?"

I fought to keep control as untold grief washed over me. "She might."

"Now, now, we know little yet," Mrs. Higgins comforted me. "She's young and strong. She can pull through this. I know she can."

"How did Truesdale even activate her?" Bill wondered.

"It could've been anything, Bill. A text, a phone call, or someone could have walked right up to her and said a code word and told her to follow him."

"Len, we've got to stop this woman!" Bill vowed.

"How? Last time she used Teddy Santos, and for all I know, he's still programmed. Who can we trust? How far do her tentacles reach?"

"Len, I'm pulling in the FBI New Jersey Task Force," Bill intoned. "We have to get a bead on this woman."

I nodded. Gabe Petrie and the Task Force had resources far beyond the limitations of MPD. Bill was a former FBI agent and would have intimate knowledge about just how deep they could look, but I had my doubts that even they could help in this case.

A doctor approached the three of us, and Bill and I stood. He was a brown-skinned man whose homeland was probably India. He had straight, dark hair, brown eyes, and he looked us over in a very businesslike way.

"You're here for Ms. Emery?" he asked with just the hint of an accent.

"Yes, Doctor. I'm her fiancé," I disclosed. "Leonard Wise."

He inclined his head, and we stepped aside from the others.

"I'm Doctor Burman. Are you the father of the child?" he asked quietly.

"Yes," I croaked, surprised that my voice sounded so hoarse. "Is she — I mean, is the baby—"

Words failed me.

He eyed me as if I might be the reason she had ended up here. "She has cuts and abrasions on her body. Can you explain that?"

I could have told him the truth — that she had tried to shoot me and my landlady while in a fugue state — but I didn't think it would help. "She fell against a china closet and broke the glass. We got her right here."

He looked at me seriously, probing for any falsehood. "She lost the baby."

My legs had no strength as my vision grew dim. I felt Bill's powerful arms under my armpits, and he lifted me and guided me into a chair. For a big man, he moved fast, and I was thankful for it.

"Are you all right, Mister Wise?" Doctor Burman asked, as I tried to clear my head.

"*Doctor* Wise," Bill stated plainly. "He has a medical degree."

Burman nodded. "And who are you?"

"Police Lieutenant William McGee. I'm also a friend."

"Anything you have to say, you can say it in front of me, too," Mrs. Higgins demanded, her chin raised proudly. "I'm family."

He frowned at this, but wisely did not confront Mrs. Higgins. "I don't want to go into detail, but someone forced a foreign object into Ms. Emery's uterus, hours ago."

Mrs. Higgins gasped, and her hand went to her mouth.

"From the damage and the angle, it appears to be self-inflicted," the doctor proposed grimly. "She did a lot of damage to herself."

It was a good thing I was sitting.

He eyed me suspiciously. "I have to ask — did you and Ms. Emery have a fight?"

"No... no..." I stumbled. "She had finally agreed to marry me."

"It was a celebration dinner we were havin'," Mrs. Higgins added.

The doctor watched me. "You wanted the child?"

I fought back tears. "Very much."

"I'm sorry," the doctor apologized. "But it appears she had other ideas."

I fought to keep control of myself. "Will she be all right?"

"She'll live, but I have to be honest, she might never have children after this."

I fought to stay centered.

"I also am recommending a psychological profile. You say that she agreed to marry you and then she did this to herself? We need to have her mental state reviewed before we can release her."

I surged to my feet, fury racing through me, clearing my mind and giving me the power I needed to keep going. "I have to see her. Is she conscious?"

The doctor seemed a bit surprised by my sudden change. "I'll check." He stepped away.

I glared at Bill. "Call Petrie and any connections you have, Bill. Find out whatever you can."

He nodded, but there was suspicion in his eyes. "What are you going to do?"

"I'm going to see Jyanette," I said, my rage giving me the strength to go on. "Then, I'll do what I have to."

He and Mrs. Higgins exchanged a look. Bill rose, and without another word, headed out.

"Doctor," Mrs. Higgins spoke quietly to me. "What *are* you going to do?"

"I'm going to stop the person who did this," I vowed, not allowing the grief to overwhelm me.

"A noble intention," she responded. "I hope you plan to keep it that way."

"No, Mrs. Higgins," I fumed. "I intend to do whatever is needed. I intend to bring Emma Truesdale down, and if possible, with my hands wrapped around her throat."

"Doctor," she spoke firmly, as if she were calming a child. "Ye're angry, and ye're hurtin', but when you seek revenge, you dig two graves, and one's for yerself."

I looked over at my landlady, and I could see fear for me in her eyes. Or possibly fear of me.

"I'll do whatever it takes to stop her," I swore.

Doctor Burman came back into the room. "You can see her, but only for a few minutes."

I calmed myself. "That will be fine."

He told me the room number and stepped away, busy with the next emergency.

Mrs. Higgins put her hand on my arm. "Do you want me to come wi' ye, Doctor?"

"Thank you, Mrs. Higgins. But this has to be between me and Jyanette right now."

"I understand."

I walked down the wide hallway briskly, the anger and desire for vengeance overcoming any of my weaker emotions.

I stepped quietly into Jyanette's room. She was in a bed just under a window that showed a view of the parking lot. Her skin tone was sickly, almost a dark-beige color, and it frightened me. There was an IV that snaked through a tube into her arm, and machines beeped and hissed.

She had bandages on her arms and on her forehead for the cuts from the broken glass. Though I was sure they had not needed stitches, the white gauze against her dark skin reminded me of the horrible violence of the night.

I sat in the chair near the bed and reached up gently to take her hand. Her eyes opened halfway, and she gazed at me. I sensed that the barrier that had been in her mind was no longer there.

"What happened?" she asked.

"What do you remember?"

"Us at the diner, this morning. Then I was in court. After that, it all gets pretty misty, like a dream."

I nodded. It was typical of Vanya's programming to make the victim forget the contact point, so that they could use the same technique in the future.

Her eyes welled with tears. "They told me I lost the baby."

I fought to keep control, but all I could do was nod.

"They think I did it to myself," she lamented.

"It's what it looked like, Jyanette," I told her as gently as I could.

"It's not true," she seethed. "That was my baby — *our* baby. I wouldn't do that to our baby."

"Emma Truesdale got to you and created a scenario where you believed Mrs. Higgins and I were planning to steal the child from you."

She frowned. "What? That's crazy."

I took a deep breath. "You tried to shoot me with your handgun, and then you fired a shotgun at us."

Her eyes grew wide. "A shotgun? Where did I get a shotgun?"

"Bill is working to track that down."

She nodded and saw the look in my eyes. "What are you going to do?"

My mouth became a hard line. "I am going after her, any way I can."

She nodded gravely. "If you do, I want you to do something for me."

"Anything."

Her jaw set, and a look I had never seen appeared in her eyes. "I want you to kill her. No trial, no mercy, nothing. You kill her. For me."

I nodded and spoke through clenched teeth. "I will."

In the glove compartment of my van, I extracted an old-style flip phone I'd been gifted the previous spring. I kept it buried there like a loaded gun, occasionally plugging it into the van's power port just to ensure the battery didn't die in case I ever needed it.

To kill a monster, you call a bigger monster.

I flipped the casing open, the small screen bathing the dark cabin of the van in a sickly blue light. There was only one contact saved in the memory. I hit *Send* and pressed the plastic to my ear.

The line clicked after two rings. A woman's voice, crisp and utterly devoid of emotion, answered. "International Shipping. How may I direct your call?"

I didn't waste time with pleasantries. "This is Doctor Leonard Wise. I was told that if I ever needed help, I should call this number." I took a breath, my pulse thudding in my fingertips. "I need assistance."

A heavy silence followed — the kind of silence that happens when a machine is deciding whether or not to crush you.

"Keep the phone on your person," she finally said. "Someone will contact you within twenty-four hours."

The line went dead.

I stared at the blank screen. I had just reached out to Anthony Marconi, a criminal whose shadow stretched from the docks of Staten Island to the islands of Maine. He was a predator who viewed murder as a logistical necessity, a kingpin who didn't believe in forgiveness.

But he believed in debts. And he owed me a massive one.

6. AN EYE FOR AN EYE

I swept up the debris in my bedroom, desperate for a drink. Anything would do: wine, beer, brandy, or any variation.

As an alcoholic, I was constantly in a state of recovery. My most recent stumble was after Jyanette had broken up with me months earlier.

The day I got out of the hospital, I went immediately to a bar and began knocking back brandy. Fortunately, McGee found me and stopped me, but only after I was long past legal intoxication.

I could not allow myself to lose my edge or to give in to weakness, so for now, I focused on sweeping.

At 11:00 p.m., the flip phone in my pocket rang. I stepped outside through the exterior door in my sitting room and gently shut the door behind me. The night was cool, and I stood in the house's shadow, looking up at the full moon.

"Who's this?" a gravelly voice asked. I recognized him as one of Marconi's bodyguards, who was also his enforcer, nicknamed

Pete. He was not one of my biggest fans because at our first meeting at a motel in Maine, I'd bested him and his associate when they attempted to intimidate me.

"It's Leonard Wise," I said.

There was a grunt of recognition, then the phone went quiet.

After a moment, I heard a distinct voice. "Hello, Doc." I immediately recognized Anthony Marconi. "I understand you need help."

"Yes, if it's not too much to ask," I said, never sure how to conduct myself with the crime lord. At our first meeting, I came across as a smartass because I thought it might be a way to get past his defenses. That was before he had a Portland city detective shot down right in front of me.

Since then, I had rescued his niece from a drugged-out killer who wanted to use her as a sacrifice to empower a demon.

The usual stuff I dealt with.

"Tell me what you are looking for, and I will tell you if I can help. I should let you know, I am aware of the incident in your home tonight."

For a moment, this revelation stunned me. How did he know? It might have been on the news, but there was little information forthcoming. Bill clamped down on the officers so that nothing could leak to the press.

"How—?"

"Let's just say I keep tabs on you, Doc."

That was probably as much as he would ever tell me.

"They recently released a woman from Ancora Psychiatric Hospital, Emma Truesdale. She's trying to kill me and the people I care about."

"She's a threat to you?" he asked.

"She worked with a woman who controlled minds named Anika Vanya. She knows how to program people and send them out as weapons."

"Which explains the gunfire at your place of residence, I assume?" he stated, undisturbed.

Sometimes, it helps when you speak to someone who is used to dealing with violence.

"I need to track this woman down and stop her, permanently."

"I got that. You'll excuse me if I make a few observations?"

I frowned. "Um… sure."

"I know you're good at watching your back, but I would advise you to have protection."

The idea of having one of Marconi's looming bodyguards did not appeal to me. "I don't know—"

"Trust me, *I* know. You worked with Darren Ward to find my niece a few months back. Did the two of you get along?"

Darren Ward was a Staten Island private investigator whom Marconi had asked me to work with when his niece went missing. He was formerly in the NYPD, and at first had the opinion most cops have about psychics: that we were a waste of time. As the case progressed, I slowly convinced him I knew what I was doing, and we developed a respect for each other.

"Yes. Got off to a poor start, but in the end we worked well together."

"Good. He'll be at your house tomorrow, and he will accompany you wherever you go."

I bristled at this. "Mister Marconi, I don't think I—"

He cut me off. "Look, Doc, you just told me you are up against someone who can control other people. To be honest, if it was anyone but you, I would say you're paranoid. But I've seen what you can do. So, in your case, I believe you."

"But I don't—"

"Which means, you gotta have someone with you who knows how to handle an unexpected threat. If you want me to track down the broad, then you gotta have a bodyguard."

I could see it was pointless to argue with the man, and more than that, he was probably right. Despite my exploits with the Mountainview Police, I was an academic, a college professor. When I took on Vanya, she'd been able to put a drug in my soda that allowed Emma Truesdale to get into the dorm where I'd been living and program me. If Emma had access to Vanya's drugs and her techniques, a programmed minion could pull off the same trick, but not if I had a bodyguard.

Plus, Darren wasn't a bad guy, knew how to use a gun, and was quick and strong.

"I guess you're right."

"See, you ain't so dumb, Doc. Now, once I find this lady, do you want to know where she is, or do you want her taken out?"

The realization hit me with the force of a physical blow: asking this man to end a life was just another line item on a ledger. Marconi's offer to eliminate Emma was as casual as a man ordering a sandwich at a deli.

Ice-cold doubt flooded my veins.

"Doc," Marconi's voice crackled through the receiver, sharp and impatient. "It's a simple question."

"I—I—" The words caught in my dry throat, then the dam burst. A raw, jagged rage tore out of me, the ferocity of it shaking my own ribs. "My girlfriend was pregnant! That bitch killed my child!"

Marconi didn't flinch. There was no intake of breath, no momentary lapse in his predatory calm.

"I see," he said, his voice dropping into a register of grim professional courtesy. "I'm sorry for your loss, Doc. Consider the situation handled. Darren will be there at eight a.m."

The line clicked shut.

I stood out in the open air, shaking so hard I could barely grip the phone. Tears burned tracks down my face, and a primal urge to smash something — to break the world the way it had broken me — surged in my chest.

Where was my compass? My sense of gravity? I looked at the woman I loved and vowed I would kill Emma. Now, I'd outsourced the job to a professional executioner.

I stared at my reflection in the dark glass of my sitting-room window, hardly recognizing the man looking back. Was this the only way to neutralize a shark like Emma Truesdale? Or had I finally stepped off the edge, sliding down a slope so slick that there was no difference between her soul and mine?

To say I slept fitfully would be an understatement, and hardly surprising. I kept dozing off, then the image of Jyanette with the shotgun would appear. There was that loud, world-ending explosion, which forced me awake in the darkness of my bedroom.

I finally got out of bed at 7:00, after the memory of Jyanette in the hospital bed appeared in my dream. *"I want you to kill her. No trial, no mercy, nothing. You kill her. For me."*

I showered and dressed. Mrs. Higgins was sweeping up remnants of destroyed plaster and woodwork in the hall outside my sitting room. She was using a broom and a dustpan, and there was an industrial-size trash bag sitting on the floor for her to deposit the detritus.

"Oh, yer up then, Doctor," she said. "I can run the vacuum cleaner now."

"How can I help?"

She exhaled in exasperation. "If you could go through the china cabinet and see what we can save. I don't have the heart for it."

"You collected that china for years," I murmured, and reached out to touch her arm. "I'm so sorry, Mrs. Higgins."

She looked at me. "Yerself and Jyanette lost more than a few *chotchkes*."

I pulled back and couldn't fight the smile. "*Chotchkes?* Mrs. Higgins, since when do you know Yiddish?"

She shrugged. "Yer mother and I talk."

"I guess I should call them, let them know I'm all right," I sighed.

"I talked to yer mother last night," she explained as she dumped a dustpan of debris into the nearby trash bag. "But it wouldn't hurt for you to call her occasionally."

"I see she has been training you in Guilt 101 as well."

She raised her chin. "Only when necessary."

"Okay, I'll call, I'll call," I replied and headed down the hall. Normally, I'd be concerned that my mother and Mrs. Higgins were holding secret planning sessions without my knowledge, but I honestly had no desire to deal with my parents today. They were good, well-meaning people, and I loved them. But it was hard to explain that the woman I adored tried to shoot me and that I had forgiven her because it was someone else's fault.

The mental gymnastics were too much for me, and I was living it.

I stopped by the kitchen door and called back to Mrs. Higgins. "Is it all right to have a guest for the next few days?"

"Who?" she shouted.

"Darren Ward. He's a private eye, and he's going to be my bodyguard."

She went back to sweeping. "That's an excellent idea, Doctor. Can ye afford him?"

I wanted to say that I wasn't paying him myself, but then I would feel obligated to explain further, and Mrs. Higgins had a way of asking probing questions I didn't want to answer.

Instead, I just hollered back, "He'll be here at 8:00."

I went into the kitchen for coffee. Once the cup was in my hand, I pushed open the damaged door into the dining room.

The remnants of our attempt at a dinner party were before me. The overturned table lay against the shattered front of the china cabinet. Smashed dishes lay about, both on the floor and in the cabinet, with broken glass everywhere. We were lucky the knocked-over candle hadn't started a fire.

Or that neither of us got shot in the head.

I saw the vase on the ground, smashed, and the roses lay on the floor. The water had dried up. There were a few drops of blood on one flower, as in my vision at GSU, and the struggle trampled the other flowers flat.

I picked them up and threw them away in the kitchen.

I checked the table and tried to stand it up, to no avail. I had pushed it over in an adrenaline-fueled moment, with my life in danger, and with the power of my good leg. Setting it aright was another matter altogether.

I looked at the spot where I had been sitting. The chair was missing a chunk of the top rail where a bullet had obliterated it.

If I had moved a little slower...

Since I couldn't begin cleaning up the dining room until I had help, I pulled out my smartphone and hit the button for my mother.

My parents still had a home phone, and my mother avoided a cellular phone, although she understood how useful they could be.

She picked up on the second ring.

"Hello?"

"Mom, it's Len."

There was an exhale on the other end of the phone, as if she'd been holding her breath since my last phone call.

"Nice of you to call your mother. If it weren't for Margery, you could be dead, and I wouldn't know, *keinehora*."

After mentioning death, my mother had used a Yiddish phrase to ward off the Evil Eye. I often would kid her about it, but with the people I was facing, I took all the help I could get.

"Mom," I replied, trying to stay patient. "It's been a rough night. I'm fine, but there are bad people after me."

"Margery said something about your girlfriend shooting at you. Have you gotten yourself into an abusive relationship? I told you, settle down with a nice Jewish girl—"

I felt a headache starting. "Not now, Mama. I just wanted you and Pop to be careful. These bad people are going after people I know, so I want you to be on your guard."

"Your brother and sister never have things like this happen."

"Tom is a magician—"

"Who is dating a Jewish girl… your old girlfriend," she said to make a point.

"As you mention every time I call," I said, fighting now to keep my anger in check. My twin brother, Thomas, was a successful Las Vegas performer. Last Thanksgiving, he'd started dating an old girlfriend I knew in high school, Julia Tannenbaum. She had moved out to Vegas, and from what I knew, they were now living together. This was the last thing I needed today.

"And Rayna is a homemaker and mother," I said, familiar with the litany. "I work with the police, and sometimes I anger bad guys."

"If you'd become a surgeon, like your father, none of this would have ever happened—"

There was a knock at the front door. I thanked my lucky stars that I now had a way out of this conversation.

"Mama, it's the door. I have to go," I said. "Please be careful, maybe go out of town for a few days."

"Very well," she huffed. "You know I love you, Lenny."

"I know, and I love you too, Mom. I promise I'll call when this is all over."

I walked down the hall and into the vestibule. I put the phone away and opened the door to Darren Ward.

He was at least six feet tall and solid, not bulky, but I knew he could handle himself. Dressed in a gray suit, but no tie, his short blond hair was white at the temples. I glanced past him to see a small foreign car in the driveway. It was a white hatchback and so nondescript that I realized it was the perfect car for a PI.

"Thanks for coming out, Darren," I told him. "I appreciate it."

He came through the door and held out his hand for me to shake. I moved my cane to my left hand to comply, and as he stepped into the hall, his eyes roved around the space, taking in data. "Heard you have a problem. I have to tell you, one look and I can see that."

"Bullet holes in the woodwork?" I asked.

"The smell of nitroglycerin, sawdust, and graphite still in the air."

I stared at him blankly.

"Gunpowder, Len. Who did this?"

"My girlfriend."

"Remind me not to piss her off."

"You want coffee?" I offered.

"That'd be good. It would give me a chance to look around, get to know the place, find the weak spots."

We stepped into the hall just as Mrs. Higgins came up with a bag of rubbish.

Ward bowed his head and said, "Ma'am."

"Ooh halloo, I'm Mrs. Higgins. Ye must be Mister Ward. I understand ye'll be staying with us for a few days."

"If that's all right with you, ma'am. I have a bag in my car."

"We have plenty of room. It would be nice to have a bit o' protection after all this."

"I'll do my best, ma'am."

All three of us went into the kitchen, and I got a mug for Darren. "How do you take it?"

"Black is fine."

I handed him the mug. "Could I ask you to help me lift a table back into its correct place?"

"Only if you give me the rundown of what happened here and tell me what I'm protecting you from."

We went through the other swinging door, and Darren looked at the damage and the hole where the back of my chair had been. "Your girlfriend, huh?"

"She literally wasn't herself."

Together we lifted the table back onto its twin pedestals, while I went through the story of how I came to confront Anika Vanya, my meeting with the Stollers, and my investigation into the death of their son, Harold.

As I spoke, I got the broom and dustpan from Mrs. Higgins and swept up the debris while she used the vacuum cleaner down the hall.

Darren just observed and listened to my story.

By the time I had finished getting the broken glass and damaged crockery out of the china cabinet and brought the rest into the kitchen to load into the dishwasher, I had gone through the entire story.

I felt tired from recounting the tale, but Darren seemed to absorb it all like a sponge.

"What do you have for the rest of the day?" he asked.

"I have a meeting with Lieutenant McGee at Mountainview Police, then at 1:00, I teach a class at GSU. After that, I am visiting my girlfriend in the hospital."

"The one who tried to shoot you?"

"None other."

"Good thing I'm going with you," he stated plainly as he finished his coffee.

"I don't know if you're allowed in the police station."

"Not for the briefing. You might be a civilian consultant, but I am not cleared to hear anything they might tell you. I'll wait in the lobby."

"Or you could stay here."

He didn't blink. "I'm your shadow, Len. Get used to the dark."

I didn't argue. I couldn't. He was right, and the weight of that realization settled into my gut like lead.

For the first time in my life, I didn't just feel threatened — I felt hunted. As I looked at the man sworn to protect me, I knew the truth: I was walking into the most dangerous hours of my life, and a shadow was the only thing I had left to lean on.

7. ILL WILL

"And that's everything we have on the current whereabouts of Emma Truesdale," Bill concluded.

We were in the big conference room at the Mountainview Police Department. It was a plain, white room with industrial carpeting and a long table that could seat ten. They previously had a door that opened directly to the lobby, but they removed it during security upgrades following an attack on the building.

Bill had just finished recounting all the data they'd been able to track down on the Ohio killing. He had illustrated the driving route that they believed Emma Truesdale had used to get there from New Jersey. On a map he projected on the screen at one end of the room, it showed the place where Emma had abducted Aubrey and the location where a passerby had discovered her body.

I arrived about 10:25 a.m. and, to my surprise, Gabe Petrie walked in at 10:30. I knew Bill had put a call in to him, but I didn't know he would get involved this quickly. He's about five feet eight with a receding hairline, with an impressive widow's peak. He was a powerfully built man, and although we had butted heads in the past, he was good at his job and committed to the FBI.

We also had McGee's aide-de-camp, Officer Ben Galland. He was a clean-cut officer with movie-star looks, a firm jaw, and his blond hair was in a short crew cut. Detective Sergeant Tice filled out our little group. He was also an excellent choice, as he could disseminate any necessary information to the other detectives, as well as the uniformed officers.

Gabe stood and cleared his throat as McGee sat. "I'm only allowed to share certain details, but I can tell you this: they abducted Aubrey Andrews from a jogging path she went to daily, which suggests she was being observed by someone who knew her habits."

"So Emma had a confederate in the area or sent an asset ahead of time to do the legwork," McGee theorized.

Gabe nodded. "Yes. From the preliminary blood and tox screening, they took Aubrey down with a dart using a powerful animal tranquilizer."

"Jeez," I hissed.

Gabe went on. "An FBI team examined the site of her abduction after her disappearance, and from footprints and evidence, they reported three people loaded her onto a van. We believe a fourth person was driving the vehicle, possibly Emma Truesdale herself."

"Have you located this van?" Tice put in. "Maybe caught video of it near the scene?"

"We have not," Gabe responded. "Eliminating rental vans local to the Columbus, Ohio area, we are working from the theory they had driven the van she used from New Jersey."

"What kind of vehicle was Truesdale in when she left Ancora?" McGee asked.

Gabe nodded. "We've collected video footage at Ancora, but we have neither identified her driver nor the vehicle. It was a nondescript white hatchback."

"How did they get her up on that billboard?" Tice wondered.

Gabe shook his head. "Well, there's no video surveillance of that area, which may be why they chose it. That, and the obvious symbolism. What we know is that they deactivated the lights on that billboard that night. They kept Aubrey drugged and unconscious with the same animal tranquilizer. The team carried her up and nailed her up there about midnight. She bled out by morning." He paused before he added, "I would like to believe she never regained consciousness."

I clamped my teeth together to control my outrage. I hoped she hadn't woken up either. It was a terrible way to die. I still remembered the bubbly young lady, so full of excitement about life. Did she even know why they tortured her to death and by whom?

And her crime? She shot a psychopath who lunged at her and would've killed her. Anika Vanya had reached beyond the grave to continue to destroy lives.

Gabe sat down and looked at me. "Are you going to explain what happened at your house last night?"

I took my cue and stood. "Assistant District Attorney Jyanette Emery had sought therapy from Doctor Anika Vanya after she divorced her husband. I believe the doctor programmed her. Vanya had used her when she attempted to eliminate me in the past."

Gabe interrupted. "I think we all read the file, Doctor."

"I wanted to make sure everyone was aware of the facts. Since Vanya was dead and Truesdale incarcerated, Ms. Emery saw no reason to be deprogrammed."

"We now know that was a mistake," Bill added.

"Ms. Emery and I were dating, but you may not know that we had broken up in June," I announced, and then pushed through the next part. "Not everyone in this room is aware that Ms. Emery was pregnant."

All heads snapped up to gaze at me.

"Through some kind of mental program instigated by Emma Truesdale, Ms. Emery believed that I and my landlady were attempting to steal the child from her. I do not know the intricacies of this false narrative, but she... damaged herself, and then came to my house to shoot me with her legal concealed-carry weapon and a shotgun."

"Is she going to be okay?" Tice asked, and there was genuine concern in his voice.

I couldn't meet anyone's eyes. "She lost the baby and is in serious but stable condition."

I sat down and looked at my hands. I felt embarrassed that I had to reveal so much. People who are victims of crimes have to go over private details about themselves, leaving them feeling exposed.

It explains why so many crimes go unreported.

McGee took charge again. "We tracked the serial number of the shotgun. A man named Martin Hodges purchased it legally in Pennsylvania."

Galland touched a key on the laptop, and the image of a gray-haired man with a mustache appeared on the screen. He was Caucasian and looked like the sort you would meet at a neighborhood cookout.

Bill went on. "So far, we haven't been able to get in touch with him. I spoke this morning to his employer at Endress Auto Supply, where he is a sales associate. His employer, Mister Endress, told me they haven't seen Hodges all week. No phone call, no explanation."

Galland raised his hand to draw attention. "Since this case broke yesterday, I have recovered our clone of the hard drive taken from Dr. Vanya's office. From her office records, I can tell you that Mister Hodges was formerly a resident of New Jersey and was a patient of Vanya's for six months about four years ago."

Gabe huffed. "Looks like we have one of the team Truesdale is using."

I interjected. "I spoke with my TA, Teddy Santos, yesterday about the theory that Vanya left some kind of online database with the names of programmed people and the codes to activate them. This way, she or Truesdale could access them from any location. Galland, have you been able to look into that?"

Galland flushed a bit at my mention of Teddy, then he frowned. "No one brought it to me, but it is a logical idea. It could explain how Truesdale picked her team and gave them assignments so they would be where she needed them to be ahead of time."

Tice frowned. "If it's an online database, how can you trace it? It won't be on the hard drive you have."

Gabe smiled. "If we access her web history, it should point you in the right direction. If she was compiling a database, that would require frequent visits."

Heads nodded all around the room.

Gabe went on. "We have had agents visit Ancora, and we have taken Doctor Harold Veller into protective custody. We also have a team working on the computer in his office, but it appears the good doctor erased the hard drive immediately after he released Truesdale."

"Under orders from Emma, no doubt," I countered.

"He has no memory of doing it," Gabe confirmed. "But our guys are working to restore the data, and maybe we have a few other tricks to see about the browser history. I'll tell the technicians to focus on looking for that database."

McGee turned to Galland. "We also need the names of any patients that went to Vanya over the last five years, and as much contact information as possible."

"I am currently compiling that, sir," Galland told him. "I'll email Agent Petrie and Sergeant Tice as soon as I finish."

"That'll help," Tice grumbled. "But how do we cover them all?"

"We don't," McGee ordered. "We locate them. If they are unavailable, they might be part of Truesdale's team. Galland, keep an eye out for anyone in law enforcement or that has a military background. They would be the most dangerous to us, and the most useful to her."

Gabe considered this. "Good! Now, after this meeting, I want to organize an FBI team to work on a plan to go after her."

"Well, that's—" Bill began.

"We don't need to," I interrupted, and all eyes turned to me. "She is coming to *us*. Bill and I are the ones she wants — me most of all."

Everyone around the table was silent, as they knew it was true.

As my class ended and my students filed out, their attention now shifting to their smartphones instead of me, Darren stood up from his perch in the last row of the room.

My classroom in Williams Hall was large because of the interest in parapsychology. It was a "stadium-style" facility, where I was at the lowest point, with a large wooden desk in the center where I would lecture. There was an interactive "smart board" behind me, with a keyboard and mouse at the desk. The students' seats rose upward, giving me an easy view of the young people in my room, not that they made eye contact with me, as most had laptops or tablets in front of them to take notes.

"Interesting lecture," Darren said as he climbed down the last step. "I wasn't aware that the Spiritualist Movement was as big as it had been."

I nodded. "Especially in the 1890s when it was at its zenith. It was a worldwide sensation in the day and filled with charlatans. Even so, it helped create many of the controls and technology we use to research phenomena today."

We wandered out of the room and into the parking lot where my van waited. It was another glorious fall day, as if nature were trying to make up for all the darkness I faced.

We continued to discuss the trappings of the spiritualists as we made the short drive to Mountainside Medical Center.

"Maybe you should stay in the waiting room," I told Darren.

"I'm going to be stationed right outside the door of the room," he said.

"But—"

"She is the woman who tried to kill you."

I exhaled with annoyance. He was correct; she attempted to murder me, but it was still Jyanette.

We headed into the hospital, received our visitor passes, and walked down the hall to Jyanette's room.

At the doorway stood an African-American uniformed officer. She was about five feet tall and sturdy, and I knew that most of her weight was pure muscle. Tylissa Booker had dreadlocks that were arranged behind her head, tucked beneath her hat.

"Tylissa, what are you doing here?"

"Hey, Len!" she said, delighted to see me. "We're monitoring Ms. Emery to make sure no one gets to her. They chose me because I got deprogrammed by Doc Yearling last year."

"Is this round-the-clock?" I asked.

"Sure is. My relief is coming in at midnight. How are you holding up?"

I inclined my head towards Darren. "I've got my protection."

Tylissa nodded in approval, with maybe a brief glint in her eye. "I see you do."

Darren smiled and held out his hand. "Darren Ward."

"Sorry, where are my manners? Darren, this is Tylissa Booker, Officer Booker."

They were still shaking hands. "It's a pleasure," he said with an intense look at Tylissa.

Tylissa eyed him up and down and purred, "It could be."

These two seemed more interested in each other than me, so I went into the room and sat in the chair next to Jyanette as Tylissa and Darren murmured to each other in the hall.

Jyanette's color was still off, and she looked drained, but I got a wan smile when she saw me.

"How are you feeling?" I asked.

"Weak," she said, and nodded her head at the door. "Who's the muscle?"

"Darren Ward," I told her.

"The PI?"

"He's my bodyguard," I confessed.

She made a sound of derision. "He didn't help much when you got beaten up in Staten Island."

"He wasn't there when I went up against that cult leader. If he had been, I might've come out less damaged."

Jyanette glanced over at him. "How can you afford him?"

"Someone else is paying for him."

"Marconi?" she gasped.

"I needed some help. He owed me a favor."

"Len, you told me he's a criminal."

I lowered my voice. "I would bargain with the devil himself if he could keep you safe."

Her mouth was tense, but she understood.

"You're not looking at your phone, are you?" I asked.

"Can't. The police took it as evidence. I miss it."

"You'll survive. You know I have an idea."

"Do tell?"

"You could stay with us while you recover. We have plenty of room, and Darren would be there to turn back any invaders."

"Would it be in your room?" she asked, her eyebrows raised.

"I don't think you're up for that," I smiled.

She sighed. "I'm not. They had to put stitches up inside me."

"Yeow."

"I agree. I just think that I can't do stairs."

I nodded. "You can take my bed and I'll sleep upstairs."

"You aren't much for stairs either, Len," she reminded me, with a glance at my paralyzed right leg.

"I can do them. It just takes longer." I reached into my pocket. "I brought you a little something."

"What is it?" She frowned. I pulled the jewelry box from my pocket, and a dark expression appeared on her face. "That's not —"

I smiled. "Yes, it is." I opened the box, and the ring with its tiny diamond sparkled up at her. "Jyanette Emery, will you—"

"Don't say it," she gasped as a flood of tears fell down her cheeks. "Please, don't say it."

Confused, I shut the box and put it away. "I thought that's what you wanted?"

"What do you mean?" she croaked, eyes still wet.

"When you agreed to come to dinner, you told me you wanted to marry me."

She looked at me, afraid. "Len, I don't remember any of that. That was after someone else took control."

I grimaced. Of course, that was the case. I had forgotten and just wanted to make Jyanette happy.

"Sorry," I muttered. "I should have figured that out."

"It's not something I can talk about right now, Len."

"Sorry," I murmured again. "You could still stay with us."

"They won't release me for days, and my parents are coming up tomorrow. They're going to stay at my place and help me with household tasks." She paused for a moment before speaking again. "How is Mrs. Higgins' house?"

"Shot up. Fortunately, it's mostly cosmetic damage. Mrs. Higgins lost a lot of china."

"I'll never be able to show my face to Margery ever again," Jyanette bemoaned.

"She's just glad you'll be all right."

"I spoke to the doctor," she murmured in a tiny voice. "He thinks I won't be able to have children after this."

I nodded. There was truly nothing I could say.

"I'm tired, Len. Let me sleep," she said after we had been silent for a long while.

"One thing hasn't changed, Jyanette. I still love you," I whispered.

"I know," she replied. "Thank you."

I went out in a daze, and Darren appeared at my side with a hasty goodbye to Tylissa. I trudged down the hall toward the parking lot.

I know little about women, I confess, but when you tell your lady, "I love you" and she answers, "I know," you're not in a good place.

Darren and I got back into the van, and I drove off, headed for the house. As I drove, I heard the chime of a text on my phone but I ignored it. Once we pulled into the driveway, both Darren and I exited the vehicle. He headed to his car to get his overnight bag, and I grabbed my leather messenger bag with my laptop and some papers I had to grade.

I checked my phone, and there was indeed a text waiting, it read:

Len, It's Kate

Something is wrong.

I frowned when I read this. It was a pretty strange and cryptic message and very similar to the odd email she had sent. I immediately phoned the number, and it picked up on the first ring.

"Yearling."

"Kate, it's Len."

There was a pause. "To what do I owe this call?"

"I thought it was the best response to your text."

"What text?"

I spoke it aloud to her, hoping it jogged her memory.

"Len, I didn't send you that text."

"You're kidding," I said.

"No, I didn't, and I don't have a record of it on my phone."

"Well, it showed up on my phone," I said, curious at this response. "That's why I'm calling."

"I have no explanation, Len," Kate said, and gave a sigh, changing the subject. "How are you doing? Gabe told me what happened at your house."

"It's been a tough day. Keep on your guard, Kate. Since you've deprogrammed people, you might be a target."

"I sincerely doubt that, Len. But I'll watch my back."

"Do that."

I ended the call, more confused than I was before I made it.

"You okay?" Darren asked, the weight of the duffel bag settling effortlessly over his broad shoulders.

"Fine," I lied, sliding the phone into my pocket.

We headed toward the front door, but my mind was stuck in a loop of the last ten minutes. Kate had emailed and sent the text with the same cryptic message. And then she claimed total amnesia.

The medical professional in me searched for an excuse — trauma, a glitch, a fugue state. But as someone who had survived Anika Vanya, I knew better. This wasn't a lapse in memory; it was a breach.

Something had burrowed its way into Kate's life and recovery, and I needed to find out just what was going on.

8. RETALIATION

"Mrs. Higgins, that meal was fantastic." Darren leaned back from the kitchen table with a contented sigh.

"I felt bad about offerin' ye leftovers, but since we din't eat the food last night, I thought it was a pity to let it go to waste."

"It was a triumph, Mrs. Higgins," I praised her. "You outdid yourself. I wish Jyanette had enjoyed this fine meal."

"How is the dear?" she asked.

"Better. Her parents are coming tomorrow."

"And she turned down Len's proposal," Darren added.

If looks could kill, the glance I gave Darren should have at least beheaded him. "Was that necessary?" I fumed.

"She did what?" Mrs. Higgins sputtered.

"We had crossed signals, Mrs. Higgins," I said. "Apparently, when Jyanette said 'yes' it was because they had programmed her to do so."

Mrs. Higgins looked at me with pity. "Oh, Doctor, that's just not fair."

My jaw tightened. "I know." Turning to Darren, I asked, "Why?"

Darren shook his head. "All of us need to know what is really going on. Look, Leonard, if you are going to get through this, you have to be honest about it. About all of it."

I wasn't happy, but he had a point.

I rose. "I have papers to grade, and I need to review my lesson plan for tomorrow."

Mrs. Higgins popped up as well. "I'll show Mister Ward where he'll be sleeping."

Darren was the only one who remained seated. "I think I should sleep on an air mattress in that office of yours, Len."

I frowned. "Is that necessary?"

"There's a separate entrance. Your adversary might know where you sleep. From a tactical point of view, if I were going to stage a hit, that would be the place I'd strike. It has quicker access to you, and help wouldn't be able to get there quickly."

I considered this. "I have a better idea. Why don't you sleep in my room, and I'll sleep upstairs?"

"Better," Darren agreed.

"The best option is that we all sleep upstairs and leave yer room empty," Mrs. Higgins put in.

Darren and I exchanged a look.

Mrs. Higgins went on. "It's the best defensive position, as any attacker would have to get up the stairs to get the doctor, and, Mister Ward, ye'll be nearby, but ye get to sleep in a bed."

Darren's lips jutted out in thought, and then he said, "I have to admit you're right, Mrs. Higgins."

"Let me get my papers," I said.

Darren was up and by my side. "What do you need to grade them?"

"Just my bag and my laptop."

"Good. I saw you put the bag down in the hallway. Get them and you can set up in the living room. I honestly don't want you alone at a separate end of the house. You're just too vulnerable."

I nodded. I guess I needed a "siege mentality" these days. After the destructive encounter with Jyanette, I had to let go of my comfortable belief that my extra senses would always protect me.

I believe psychic warnings come to me because the intention of a person who wants to do me harm creates mental energy. Since they direct this negative mental energy at me, my mind can tap into it, and I get a warning.

A perfect example was the flower box with the shotgun. They had activated Jyanette to attack, and it focused her mind on the flower box and the weapon inside. My mind interpreted this to warn me with a buzz when I picked up the flowers that I had bought.

I didn't get any other warning signs because, since Jyanette was not operating on her own thoughts but in a program, she didn't produce the mental energy that I could detect.

This was the problem with the hypnotized people that Emma Truesdale sent at me. The programming blocked me from being able to read them.

This put me at a tremendous disadvantage.

I grabbed my messenger bag, which had the papers and my laptop, and under Darren's watchful eye, I went to the living room.

The living room has all the original chestnut paneling and is directly in front of the entrance vestibule. It has a huge tiled fireplace and built-in bookcases of darkly stained wood. I sat on the sofa and pulled out the papers.

"I'm going to help Mrs. Higgins clean up," Darren reported.

"You don't have to do that," I told him.

"I want to. Do me a favor, try not to get killed for a few minutes." He grinned and headed back to the kitchen.

I looked at the papers in my hands. I was planning to grade them and get them out of the way, but I really didn't need to finish them until next week.

I put them aside and attempted something. Although I couldn't receive the mental intention of the programmed minions, Emma Truesdale's mind would focus on me, and maybe I could use that.

I couldn't actually reach directly into her mind unless we were facing each other, but perhaps in a deep meditation, I could get some kind of reading.

I closed my eyes and focused on my breath to bring my mind to a lower level.

In… out, in… out.

The aim was to let things come to me instead of attempting to force them. I envisioned Emma Truesdale from memory. I focused on the last time I had seen her, when she was in a cell, and she dropped all artifice. Her straight brunette hair that fell to her shoulders, her thin face was attractive, despite her pinched features.

Memories flowed through my mind: Emma in the holding cell. Emma at Harold Stoller's house, accusing me. She and Vanya in the basement of the abandoned slaughterhouse, pointing a gun at me with glee.

I relaxed, allowing the memories to flow through me without getting attached to a specific one. I just had to let the pictures flow through my brain.

There was darkness, and a light that was hazy and undefined. I relaxed and just tried to be open, with the images of Emma Truesdale as my touchstone.

All at once, my vision cleared. I was looking out the front of a vehicle through the windshield as it moved along. I appeared to be riding in the passenger seat, and there was someone else driving.

It appeared I was doing "remote viewing." That is the practice of seeing impressions from a distant target. I had studied the concept with my mentor, Doctor Fritz Kohl, and even done it in the past. But usually only with someone with a strong psychic ability. To pinpoint my specific target like this surprised me.

Since the eyes through which I observed the scene were looking directly ahead, I could not see the driver, but we were riding in silence. That made sense. If the others in the van were hypnotized drones, Emma would probably only speak as a command. Other than that, the obedient assistants remained silent until someone ordered them to respond.

"Do you think this is a good move?" I heard Emma say.

Since I was seeing from Emma's point of view, as best as I could tell, I assumed I was inside her head. Her voice sounded odd. It seemed to take place all around me, as opposed to hearing a person speak where the sound comes from a specific location.

The driver spoke in a gravelly voice. "It is necessary. We must keep him off-balance, distracted."

Emma's eye glanced over at the speaker, but I saw little. The road wasn't well lit, and the reflection from the headlights showed a female silhouette, but that was all.

Emma spoke. "It surprised me he survived the woman's attack."

The driver chuckled. "It pleased me they both survived. How else can we continue to inflict pain if they're dead?"

Emma looked straight ahead as the vehicle turned down a familiar cul-de-sac. I recognized the road, and I saw the van pull over to the curb two houses down from Mrs. Higgins' house.

The eyes shifted to a man in the back.

"Todd!" Emma barked.

A man leaned forward, dressed in black with a SWAT-style bulletproof vest and some black makeup smeared on his face to help cover his Caucasian features.

His eyes looked dead.

"Yes," the man responded.

"Do you remember what you needed to do?" Emma said.

"Do I?" he replied with absolutely no emotion.

The driver chortled. "You think you'd know how to give commands by now."

When I last encountered Emma, I had learned that when you dealt with a programmed person, you could not ask questions, as it required a conclusion and therefore independent thought. You always had to phrase things only as an order to be obeyed.

Emma's eyes stayed on the man, ignoring the driver. "I told you the mission. Tell me if you recall it."

"I recall my mission."

"Good. Tell me if you know the target and the goal."

"I know the target and the goal," he dutifully repeated.

"Excellent. Anyone who tries to stop you, remove them. You must complete your mission as ordered. Tell me if you understand."

"I understand."

"Good," Emma told him. "Deploy."

The side door of the van opened, and by the light from a nearby streetlamp, I saw the van was a big one with multiple seats. There were at least four other people in the vehicle, though I only got a glimpse of their silhouettes.

My attention went to the large rifle that the man picked up. It had a slim barrel with a large tube at the end, which could only be a silencer. On top of the rifle was an optical scope, and the lens reflected the streetlight with a green hue, suggesting that it was a night-vision scope and would allow him to see in the dark.

The man stepped out of the van, and the door slid shut.

Trying to stay calm, I fought to pull myself up out of the vision. I'd gone pretty deep, but by returning my attention to my breath, I concentrated on speeding up my respiration, which brought me quickly out of the trance the way my mentor had trained me.

I gasped as my eyes opened, leaving me a little light-headed, but I was back in the living room. I used my cane to push myself up, but my limbs felt heavy and clumsy, as if I'd just reentered my body and didn't know quite how to operate it. How long had I been meditating? I thought it had only been a few brief minutes.

I moved to the hall, walking with more assurance as I recovered from the mental journey. I pushed through the door into the kitchen.

There were Mrs. Higgins and Darren; she sat at the table and he stood. He was holding a cup and saucer, probably tea, and my landlady had a small cordial glass in front of her filled with port. She would call it "a wee dram" when she indulged.

"Trouble," I croaked.

Darren put the cup down on the table and reached into his sports coat to extract a rather impressive handgun. "What is it?"

"Sniper," I explained. "On his way…"

"How do you know…" Darren began, then with a glance at Mrs. Higgins, he sighed. "Never mind. From where and how soon?"

I cleared my throat, feeling more like myself. "They dropped him off about three houses down. Big rifle with a silencer and a night-vision scope. He might also have a laser scope, I'm not sure."

Without hesitation, Darren moved to the light switch on the wall and shut off the lights. This plunged the kitchen into darkness.

"You two stay here. I'll turn off the lights in the house."

"I might have a light on in my office," I hissed.

"Good, maybe that will attract him, give him a target that isn't us." Darren crouched and moved through the door into the hall. Immediately, the light coming in under the door went out.

My eyes adjusted slowly in the dark kitchen. I moved to the table and slid into a seat. Mrs. Higgins reached over and took my hand.

"It'll be all right, Doctor," she said quietly.

I looked at the sweet lady who let me share her home and murmured, "I'm just worried about putting you in danger, Mrs. Higgins."

"This is evil, pure and simple, and there was naught ye could do about it."

I shook my head. "But this sniper, he's just some guy, probably a veteran. Yet, he might kill us, and what can we do? To stop him, we'd have to kill him."

Her eyebrows went up. "Might be a good idea to carry that Taser thing with ye."

I shrugged. "Can't do much about that now. I left it in my office."

The door swung open, and Darren came back into the kitchen in a low crouch. "Lights are out except in the office."

"What should we do?" I asked.

He moved to the table to speak in soft tones. "We did the most important thing. Snipers need light and space. He's outside, and the house is dark. You say he has a night-vision scope? Do you know if he has thermal imaging or not?"

"I don't know," I conceded. "I only saw the rifle, and there was a scope with another contraption on top."

"That's not much help," Darren complained.

"Sorry, I'm a parapsychologist! I'm not trained in ballistics."

"Okay, we can't know where he is until he fires. You said he has a silencer? That makes finding him more difficult."

"We should call the police," Mrs. Higgins stated.

"I agree," I replied. "But she ordered this guy to shoot anyone who tries to stop him."

Darren let out his breath in a hiss. "This could get very messy, quickly. We really need the police."

I realized he was right, pulled my phone out of my pocket, and hit the button to call Bill.

"McGee."

"Bill, I have a situation," I whispered.

"Now what?"

"A sniper is outside my house."

I heard Bill inhale in shock. "Is he shooting at you?"

"Not yet. But I'm worried. They ordered him to eliminate anyone who tries to stop him."

"I see. May I ask how you found this out?"

"I spent a few minutes inside Emma Truesdale's head."

There was a pause. "I didn't know you could do that."

"Normally, I can't, but she's fixated on me, and I could tap into that. Any suggestions as to the best course of action?"

"Well, if we make a big show, come there with, say, three police cars with lights and sirens, it could scare him off."

I covered the phone with my hand. "Bill wants to come in with lights and sirens, scare him off."

"Not a bad plan," Darren agreed. "But if he's programmed like you said, he'll be back as soon as the light show is over. There are a lot of places to hide in this neighborhood for a pro."

I went back to Bill. "Does the FBI team have a counter sniper?"

Bill snorted. "Sure, I'll just call him on speed dial."

Darren spoke up. "Maybe all we can do is scare him away. To track down a sniper, you need to do three things: triangulate, observe, and neutralize. Otherwise, the best way is to lay down smoke to obscure his target."

"Smoke," I repeated as an idea formed. I returned to the phone. "Bill, could you send in a team, quietly?"

"I suppose. How will that help?"

"Can they hit the property with tear gas?" I suggested.

Bill considered this. "I don't see how that's better than coming in with lights and sirens. It would chase away the sniper."

"Normally," I confirmed. "But they programmed this guy to kill us, and anyone that gets in his way. If you hit the property with tear gas, it will force him to attack the house."

Darren nodded. "That might flush him out, force him to reveal himself."

I went on, "Or the gas might shock him out of his programming. Either way, it increases our odds of stopping him, hopefully without lethal force."

Darren grunted in disapproval. "I'd rather use deadly force than get shot."

Bill considered this. "It might work. I'm sure the neighborhood won't be pleased. But it is night, so hopefully anyone downwind will have their pets indoors."

"Then please do it," I implored.

"On it," Bill said, and hung up the phone.

At that moment, there was the sound of glass breaking in the hall, as a bullet smashed into the wood of the kitchen door that faced that window. The door swung open until the spring pulled it back to center.

It was strange. There was only the sound of the breaking glass and the *thwack* of the bullet as it hit the door.

Darren hit the floor, and Mrs. Higgins let out a quick, "Oh!"

I was too busy just trying to breathe.

"Everyone all right?" Darren snapped.

"Yes," I replied and looked up at the chunk missing from the door. "What the hell kind of round is this guy using?"

"Something big," Darren answered.

"How did he find us in the dark house?" Mrs. Higgins asked.

Darren moved to the cabinets for protection, his pistol pointed at the ceiling. "If he's got thermal imaging, he probably saw us as hot spots around the door."

"Or he has X-ray vision," I offered.

"How long until the cops get here?" Darren grunted.

"I don't know... minutes," I said as I moved from the table and stood against the wall, as did Mrs. Higgins. The three of us stood with our backs to the wall, trying to be as small a target as possible.

Foreboding filled the silence, and there was a heaviness in the air as we waited.

My phone rang, inciting another bullet to strike the kitchen door and knock another hole in it, as the round struck the far wall.

"Yes," I hissed.

It was Bill. "The police are in place. They're up the hill from you and are staying behind the police cars for protection."

"Good plan," I whispered.

"I also got the New Jersey State Police to send a SWAT team, and they should be there in a few minutes. We'll try to move in with gas masks."

"Got it."

"You guys stay in the house so you don't get shot."

"I like that idea," I said, and shut down the phone. I flipped the switch so that the phone would only vibrate instead of ring.

In the distance were several quiet thumps, and even in the house, we could hear the hiss of the gas as the canisters hit the ground and released their contents.

There was another shot fired, quieted by the silencer so that it sounded like a baseball hitting a mitt.

"That's one hell of a suppressor he has," whispered Darren. "Something that can shoot that big a round, and the sound gets taken down so much."

"He didn't shoot that round at us," I worried. "Do you think he's firing at the cops?"

"Could be. But if he gets a whiff of that gas, he won't be firing at anyone."

With his gun held high, Darren ducked through the kitchen door into the dining room. I followed on his heels, crouching as low as I could with my bad leg.

"Where are you going?" I whispered.

"I want to keep my eye on the front door. If he tries to break in, I want us to have the upper hand."

There are only a few windows in the long hall that face the main road in the house's front. One window was across from the kitchen door, and he had already smashed the lower pane when the two large-caliber bullets hit it.

As Darren crouched to slip past the second window, the world exploded.

The man leapt through the window, and didn't just break the glass; he used his body as a kinetic projectile, slamming through the heavy wooden frame. The wall seemed to disintegrate, spraying jagged shards of glass and splinters of aged oak across the room like shrapnel. It was a deafening noise — a thunderclap of structural failure that left my ears ringing and my lungs seizing.

In the intruder's wake, a thick haze of gas flooded the space, swirling through the jagged hole in the wall.

Time slowed to a nauseating crawl. My brain, stuck in a survival loop, fixated on the most absurd details. The man was gaunt, his face a landscape of sharp angles smeared with streaks of tactical greasepaint. His eyes were a horrific contrast — swollen and bloodshot, yet burning with the terrifying, singular focus of a zealot.

He landed in a controlled roll, the heavy tactical rifle already angled across his chest. He had used the weapon as a battering ram to lead his entry, and even before his boots found purchase on the hardwood, he was already pivoting, bringing the muzzle up to find a target.

Darren was a blur of pure reflex.

Before the assailant could level the muzzle, Darren's hand clamped onto the rifle's barrel, wrenching it upward. In the same heartbeat, he pressed his own pistol against the man's chest and squeezed the trigger. The gunshot was a physical force in the narrow hallway, a bone-shaking *crack*.

Darren had aimed for the center of the combat vest. I knew that pain — I'd taken two rounds to the Kevlar myself. It doesn't just stop you; it feels like being hit by a swinging sledgehammer. It crushes the breath out of your lungs and turns your ribs into a cage of agony.

The impact did its job. Falling back, the intruder buckled, his grip failing just enough for Darren to rip the heavy rifle away. The sudden weight transfer sent Darren staggering back, hitting the floor on one knee as he struggled to manage the bulk of two weapons.

The man in black, however, did not share our limitations. Despite the shock to his heart and lungs, he didn't stay down.

In a fluid, sickeningly fast motion, he reached for his calf, unsheathing a combat knife that caught the dim light. It was a brutal piece of steel — heavy, matte black, with a serrated edge designed to tear through more than just fabric. He gripped it upward, a killer's stance, ready to lunge it into Darren before he could find his feet.

By now, the gas was a choking wall, a chemical haze that turned the hall into a gray nightmare.

The "doctor" in me vanished. I stepped into the fog, shifting my weight and sliding the heavy metal cobra head of my cane into my left hand, gripping the shaft like a baseball bat with my right. As the assailant rose to finish Darren, I put every ounce of my desperation into a blind swing.

The metal top connected with the back of the man's head with a sickening, wet *thud*.

He slammed against the jagged remains of the window frame, the knife still white-knuckled in his grip. I didn't give him a second chance. I swung again, a precise, bone-cracking blow to his forearm. The knife skittered across the hardwood as the man finally crumpled into a heap.

Then the gas hit me. My vision went white, my throat constricting as the caustic chemicals turned every breath into a lungful of fire.

By now, the gas blinded me, and I was coughing from the irritating chemicals.

I could hear Darren cough out, "Is he down?"

I moved to our attacker, who lay still on the floor. "Yes," I croaked.

Darren moved away from the open hole that had been Mrs. Higgins' window as gas continued to seep through, and I backed away myself.

"We gotta move him, restrain him!" I shouted, tears in my eyes that made me squint. It was amazing how much my eyes hurt from just the small amount of gas that had leaked into the house.

Darren came through the fog sans rifle and put the pistol back into his shoulder holster. We both took an arm and dragged the man down the hall.

"Don't move, hands in the air," a muffled voice said from the open window, an automatic rifle pointed in my direction.

"Assailant down," I rasped, and raised my hands with my cane still in one hand. "I will open the door for your team." This short sentence made me fall into a coughing fit.

"Roger that," the man replied through his gas mask, and lowered the weapon from us.

Still coughing, I limped down the hall to get to the front door. As I pulled the door open, four men pushed past me and into the house. I fell back to avoid more of the tear gas getting into my lungs.

The last man who came through the door was taller than me by an inch and wore a suit jacket over his police vest.

It was Bill.

He shut the door and led me into the house, where we walked into the living room. That room wasn't near the broken window — either of them — and was still clear of gas.

He took off his mask. "Len, are you okay?"

I made a horrible nasal sound as I attempted to clear my throat. "Yes. Mrs. Higgins is in the kitchen, and Darren's in the hall."

"The gas is already dispersing," Bill told me and pulled something from his jacket pocket. It was a small pack of wipes, of all things. He offered me one. "Wipe your face with this; it will help."

We stepped into the hall, and Bill was right. The haze had faded, and the men were taking off their masks. I wiped my eyes carefully and could see that the team had the shooter on the floor, handcuffs affixed to his wrists.

They had also handcuffed Darren.

I spoke up. "Excuse me, the man not dressed for combat is my bodyguard."

With nothing more than a nod from Bill, a nearby officer released the shackles. Bill offered Darren a wipe. He took it and wiped his hands and face, with only a grunt in response.

A big man came up to me. He pulled aside the mask and in a large voice said, "How come I only hear your name when the shit hits the fan?"

I smiled as I recognized Claude Albertson. His red hair was graying to a light coppery color, but his red mustache was there in all its glory. He was the commander of a New Jersey State Police SWAT team and a formidable man.

His SWAT team had raided Anika Vanya's office a year earlier, and he had taken a bullet from Vanya's secretary, Amanda Prentiss. The same woman whose parents had started the lawsuit against GSU and me.

After the incident, he had returned to active duty, but our paths had not crossed until today.

"Good to see you, Commander," I said. Albertson was one of the highest grades in the SWAT ranks, that of Field Commander.

Albertson crossed his arms. "I've been talking to McGee ever since I heard about that poor girl in Ohio. Since this involved Vanya and her legacy, I asked to be his first call when anything went down."

Darren was wiping his face, and he bent over to pick up the large, threatening knife, which he offered to Albertson hilt first.

Albertson took it, frowning as he examined it. "This is not something just anyone would own."

Darren's face was stone, his eyes still red. "Ontario MK-Three Navy Knife. Usually only a Navy SEAL would carry a blade like that."

The officers had helped our attacker to his feet as consciousness returned to him. He glanced around the room, confused.

"Damn," Albertson grunted, handed Bill the knife, and stepped over to the man. "What's your name, soldier?"

"I-I'm not a soldier anymore," he stammered. "I'm retired. Sergeant Todd Masler, special forces, sir." He looked around the room again as best he could through his watery eyes. "Where the heck am I, sir?"

Albertson went on loudly. "You just attacked a house. You assaulted civilians!"

The man stiffened as the two officers held him. "No, sir! I wouldn't do that."

McGee stepped forward. "Masler, did you ever go see a therapist named Anika Vanya?"

Masler blinked at this, or it could have been the tear gas. "Yes, sir. About two years ago. My CO wanted me checked out to make sure my last tour of duty didn't mess with my head."

Bill went on. "What happened there?"

He shrugged. "She asked me some questions, and I filled out some forms."

As I watched the interaction, a part of me was saying: *Yes, and programmed you as a weapon, ready when needed.*

That's when the realization struck me: *This was too easy.*

I have learned to listen to that part of my mind.

"Bill," I called out and signaled him over.

Bill stepped away from our prisoner, and I moved with him near the outer door.

"Something's wrong with this," I whispered.

He frowned. "Bad guy trying to kill you? I agree."

"No, it's almost like they planned for him to be caught."

The frown deepened. "To what end, Len?"

"I don't know. To distract us, pull resources away from another place."

Bill shook his head, and I stared at him; the man who had stuck by me when Aubrey Andrews accused me of sexual assault. The man who fought Vanya every step of the way and ultimately helped defeat her.

It was suddenly clear to me. Bill was a person Vanya and Emma Truesdale had hated as much as she hated me.

"Bill," I gasped. "Your family!"

9. PAYBACK

When I told Bill my concern that he had left his family unprotected, he pulled his cell phone from his pocket.

I expected him to make a call; that's what I would do. But he didn't. He calmly typed a short sentence and sent the text. He then looked at me, and I was shocked that I saw fear in his eyes. "Can you come with me, Len? You and your friend?"

My vision was still blurry from exposure to the gas, but I nodded without hesitation.

Bill yelled over to Albertson. "Commander, can you finish up here and cover this location until we can get uniforms to take your place?"

"10-4, Lieutenant," Albertson joked, but then he caught the look in Bill's eye. "Everything all right?"

"Not sure. I have to check another location," Bill said. "Can you handle clean-up?"

"We can be mobile in five minutes or less, if you need us," Albertson offered.

Bill exhaled as if he'd been holding his breath. "Not sure. Please lock down this location, and get Mister Masler into protective custody, no phone, no visitors."

Albertson nodded. "I can do that, LT."

It was astounding to watch. One man was a local detective, and the other was a State Police SWAT team commander, but that didn't matter. They were both cops who respected and trusted each other to do the right thing.

The kitchen door opened, and two men aimed their weapons at a very surprised Mrs. Higgins. She held her hands up, and I called out, "That's Mrs. Higgins. It's her house."

They lowered the weapons, and Mrs. Higgins moved quickly through the crowd to reach me.

"Doctor," she fretted. "McGee has to get right home—"

"We know, Mrs. Higgins," I told her. "We're about to go."

She had a fierce look in her eyes. "Then get!"

I couldn't help but wonder how Mrs. Higgins had come to the same conclusion I did, but she does things occasionally that make my psychic abilities pale in comparison.

"Darren," I called, and the big man moved toward me. "We have to go."

He frowned. "Why?"

"This was a distraction," I said simply.

He didn't hesitate, but moved next to me. Darren, McGee, and I headed out the door to McGee's unmarked police car out on the street.

We were in Bill's police car with the sirens wailing and the lights flashing. I was in the front passenger seat, and Darren was in the back, behind the divider.

Minutes later, we were miles away as McGee came in "hot," as cops call it when they head for a location with lights and sirens going.

"What was that text you sent to Laura?" I said, referring to Bill's wife.

"Emergency code to get into the safe room," Bill explained.

I paused and considered this. "You have a safe room in your house?"

"Built it myself," Bill offered, his mouth a hard line.

"Really? Whatever for?"

Bill looked straight ahead as he drove. "For times like these."

It seemed like forever before we pulled in front of a house, a two-story structure built in the Colonial Revival style. There were street-facing windows, and the building was very rectangular. I had never been to Bill's house before.

It was kind of a shock. After all, we'd known each other for almost a year-and-a-half; we worked together; he was my friend, and he was my AA sponsor. Yet I had never met his wife, Laura, or his two boys, Elliot and Martin. I had seen photos of the boys a thousand times, but I had never been in the same room with them or met them face-to-face.

Fear rose in me that now I never would.

Bill and I got out of the car, and I opened the back door to let Darren out. We stood staring. The front door to the house was bent in and broken, as if someone had taken a battering ram to it.

Both Bill and Darren waved me back as they each pulled their weapons and moved forward cautiously.

"What do I do?" I asked.

"Read the freakin' vibrations," Darren whispered back.

I exhaled sharply, but moved behind the car. Darren had a point. I was pretty much useless in this case, and people had shot at me enough for one night. I observed the surroundings to look for the van I'd seen while I was inside Emma's head.

There was little traffic going by in the street, and I scanned the parked cars, but there wasn't any vehicle large enough to be the van.

For a moment, I wished I had a gun, but knowing my lack of expertise, I'd probably end up shooting myself.

I decided that when I got home, I would pull the small Taser Bolt from my desk and keep it on me from now on.

It was a few more minutes, and then Bill came out. He was carrying his younger boy, Marty, aged seven. Walking between him and Darren was Elliot, aged nine. The two men had put their weapons away and focused on the children.

"Where's Mommy?" Marty whined, his face against his father's shoulder.

"Somebody took her," Elliot explained, as if for the hundredth time.

"Guys," Bill spoke gently, "we have to go to police headquarters. I'm going to have to keep you there until I can get Auntie Maire up here to pick you up."

"I don' wanna stay at Auntie Maire's," Marty whined. "I want Mommy!"

He began to cry again.

"Don't be a baby. We gotta be strong," Elliot told his brother.

I thought they were both being amazing.

"Darren, Len, I need the kids up front with me. You guys get in the back."

We didn't argue. I opened the back door and Darren got in, and I followed.

Marty was still sniffling as Bill got on the radio and ordered a police car to the area, as well as asked the dispatcher to get a forensics team to his residence.

He pulled the car away from the curb and toward the center of town. "Elliot, tell me what happened, son."

"We were playing on the Xbox, last game before bed—"

"And I was winnin'," Marty added.

"Then, we heard this loud noise."

"Like a 'splosion," Marty sniffed.

"Yeah, like that. Mom comes in and says we gotta do a 9-1-1 the way we practiced. So, we head to the bookcase."

"Yeah," Marty mumbled, "with the secret room."

"We go in, and Mom tells us to hit the lever on the door like she showed us."

"It took both of us to do it," Marty said, and cried again. "But Mommy was outside."

"Did you see who came in?" Bill asked gently.

Elliot shook his head as Marty sobbed quietly.

Darren and I sat in the back seat. I hoped he didn't feel as useless as I did.

"How did you know?" Darren murmured to me. "Psychic flash?"

I sighed. "Plain old instinct. Taking down what's-his-name had been too easy. I think his 'mission' was to pull Bill from his house and keep all of us busy."

"While inflicting property damage?"

"I don't believe that shooting either Mrs. Higgins or me was part of the plan. That's why he missed us by such a wide margin."

Darren nodded. "You could be right. If he was being strategic, he would have moved to the back of the house. He could've seen us through the back windows much easier."

"Instead, he set his position in the front and shot blind from there." Darren looked forward as the streetlights flickered over his face. "My guess would be that he wanted to keep the fight out front."

We drove on in silence; the only sound was Marty's sobbing.

About an hour later, I was still at the Mountainview Police Department, sipping terrible coffee in the canteen with Darren across from me. The place was a flurry of activity, as apparently they had moved every cop to on-duty status and the place was operating under a siege mentality.

Who could blame them? The last time we fought Vanya, the building almost got blown up. Maybe Emma Truesdale wanted a second chance to do so.

I worried about what was being done to Laura. If Emma had a stash of Vanya's special drug cocktail, she could turn Bill's wife into a zombie, even as I sat there drinking coffee.

Why hadn't I thought of this sooner? Emma had sent Jyanette to kill me, so using the same technique to get Bill was obvious. Of course, from what I knew of Laura, she had never been to a therapist, so abduction was the only way to acquire her for programming.

Had they wanted the children as well, or were they only after the wife? If they had taken the children, it would have given them a stronger hand for blackmail.

Laura's fast thinking and the fact that Elliot and Marty were familiar with the safe room and knew how to secure it changed whatever the plan had been. Perhaps Laura was going for a weapon when they smashed in the door.

Bill stuck his head in the open doorway. "We're meeting in the conference room in ten minutes."

"I'll be there," I said.

"Good." McGee moved to my bodyguard. "Darren?"

The big man turned.

"We'd like you to be there, too," Bill stated.

He gazed at Bill. "Are you sure?"

Bill nodded. "We could use any extra hands we could get right now. You're pretty handy in a fight."

"It would be an honor."

With that, Bill slipped away, and Darren turned back to the table to stare at his cup.

"He's right, you know," I said as I took another sip. "You were brilliant tonight."

"You're not bad yourself, Doc. Nice moves with your cane."

After a few minutes, our cups were empty. We made our way to the conference room, which was only one door away. The room was pretty full, and I saw Albertson was there, as well as Gabe Petrie and most of the MPD officers. It surprised me to see Kate Yearling was there as well. She looked gaunt and wore a dark-gray pantsuit that looked too big on her. She wore a red hair wig. If I didn't know better, I might not have realized that it was not her hair.

I slipped in and went to Bill. "Where are the boys?"

"My sister came from Clinton and picked them up. Marty wouldn't let me or his brother out of his sight. He didn't want to be alone."

"I can understand that," I sighed.

"They'll stay with my sister until we have this handled."

I nodded and moved away as the room continued to fill. I walked over to Kate and leaned in to talk to her. She looked up from a pad where she was scratching notes.

"How are you doing?" I asked.

"Tired, but I might be some help, so here I am."

"It's good to see you." I took her hand and gave it a quick squeeze, which elicited a smile from her.

I faded to the back wall next to Darren, using my cane to lean on. All the physical activity had made my paralyzed leg ache. This didn't happen often, but I hadn't been to my dojo for a workout in a few weeks, and my body was missing it.

I glanced around the room to see Galland, Tice, as well as the entire staff. The only person missing was Tylissa Booker, and I assumed she was still with Jyanette.

Into the room walked Captain Don Harris. The Mountainview police captain was a big African-American man, tall and strong, with short gray hair and a presence you could feel.

He nodded to McGee, who spoke up.

"I am sure by now you've all heard about the attack on the home of Margery Higgins, where Doctor Wise lives, as well as my home. We believe that Emma Truesdale planned and executed these attacks, with the help of several unwitting civilians programmed to do her bidding."

Bill was not wrong, but to be specific, the people were responding to a storyline created in their heads.

As Bill talked, I wondered about the driver of the van, the woman with the gravelly voice. I knew that Emma and Anika had been lovers. Did Emma meet someone during incarceration? That might be something to look into.

Bill went on with a rough overview of the two events at my house and his, bringing in Albertson to talk about the use of tear gas at my place. Bill also brought up the fact that the assailants used a battering ram at his house.

On the screen, he flashed a photo of Emma Truesdale, apparently her mug shot, as she was wearing an orange jumpsuit.

Cops asked questions, which Bill fielded. My mind wandered a bit, and I spent my time looking around the room. I always have to keep imagined walls around my mind when in a crowded space. If I don't, stray thoughts seep into my head and it becomes a tsunami of different voices.

I let my protections down a bit to allow little snippets in, so I could get a sense of what the people were feeling.

That's got to be rough, his wife…

How does this crazy lady get people to do these things…

The doc looks okay. If somebody had shot up my house…

And the like. The officers showed concern about Bill and me, and a lot of them were angry. They felt this violated one of their own, and it would not stand.

Finally, Captain Harris stepped forward. "I want to thank the State Police and the FBI New Jersey Task Force for their aid in the events tonight. We are now all working as a team. I want communication between all parties to be open. If we work together, we can shut this down before anyone else gets hurt."

The team gave a short round of applause. Bill immediately handed out assignments to our team. Albertson ordered his men activated for the next twenty-four hours, and finally Gabe Petrie informed the group of the FBI's plans.

Everyone headed out to begin their assignments. I could see Bill was busy talking to detectives and uniforms about their tasks, so I walked over to Kate.

She had put her notebook down and was using the heavy table to push herself up. I came and supported her arm to help her up.

"Thanks," she breathed as I got her upright.

I glanced down at the notebook... and my blood froze.

Written on the page was only one sentence:

Something is wrong.

It wasn't one time, but line after line, the same thing over and over.

I looked at her as she picked up the notebook and slid it into her leather attaché and noted that she avoided meeting my eyes.

"Kate?" I requested. "Look at me."

"I don't have time for this," she said, smiling as if it were a game.

"I'm serious, meet my eyes."

She turned from me, and I gently took her arm. She glanced over at my hand, and then looked me in the eye.

And there it was, that wall I faced when I dealt with a programmed person running on instructions.

"Gabe," I grunted. "Come here, please."

Kate pulled her arm from my grasp. "That's unnecessary—"

"What's going on?" Gabe asked, coming closer.

"Kate's compromised," I countered with a glance at him.

"What?" Gabe huffed. "What are you talking about?"

"Len's lost it, Gabe," Kate answered, her attaché in front of her chest. "He's displaying the classic symptoms of paranoia."

I turned to Gabe. "She's got a wall up in her mind."

Gabe looked even more confused. "What the hell are you talking about?"

I realized Gabe wouldn't know the reference I'd just made, so I returned my attention to Kate. "Show him the notebook."

Kate laughed, but it had a strained sound to it. "It's just my notes from this session. I'll type them up for you later, Gabe."

I stepped closer to Gabe. "She wrote the same words over and over: 'Something is wrong'."

Gabe looked at me with suspicion, but then moved his eyes to Kate and put out his hand. "Let me see the notebook."

"It's just my notes," she remarked with an exasperated sigh. "And you know how bad my handwriting is."

"Kate," Gabe demanded. "I need to see your notebook." He gestured with his hand a second time.

"All right," Kate said, her voice dropping into a flat, unnerving monotone, as if she were merely checking an item off a grocery list. She reached into her attaché case with slow, deliberate grace.

The bag didn't just open; she let it slide from her grip, hitting the floor with a heavy thud as she revealed a compact semi-automatic.

"You did this to me!" she shrieked, the sound tearing through the room like a physical blade. "You bastard!"

The muzzle leveled at my chest. With her free hand, she grabbed the edge of her wig and ripped it away in one violent motion. The sight was a visceral horror — the top of her skull was a topographical map of trauma. Pale, discolored skin grafts stitched together in a jagged patchwork, crisscrossed by raised, roped scars where the scalpels had done their work.

Her face was unrecognizable. The composed therapist I'd known had been replaced by something primal; her features contorted by a hatred so vast it seemed to vibrate in the air between us.

As the barrel rose toward my eyes, Gabe snapped out of his paralysis. He lunged, his hand clamping around her wrist and wrenching the weapon toward the ceiling a fraction of a second before she pulled the trigger.

The roar of the discharge was deafening, trapped within the four walls. An overhead light fixture shattered, raining glass and white dust over us as the bullet tore through the acoustic tiles.

The room erupted into a symphony of sliding metal as every agent present drew their sidearms, a dozen muzzles suddenly centered on Kate's chest.

"For God's sake, Kate!" I yelled, stepping directly into the line of fire to shield her. "Drop it! Drop the gun!"

She glared up at me, her eyes burning with that terrifying, alien loathing. But then, as quickly as the storm had arrived, the clouds shifted. The fury evaporated, replaced by a vacant, hollow confusion. Her arm went slack in Gabe's grip.

Gabe didn't hesitate. He stripped the weapon from her numb fingers and stepped back, thumbing the magazine release as he moved. I caught her by the shoulders, pinning her arms gently to her sides. She stared at me, the anger gone, her eyes searching mine with the desperate, heartbreaking look of someone waking up from a nightmare they didn't know they were having.

"Len? What was I doing?" She suddenly seemed aware of her surroundings. "How did I get here?"

"It's okay, Kate. You're compromised, but it's all right now."

"Compromised? What do you mean?"

"Someone got to you, programmed you."

She frowned. "When did that happen? Who...?"

I shook my head. "I don't know."

Bill stepped up, and I released her arms. "Kate, what happened?"

She turned and, almost embarrassed, picked up her wig from the table where she had thrown it. With a glance at the others, she settled it over the damaged flesh of her scalp. "I'm not sure. I blamed Len for what happened to me. Somehow, I knew it was his fault."

She arranged the hair, and it was amazing she could do so without a mirror or something other than her hands, but in moments it was back in place.

By now, Darren had come around the table to stand just behind me, his expression tight with worry.

Bill sighed. "Kate, I am afraid we're going to have to put you in holding."

She was shocked. "Holding? But I'm no criminal."

"No," I explained. "You were a spy."

She turned to me. "A spy?"

"Do you remember how you got here?"

"No."

Gabe piped up. "I drove you. After you called me and insisted you come along."

"Any recollection of that?" I questioned.

She dropped her head. "No."

"Truesdale wanted you here to find out our plans, our strategies," I went on. "You're probably under orders to contact her when the meeting finished."

"That's why we need to put you in holding," Bill surmised. "If we don't, then at some point you will feel an overwhelming impulse to call her, and then forget you did. We can't risk that."

Kate nodded as the realization struck home. "You also don't know what I'm programmed to do. Neither do I, consciously." She looked from Gabe to me, and then to Bill. "You're right, I need to be locked away."

"It's for your own safety," Bill said, though his voice lacked its usual steel. It sounded like a hollow apology.

He gave a sharp nod to Galland. The young officer stepped forward, his boots crunching on the fallen ceiling tiles. "Doctor Yearling," he said, his tone softened but firm. "Please. Come with me."

Kate didn't argue. She didn't even look back. She simply turned and followed him out of the room, her movements mechanical, leaving the heavy scent of ozone and cordite in her wake.

Around us, the room breathed again. The police and the agents holstered their weapons and drifted back to their posts, the adrenaline fading into the dull hum of a crisis averted. The drama was over, but the air still felt charged.

I stood in the center of the wreckage, my eyes fixed on the empty doorway. I felt the three of them — Gabe, Bill, and Darren — closing in around me like a living shield.

"This changes everything," I whispered, my words heavy.

"How do you mean?" Gabe said, still thrown by the situation.

"They couldn't have programmed her in the short time since Emma has been out. Think about it, the most logical time to have prepared her would have been while she was in recovery and confined. In the hospital, there would have been plenty of opportunities, and an unknown person could have gone unnoticed."

Gabe nodded. "I'll have them pull her medical records, get a list of everyone who visited her."

I thought for a moment. "Look for a doctor that visited at odd hours or wasn't one of her regular caregivers."

"A doctor?" Gabe repeated.

"Or someone masquerading as one," I said, and then shook my head. "Or it could have been a programmed doctor."

"Len, what are you thinking?" Bill asked.

"I believe that if they programmed Kate during Emma's incarceration, another person trained in Vanya's techniques is out there."

10. ANIMUS

It was late, and I was all in. Gabe had set up in the conference room with Albertson and Bill, while Darren and I went back into the canteen. I wrote up notes and tried to decide on my next course of action.

My focus was to do the best I could to describe the van I'd "seen" through Emma's eyes. The problem was that, like most visions, in retrospect it had taken on the hazy quality of a dream.

Still, I focused as best I could and pushed my way through it.

Darren had been highly apologetic to me for being on the far side of the table when Kate pulled her gun. I reassured him I did not feel it was any failing on his part.

"We were in a room full of cops," I soothed. "I'm just glad they didn't take Kate out." I sighed wearily. "I've got to get some sleep. Should we bunk here?"

"Safer than the house," Darren advised. "I think a hotel would be more secure, a room paid for in cash under an assumed name."

"Is that necessary? Aren't we being a little paranoid?"

"I was there when you told Lieutenant McGee and Agent Petrie that there is someone else with the ability to program people. We need to be paranoid. I'd like you to leave your phone here."

"Why my phone?"

"If someone has gotten into the National Security Agency or Homeland Security databases, they can track your phone anywhere you go. If they have people with guns at their disposal, a raid on a hotel room would be child's play."

"Okay, give Bill your phone number and we'll head out."

"Both our vehicles are at your place," Darren pointed out.

I shook my head in exhaustion. "Damn."

"Give me your phone and your notes. I'll arrange a ride with McGee."

I handed over the hand-scribed pages. In my pocket, I felt the small flip phone I had used to call Anthony Marconi. Since I turned it off, I figured I could keep it, and pulled out my smartphone to give to Darren. "I hate to leave him when they've kidnapped his wife."

"He'll understand. If you can get some rest, maybe your mojo will work better."

He grabbed my phone and left the room.

I stared at the wall. So far, my "mojo" had accomplished little, except to keep me alive. I managed the remote viewing with Emma, but that did little except give us a warning about the sniper attack. I did not know where our assailants were or what they would do next.

Some psychic!

I tried to imagine what the situation would have been if the attack had occurred without the warning. By the time the sniper fired on us, Emma and her crew would have been in place and ready at Bill's house. I would have called McGee for help, and he would have run to assist, which would leave his house unguarded. With her assailants in place, Emma could strike the moment he left.

Because I called Bill sooner than Truesdale expected, her team was in transit to McGee's house. The timing might have been what made the difference in getting his kids to safety. Did Emma know he had a safe room? Worse, what had her unnamed accomplice found out from Kate? If they had programmed Kate for a while, she might have revealed many FBI secrets that Emma could use.

Darren was right. If Emma had another operator in the area for a month or two, I couldn't trust anyone. I only caught on to Kate because a part of her mind was trying to resist. That's why I got the email and the text from her. That's why she wrote the same line over and over; a part of her was fighting back.

"Let's go, Len," Darren told me from the doorway. "I've got a ride."

"Where are we going?" I yawned.

"You'll see when we get there."

I got up, and Galland met us in the hall near the lockers. He was in street clothes, and it was the first time I had seen him out of uniform.

"Hey, Galland," I greeted him. "You're off-duty?"

"A lot of us are shutting down, but I wanted to stay, be here for the LT," he said. "But McGee says I need to get some shuteye and ordered me home. So, I'm your driver."

"We're all tired," I agreed.

We walked out the side door, Galland using his magnetic card to unlock it. I followed him, and Darren followed me, glancing around the dark parking lot, his hand on the gun in his coat.

We made it to Galland's car, a four-door hatchback. I lay down on the back seat, and Darren rode up front. I dozed as we drove along the night-shrouded streets.

After less than five minutes, we pulled into a lot. I opened my eyes to see an illuminated sign that read "Step Back Inn."

"Step Back Inn?" I said as I sat up. "Was the name 'Hotel It'll Do' taken?"

"It doesn't scream, 'I'm hiding from zombies,' so it will do," Darren replied as he looked over at Galland. "Can you wait until I get a room?"

"Yes, sir," Galland said out of habit. "I mean, sure."

Darren got out of the car and made his way to the front lobby.

"Any luck with the hard drive?" I questioned.

"Some, nothing we can use yet. If Vanya created a website with hidden files, I haven't tracked it down. I think it keeps moving."

"Moving?"

"To different servers. It's like they know we're after them, and they keep moving the files. Or it could be they routed the files to false locations."

"How close are you?"

He forced a tired smile. "I'll let you know the minute I find something."

"Is Teddy able to help?"

"The DA has a warrant that allows us to go through the hard drive, and I cloned Santos a copy with the LT's permission."

"What does that do?"

"It doubles our ability to pursue. The way the files are being moved, I think they left a hacker in charge of them who is watching and staying one step ahead."

"A hacker?" I said, and I felt concern tug at my heart. They had programmed Teddy the last time we fought Vanya. If there were an operator in the area, could he or she have gotten to Teddy and given him orders to hide the database? And while I was at it, could they have kidnapped Galland and programmed him? If so, could Galland be the one coordinating the attacks against Bill and me?

This heightened sense of paranoia made me suspect everyone.

Darren tapped on my window, pulled the door open, and I slid out. Darren gripped my arm and helped me to my feet, my cane held firmly in my other hand. With a wave from us, Galland drove off.

We walked outside the building and to the back of the hotel, where there was a set of concrete steps. I was leaning on my cane pretty heavily, aware that fear and adrenaline had been the only things keeping me upright.

I stared up at the imposing stairs. "Can't we use the elevator?"

"Safer to use the steps, less chance of a witness seeing us. I know you take a while, and I have to warn you, we're on the third floor."

I sighed as Darren went up, but I stopped and glanced around the lot, trying to be aware if we were being observed. They could have followed Galland, but I sensed nothing out of the ordinary.

One at a time, I crept up the steps, using the handrail and my cane to speed up the process. I guess it had been a smart move to pick a room at the back, but did it have to be on the third floor?

Once on the correct level, Darren went to the door first and unlocked it with a plastic key card, and we went into the cheap room. Two double beds awaited us, and there was a bathroom toward the back, an open closet with attached hangers, and across from the beds was a dresser with drawers upon which sat a television set. Not one of the thin-screen models you might get in the twenty-first century, but a clunky one with a picture tube that shot beams of radiation into your brain.

I took off my shoes, sports coat, shirt, pants, and socks and got into the too-soft bed.

"You okay if I watch some tube?" Darren asked.

"You could do anything except play the drums, and I'd sleep through it," I mumbled.

Darren grinned. "That wouldn't help keep a low profile."

I rolled over, thrilled to be lying down at last, and soon drifted off to sleep.

The hallway of Mrs. Higgins' house had stretched into an impossible, cavernous throat. The familiar wallpaper was now a sickly, bruised purple, and the door to my sitting room — my only sanctuary — had retreated into the distance, appearing no larger than a postage stamp.

Then the sound started. A low, wet rattling.

I looked back toward the living room and felt my heart seize. A wall of bodies was shuffling out of the shadows, moving with a jerky, disjointed gait.

It was everyone — McGee, Galland, Teddy, even Mrs. Higgins. Kate was there too, her scalp still a patchwork of raw grafts, and Darren, his broad shoulders slumped and useless.

"Help me," they croaked, the words bubbling through throats filled with fluid. "Help... us..."

They weren't merely dead; they were a collective of the damned. Their skin was the color of curdled milk, translucent and slick with the film of the grave. I watched in frozen horror as a piece of Mrs. Higgins' cheek sloughed off, hitting the floor with a soft, sickening *thud*.

I stepped back, my hand instinctively reaching for the heavy cobra-head of my cane. My fingers grasped empty air. I looked down and gasped; I was standing tall, balanced on two perfectly whole, healthy legs.

I turned to flee, my stride long and powerful, but the hallway was a treadmill of nightmares. No matter how fast I ran, the door remained miles away.

Behind me, the sound of dragging feet grew louder. The stench hit me first — the cloying, sweet rot of a sun-bloomed corpse. I could feel the cold, skeletal pressure of their fingers grazing the back of my neck, their jagged nails catching in my shirt.

I lunged for the door handle, screaming—

And sat bolt upright in the hotel room.

The sun was shining through the window, and Darren was sitting on the corner of his bed, holding the twenty-four-inch blade from my cane in his hand, testing the edge with his thumb.

He didn't look away, but spoke with his eyes on the blade. "Welcome back. You didn't tell me you had this."

I was breathing hard from my frightening dream. "You didn't tell me you were planning to go through my things."

I observed him and realized I had not made direct eye contact or attempted to reach into his mind. What if Emma's partner had gotten to Darren and programmed him? I didn't have my regular phone. No one knew where I was except Galland, and Darren was holding my only weapon.

"I saw the catch, and I wanted to see what it was for." He grabbed the shaft and returned the sword to its home. He placed it on top of the blanket that lay on me. "I've already showered. I'll get coffee; you get clean."

I nodded in agreement, relieved.

The shower was a rather disappointing, cockeyed spray, but the water was hot. I cleaned myself and used a pocket comb to put my hair in order. I glanced at the stubble on my chin in the bathroom mirror.

Once cleaned and dressed, I moved to the window and pulled the shade aside to see what the weather was like. It was clear, but looking outside, I received another surprise. Across the street there was a graveyard, known as Endless Vista. Actually, it was a "memorial park," the politically correct term now used.

In those beautiful grounds, a block off Route Three was where the grave of my long-deceased fiancée, Cathy, was located. It had been months since I'd visited.

In that moment, I desperately wanted to go there.

I sat on the bed and controlled my impulses until Darren had returned. He brought coffee and an egg, something-or-other he'd rustled up at a McDonald's within walking distance.

I sat on the bed in a shirt and pants and ate. I used a washcloth that I had dampened to remove the debris from my jacket, but it seemed a pointless task. Both my clothes and Darren's were worse for wear from the attack.

"How do we get back to Mountainview?" I asked.

"I'll get us an Uber. They'll drive us back to your house. There we can get our cars."

I nodded. "Good plan. I'd like to call Mrs. Higgins."

He pulled out his phone, hit a button, and handed it to me. "Here."

The display read "Mrs. Higgins" and was ringing.

She picked up on the second ring. "Halloo?"

"Mrs. Higgins, it's Leonard."

"Doctor! Where have ye been?"

"Darren thought it would be safer to go to a hotel."

She considered this for a moment. "Aye, that makes sense. Did you get some sleep, at least?"

"A little. How about you?"

"Enough. There were two foine officers watching the house the whole noight. I've been getting plastic over the windows and trying to clean up."

"Darren and I are coming over for our cars, and I'd like to change clothes."

"That will be foine, Doctor. See ye then."

I ended the call and handed Darren the phone. He played with the screen, and I imagined he was using an app to get the car-share ride we needed.

"McGee texted me that there's a 10:00 a.m. meeting at Mountainview PD."

"What time is it now?" I questioned as I took another sip of coffee.

"8:30."

I rose. "Then we'd better get to it."

An hour-and-a-half later, with both of us in fresh clothes, Darren and I were back in the MPD conference room with most of the people from the previous night. Albertson was missing, and I assumed his duties with the State Police took precedence, or he was out pursuing a lead.

Gabe Petrie was there and didn't look happy.

I approached him and lowered my voice. "How's Kate?"

"Still in holding," Gabe sighed. "This morning, CeeCee escorted her to the police locker room for a shower and returned her to her cell without incident."

"Well, that's good, I guess."

"She's being moved to the mental ward in Morris Plains this afternoon. Involuntary commitment."

"Is that necessary, Gabe?" I asked, concerned.

"Dammit, how do I know? Until we have a clue what's going on or what they ordered her to do, we can't have her walking around free."

"Can I talk with Kate after the meeting? Perhaps I could get some insights from her."

"You have my blessings," Gabe said. "Could you deprogram her while you're at it?"

"Sorry, not in my skill set."

When I had broken Aubrey Andrews' hypnotic conditioning created by Anika Vanya, I had an advantage. Bill and I accidentally discovered her key, and I knew Vanya used poems from *Alice In Wonderland* as locks. I had looked up several poems on my phone until we found the one that worked. I had no clue what key or lock they had used on Kate, and I was sure it would no longer be from Alice.

Bill came into the room. He'd obviously showered and shaved, combed his hair back, and his face was without stubble. He was wearing the same clothes as yesterday, so he must have just caught a few hours of sleep in one of the three bunk rooms.

He called the meeting to order. "Overnight, the FBI made progress on identifying the vehicle used by the team that attacked my house." He looked over at Petrie. "Gabe?"

Petrie stood. "The FBI spent the night canvassing neighborhoods between the house where Doctor Wise lives and Lieutenant McGee's residence. We have located video of the vehicle we believe the assailants used."

He turned to Galland, who was sitting with a laptop in front of him. Petrie nodded at him, and a video appeared on the screen. It was the front of a store with the camera aimed at the sidewalk and the street behind it. A van went past quickly, and I tried to watch it, but it was little more than a blur.

Galland hit a few keys, and the video repeated in slow motion. A long white van passed. It was the style of a minivan, but much longer, even more than a commercial van. There were four panes of glass for the back and a side door that opened out; not a sliding one like my smaller van used. It appeared to be the correct size for what I'd seen. A woman who might have been Emma Truesdale was in the passenger seat.

"We were lucky enough to get it at a traffic camera," Gabe added and nodded to Galland, who did his keyboard magic and the image changed.

Now we were looking down at an intersection as the van drove up to it. The windshield appeared dark, and we couldn't see into the vehicle. Worse, the license plate was nothing but a dark black rectangle. We couldn't read the license plate numbers at all.

"Best as we can tell," Gabe continued, "the vehicle had some kind of privacy panel over the plate. This allowed it to be seen by anyone on street level, but with an elevated camera, it hides the plate number. The vehicle has a tinted windshield, which is illegal in this state, so we couldn't get a photo of the interior or the driver. In fact, the only windows not tinted were the driver's side and passenger's."

"Convenient," Darren mumbled to me. I nodded in agreement.

"What we found out is that this is a 2015 Ford 350 XLT. We've sent this information to the state police, and there is now an APB on vehicles matching that description. They also are searching through registrations for owners of this specific vehicle in the Garden State."

Bill spoke up. "So far, the State Police have had no success, either finding an owner or the actual van. Troopers are checking hotel and motel lots, in case the suspects have gone to ground. There is little we can do if they have a private space."

Petrie turned to Galland. "Next photo, please."

Galland hit another key, and our attacker from the previous evening appeared on the screen in a mug shot.

Petrie went on. "This is Todd Masler, formerly a sniper and Navy SEAL assigned to Special Forces in Afghanistan a few years back. He was in a one-time therapy session with Doctor Anika Vanya two years ago. At least he only remembers one session. He was a highly trained sniper and a recipient of the Bronze Star Medal for saving his entire team from an unexpected attack. He's married, has a two-year-old child, and has no criminal record of any kind. As far as I can tell, not even a damn parking ticket."

Bill nodded. "This is a common theme we are dealing with. Emma Truesdale uses ordinary people as weapons."

I piped up. "Or people we know and trust, like Kate."

A murmur of agreement went through the room. It was fine to speculate how the people under Truesdale's control acted, but they had all seen Kate last night, and that made it very real.

Bill nodded, and Petrie sat down. "We appreciate the FBI's involvement with this case. Doctor Wise brings up an excellent point. I asked Detective Sergeant Joseph Tice to question the overnight staff at the hospital where Kate Yearling was recuperating. Tice, can you share what you found out?"

Tice stood, and he honestly looked like he hadn't slept even the five hours that Darren and I got.

He held up his detective's notebook. "From my interviews with the overnight staff at Mountainside Medical Center, we found a couple of irregularities that were included in their reports but not followed up on by the hospital authorities." He cleared his throat and went on. "A Doctor Kay Naniava visited Yearling at 9:00 p.m. on two subsequent nights. Doctor Naniava showed appropriate Mountainside Medical Center credentials and a copy of what appeared to be a referral from Kate's surgeon."

I quickly pulled a sheet of paper from my computer bag and jotted the name down.

Tice peered around the room, then his attention returned to his notebook. "This Naniava person visited Doctor Yearling from 9:00 p.m. until midnight for two consecutive nights. She told the nursing staff that she was doing a psychological assessment of the patient and they were not to be disturbed."

"Is that how this phony doctor kept the staff out of the room?" Bill asked.

Tice shrugged. "They had no reason to doubt her. During her convalescence, many specialists saw Doctor Yearling, and from what the staff told me, they would show up at all hours of the day and night."

I considered what Tice had reported. Someone could have programmed Kate in those two days. After all, Vanya had programmed me in one night. The deep hypnotic preparation that Vanya had used for her people usually required multiple sessions, over time, to set the training in place. This suggested that it might have been someone new to the process who was in a hurry. This may have been what allowed Kate the chance to fight it.

After Tice finished, Galland told the group that he was getting close to finding the location of what he believed was the hidden database that Vanya used with all the information of her programmed people.

One of the other detectives reported that they had found fingerprints at the McGee residence, and they were being run through the national databases.

After an hour, Bill gave everyone their assignments, which were to find the van, dig for any new information, and be ready to move on a moment's notice.

As the room cleared, Bill held up a hand and asked me to stay. I waited until the room emptied, and then he sat next to Darren and me.

Bill spoke in a low voice. "Len, can you find out anything? I mean, in your special way?"

I nodded. "I can try, but I'll need someplace secluded."

"How about one of the bunk rooms?" Darren suggested.

I nodded. "Only if you wait outside. I might need someone to wake me if I accidentally fall asleep while meditating."

Darren nodded.

I went on. "Before I try that, I want to talk to Kate for a few minutes. Since she's not running on her program—"

"We hope," Darren mentioned cynically.

"She might have a memory of the person who programmed her, this Doctor Naniava that Tice talked about."

"Anything that you think will help, Len," Bill asserted, his jaw tight. "We are really at a loss here. I need whatever edge you can give me."

I nodded. There was so much not said between us. The woman he loved, the mother of his children, was in danger. We'd already seen the amount of compassion these monsters had from what they had done to Aubrey and Jyanette.

Pushing myself up with my cane, I said, "I will do everything in my power to get Laura back to you, Bill."

I made my way out of the conference room and into the hall, heading down to Kate's holding cell with Darren on my heels.

Darren had come in handy the last few days, and I was grateful Marconi had hired him for me.

I stopped at the processing office window. Officer Andrew Hastings sat at the desk, working on a computer in front of him. I tapped on the window, and he slid one half of it out of the way.

"Hey, Drew. I need to talk to Kate Yearling," I said.

"You want to take her to interrogation?"

I considered this. "It would probably be better if I just spoke with her through the bars."

He nodded. "You mean, since she tried to shoot you last night? I was there. Pretty scary for a few minutes."

"Don't I know it," I agreed.

"She's in Holding One. Let me know if you need to open her cell or anything."

"Thanks, Drew," I stepped through the large, open doorway to the holding cells. I turned to Darren. "Can you wait here?"

"How about I get coffee?"

"It's your stomach lining," I teased.

He smiled and headed back up the hall to the canteen. I moved over to Holding Cell One. The other two cells I passed were empty, but they would fill once the weekend hit. My focus was on staying alive until then.

Kate got up from the bed and moved to the bars to meet me. I didn't put my hands on the upright metal rods, as I was still unsure what they programmed Kate to do. She didn't have a gun, but she had teeth and fingernails. Instead, I leaned on my cobra-head cane with both hands.

"How are you feeling?" I asked.

"Like a lab rat on speed," she complained. "All night, I've had an overwhelming desire to make a phone call. I don't know to whom, or what I would say to them."

"It's part of your programming."

"That's what I figured. You hear? They're moving me to the psych ward."

"I'm not happy about that," I told her.

She sighed. "It makes sense. If I were in charge, I'd do the same thing. Any idea how they did this to me?"

"Detective Tice talked to the night crew. They said a therapist came to your room at odd hours, but had the correct paperwork. Do you recall a Doctor Naniava?"

Kate shook her head. "Not at all." She considered it for a moment. "But when you said her name, I got a weird feeling, like spiders creeping up my spine."

"Kate, with your permission, I'd like to get into your mind."

"Do you think you can? You told me you couldn't connect with programmed people."

"That's because Vanya would command them to resist. I might run into that with you as well, but if you willingly give me permission and try to open up to me, I might have more success."

"Do you think you can undo the program?"

I shook my head. "Kate, I don't have your training or your expertise. But if I can get in, I might help."

She nodded. "How many times did this fake doctor visit me?"

"Twice," I recalled.

She thought about it. "This Naniava person would have to work quickly and quietly. I can only hope the program isn't too ingrained."

"That's what I thought. Do I have permission to reach into your mind?"

"What's left of it," she joked.

"Kate, agree verbally. You know as well as I do that the subconscious mind takes everything literally. It will only work if you give me consent."

She took a deep breath, and her hands grabbed the bars tighter. "You're right, of course." She let the breath out slowly. "Very well. I give you permission to enter my mind."

I lowered my head and closed my eyes as I focused inward, calming my own thoughts and letting go of the fear, the tiredness, and any distractions.

I opened my eyes and raised my head to look at Kate through the bars. Our eyes met, and I felt her mind open to me. There was surprise and some resistance. I have been able to force my way into minds in cases of extreme emergency, and although this was definitely an emergency, I moved slowly to allow her to let me in at her own pace and at her own speed.

Memories flashed by: a class in medical school, a date with a young man, a skinned knee in the third grade.

There was little rhyme or reason, as this was just a jumble of momentary recollections that all of us have. It is also one of the defensive techniques our minds create to distract an invasion.

I could sense it the farther I went, a dark spot that was trying to hide behind memories of loved ones, meals, everyday activities, but I felt it.

The part that was hidden.

I pushed a little more, gently at first, to let her open up to me. I felt her mind give a little, and I was in a hospital room.

I was both watching and seeing myself, my body, walk into the room. My perspective was from Kate's point of view, although it felt like it was mine.

"Len," Kate's voice said, "what are you doing here?"

"I can't stay away from you, Kate," the Leonard Wise in the vision told her as he went down on one knee and pressed his lips to mine.

That felt weird. Me kissing myself.

This shocked me and I wanted to pull away, but I didn't. I knew what this was. Emma Truesdale was familiar with my ability to reach into minds. I was sure whoever programmed Kate planted a mental trap to embarrass or confuse me if I attempted to read her.

I kept pushing through, and the scene quickly changed from G-rated to nothing short of X as the Leonard Wise who wasn't really me kissed and undressed Kate. Then, professing love, he pulled off his own clothes and got on top of her.

That was when it shifted.

The error I had seen was that my doppelgänger had two perfectly good legs, which broke the illusion. The face faded to mist, and I saw a woman in a white lab coat walk into the room.

Kate's previously removed hospital gown had reappeared, as well as the bedcovers, and the woman injected something into Kate's IV.

My point of view only allowed me to see the chest of the white lab coat and lower, and the doctor was wearing hospital scrubs under the lab coat.

"What is it, what did you give me?" I heard Kate's tired voice say.

"Something to help you sleep," the doctor responded in a gravelly woman's voice.

One that was familiar.

The doctor sat in the chair next to the bed, and I could clearly see the name badge with the photo ID. On it, printed in large letters, was the name:

Naniava, Kay

As she moved lower into the chair, I felt my heart skip a beat as her face came into view.

There was no mistaking that face. It had tortured my nightmares, and I recalled her smirking at me with a look of superiority. I remembered her holding a gun pointed at me, ready to kill me.

Blonde hair, shoulder-length, a heart-shaped face, and her mouth almost like a little bow. Those eyes filled with excitement over what she was about to do.

She leaned forward and whispered, "You and I are going to be great friends."

Sitting in the chair, leaning in, was none other than Doctor Anika Vanya.

11. REQUITAL

I pulled myself out of Kate's mind, shocked by what I'd seen. Kate blinked at me, her mouth agape.

"That felt odd. What was with all that sexual stuff?" she asked. "Did you put that in there?"

"No, it was a distraction to stop me." I panted as if I'd run a marathon. "I've got to get to Bill."

I turned and used my cane to help me make long strides. It had been Vanya; I was sure of it. Vanya was still alive, and her voice differed from what it had been when I last confronted her. It might have something to do with her getting shot in the chest, giving her vocal quality a gravelly tone. In that short connection, I recognized where I had heard her before: in the van the previous night.

Anika Vanya had been the driver of the van when I had remote-viewed Emma.

Kate had seen the memories at the same time I experienced them, but since she had not met Anika previously, she did not know her true identity or its significance.

I made my way down the hall, and Darren leapt to his feet to follow me in my headlong dash to Bill's office.

I stopped to peek into the conference room, and there was Bill talking to Agent Petrie. I went in, and Darren came to the doorway to see if I needed him.

"It's Vanya," I gasped.

Bill stared at me in disbelief. *"What?"*

I paused and took several deep breaths. "Vanya is the one that programmed Kate. She's alive."

Petrie frowned at this. "Look, Doc, I have seen the file and Anika Vanya is deceased—"

"The file is wrong," I argued. "Bill, we never saw Vanya's body, never saw autopsy photos."

This annoyed Petrie. "I told you! I've seen the reports of Vanya's death. People that I know signed off on it…"

"Were there photos?" I insisted.

Petrie considered this. "No, but why does that matter?"

"Don't you see? It makes sense! Vanya's alive; she's been working with Truesdale. While they kept Emma locked up, Vanya was laying the groundwork for all of this."

"Are you sure?" Bill frowned.

"Didn't you hear me?" Petrie asserted. "I said I've seen reports, with names I know and trust on them!"

"Isn't it possible those were fakes?" I badgered. "All it would take is Vanya manipulating one person to send reports with names you know. Did you check with the people listed on the reports you received, or did you just file them?"

Petrie considered this for a moment. "I... reviewed them. They actually went through the office when Stan Frazier was in charge."

I nodded. I worked with Stan, and he was first-rate, but like Petrie, he saw reports that listed Vanya dead and saw no reason to follow up. "Also, the name Tice got from the night staff, Kay Naniava? It's an anagram of Anika Vanya. She was toying with us, leaving clues so that eventually we would know it was her."

"To what end?" Bill wondered. "I mean, we all thought she was dead. Why not just head off and start a new life, set up shop elsewhere?"

"Revenge," I explained. "Bill, we stopped her, took everything from her. She lost her clinic, her inheritance from Harold Stoller, her standing as a renowned therapist, everything."

Bill stood there as the realization washed over him. "So, she wants to take everything away from us."

"And publicly, like Aubrey's murder."

After a moment of silence, Petrie piped up. "What can we do?"

"In the immediate," I suggested, "get Galland to go through that hard drive and see if there are records of properties owned by Vanya, Unique Therapies, LLC, or the Lighthorn Foundation—"

"Is that the dummy charity that Vanya set up?" Bill asked.

"Yes. Real estate records might point us to a place where they ran to ground and where they might hold Laura."

Petrie nodded curtly. "I'll talk to Galland. I'll also speak to a few people I know, see if I can get confirmation on the reports I saw." He headed out the door.

"I'll call Evidence. They have the physical files we got from when we raided Vanya's lawyer," Bill announced. He reached into his pocket and pulled out a phone, which he handed to me. "You might need this."

"Thanks, I forgot about it." I took the phone.

"I charged it," Bill added as he stepped out of the room in search of his aide.

I went to slip the phone into my pocket, but the vibration against my palm stopped me. The display read that Mrs. Higgins was calling.

"Hello?" I answered, my voice tight.

"Doctor, I just thought I'd be checking in with ye," she said.

I exhaled a long breath I hadn't realized I was holding. I leaned against the wall, decided to keep the news of Vanya's resurrection to myself for now. "Just chasing leads, Mrs. Higgins. Nothing much to report yet."

"I'm worried sick about McGee's wife."

"We all are."

"And I wanted to thank ye for being so prompt," she said quietly. "For sending those men to repair the windows."

The blood drained from my face so fast that I felt lightheaded. "Men? What men, Mrs. Higgins?"

"The ones who are here now. They're already fitting the new frames."

I lowered my voice; the words coming out in a sharp, frantic whisper. "Mrs. Higgins, listen to me carefully. Get out of the house. Walk out the front door and don't stop."

"What? Whatever for?"

"I didn't send anyone. I didn't order any windows."

"But the paperwork they had, Doctor... it looked so official..."

"It's fake. It's all a lie."

"I see," she said. Her voice didn't waver, but the sudden shift in her tone told me everything. She did not show any fear; someone was in the room with her.

"Are the police still in the cruiser out front?" I asked, my heart hammering against my ribs. "Call them. Tell them to move in."

She continued as if we were discussing the weather, her voice unnervingly pleasant. "Well now, I dinna know where those boys have gone off to just this second."

Sweat broke out across my forehead. They had pulled the cops. They had cleared the board.

"Well, yes," she said, raising her voice slightly. "I think I'll just go out front and see how the windows look from the front of the house, Doctor. If you'll excuse me."

I heard the rhythmic *thump-creak* of her footsteps — slow, unhurried, a masterpiece of a bluff. She was moving toward the exit, playing the part of the dotty old landlady to the end.

I heard the heavy oak door groan on its hinges. She called out, presumably to the street, "Well now, I just want to see how this looks from the outside — *oh!*"

The sound cut off.

"Mrs. Higgins? *Mrs. Higgins!*"

"She's fine," a man's voice spoke into the receiver. It was a cold, flat baritone that sounded like a shovel hitting dirt.

I froze, the air in my lungs turning to stone. I forced a sound past my vocal cords. "Who the hell is this?"

"We have the old lady, and we have your assistant," the voice said, devoid of any emotion. "We'll be in touch."

The line went dead.

I collapsed into a nearby chair, the phone trembling in my hand as I stared at the black screen. I had been a fool. Vanya and

Truesdale weren't just coming for me — they were dismantling my world piece by piece. They wanted a spectacle. They wanted to hurt the people I loved in the most public, devastating way possible.

A terrifying thought took root. Vanya desired more than a quiet kidnapping. She'd want a finale. Her biggest desire would be to blow them up in the MPD, bring down the building, and kill my loved ones.

My loved ones!

I was up and moving toward Bill's office. Darren had been looking at his smartphone, and raised his head as I walked by. He followed, all his attention focused on me.

I pushed into Bill's office without knocking, and Darren stayed a few feet back from the doorway. Bill was on his office phone, saw I was distraught, and said, "Hold on a minute." He then covered the mouthpiece. "What's up?"

"Jyanette! Is she still being guarded?"

"Yeah, Albertson sent a state trooper."

"Check on it! Now!"

Bill nodded and uncovered the phone. "Gotta call you back." He hung the phone up in its cradle and pulled out his cell phone.

"And check on your kids!" I said as I headed out of the office and back down the hall.

"What's up?" Darren said, hot on my heels.

"I have to find Petrie!"

"He's in the computer room with the blond guy."

I moved to the data center where Galland was working. Galland had a monitor, keyboard, and wireless mouse in front of him, and Petrie was looking over his shoulder. The computer tower was out from under the desk and had a portable hard drive jerry-rigged into the system with wires that went into the back.

Petrie saw the look in my eye. He stepped away from Galland to meet me. "What?"

"They've got my landlady."

"How?" he thundered and instantly brought his voice down. "There were state troopers on the site."

"I don't know. Somehow they got called away. The men claimed to be window repairmen. They had paperwork signed by me."

"Damn!" he cursed, and glanced over at Galland. "We're tracing some properties, and let me tell you, Vanya and her companies owned quite a few."

"I have to go home, see if I can find anything."

"Don't go alone. You need backup."

I glanced at the doorway where Darren stood. Petrie's eyes followed mine, and I said, "I've got that."

"You keep me informed of anything you find, Wise," Petrie said quietly but with tension. "You have a nasty habit of going off and playing hero."

I returned the stare. "Just make sure that there is protection for McGee's kids."

"Aren't they with their aunt?"

"I thought my landlady was safe."

He nodded grimly. "I'll make sure there are assets in place."

"Only people you know," I reminded him. "We don't know who we can trust."

"We might know soon," Petrie said and leaned in closer. "Galland thinks he's close to finding that database."

"Really? I was sure she moved it."

"She did, but Galland is like a bulldog going after it. He's tracking the digital footprint."

"Okay, stay in touch," I said.

"Got it."

I headed through the door, and Darren Ward was at my side. "They grabbed Mrs. Higgins?"

I nodded. "And from what they said, they picked up my TA, Teddy Santos." I stopped in the hallway and extracted my phone to bring up Santos' number. As Darren and I stood in the hall, I heard the phone ring, and then go to voicemail.

I pocketed the phone. "No good! We should try to—"

At that moment, down the hall from us, there was the buzzing sound of the lobby door being opened, and I watched as several men in black suits entered the secure area.

"Federal agents!" the first man shouted. He was a tall Caucasian man with a short haircut, sunglasses, and a thin body, but he looked quite fit. Right behind him was an African-American man, also with a short haircut, but he was bigger than the first man. They wore matching black suits and held their credentials aloft.

I couldn't help but wonder why they were wearing sunglasses inside.

Another pair of men in black suits carrying large briefcases followed the first two men.

Their loud voices brought Petrie out of the computer room without Galland. McGee, Captain Harris, and CeeCee Carter all moved into the corridor. CeeCee was saying to the captain, "I couldn't stop them. They said I either open the door or they would break it down."

"What the hell is this?" Petrie bellowed.

"Department of Homeland Security," the taller black man said. "We are now heading this operation."

Petrie began. "What? But this is a joint FBI, state, and local—"

Harris interrupted, his voice much louder and more resonant than Petrie's. "You do not have the authority to circumvent a local investigation without the proper—"

The white man held out a piece of paper. "You are wrong, sir. There is sensitive data that could compromise national security."

The taller African-American gentleman inclined his head to the two other agents, and they moved as one unit into the nearby conference room.

"Sensitive data? What are you talking about?" Petrie demanded.

"You have copies of a hard drive that was used by one Anika Vanya," the man insisted. "We were unaware copies existed until there was activity on certain online accounts."

Captain Harris moved to the men. Although the agents were fairly tall, he seemed to tower over them. "Let me get this straight. You had *us* under surveillance?"

"Yes, sir," the white man said. "Agent Johnson and I kept tabs on the situation involving Emma Truesdale."

"That woman kidnapped my wife," McGee growled.

"Allegedly," Agent Johnson responded, unimpressed by McGee's demeanor.

I could see the reflection off the two men's sunglasses and I considered this for a moment.

Sunglasses... so no one could see their eyes.

Their eyes...

Darren and I had been standing near the locker room, and I nudged him with my elbow. We moved down the hall behind us to the side exit as the arguments went on.

Petrie was yelling, "It's pretty strange that I called to ask about some reports not a half-hour ago, and you guys show up, all 'federal agent' on us."

Captain Harris was adding to the melee. "I want to see that warrant, or whatever you are waving around here. I am the captain of this department, and I—"

We had reached the side door, and I waved my magnetic ID which made the door open, and Darren and I stepped outside, just as I heard Agent Johnson say, "We are going to want to talk to that consultant of yours—"

As fast as I could go, I moved to the van, Darren at my heels. "You should ride with me," I said.

"What was all that?" Darren said as he pulled open the passenger door. "Homeland Security? How the hell did they get involved?"

I started the vehicle. "They might not be. Those two guys were wearing sunglasses."

Darren shrugged. "A macho choice to add to the intimidation."

"And a way to prevent eye contact," I responded as I drove from the parking lot.

"You mean, you think Vanya sent them?"

"Vanya is alive, and somebody had to get her medical attention after Aubrey shot her, as well as a place to recover. Vanya has done some work for the government, and knowing her habit of programming people who might come in useful, it seems likely that she could pull strings in high places."

I was probably driving faster than I should have, and Darren finally said, "You need to stay calm."

"How can I stay calm? They took Mrs. Higgins out of a house that is supposed to be guarded, and now these 'men in black' guys have taken over MPD, so we have effectively lost our backup. How can any of us be safe? What if they got Jyanette again?"

Darren considered this. "I doubt they could steal her right out of a hospital, Len."

I shook my head and forced myself to drive slowly. "It's not that. She's programmed. All they have to do is get her on the phone or send someone in to say a few keywords, and she'll walk right out."

Darren frowned. "But she's hurt."

"That doesn't matter. Vanya's training makes her orders the most important thing. And now that I know Vanya has been around for months, she could have met with Jyanette and doubled down on the program, told her to do anything—"

I stopped talking as the realization hit me.

"She could have ordered her to break up with me," I stated simply.

"What?"

"It's possible. It was only a few months ago. She could have commanded Jyanette to break up with me for the sole reason of getting me out of the picture, so she could program her deeper, build the commands to give Vanya total control. If Jyanette and I had been dating, we would have spent too much time together. By breaking us up, she had ample time to get her alone."

My phone rang, and I blanched. The car had a Bluetooth connection, and the dashboard display showed it was an unknown person. I hit the virtual button on the console to answer it.

"Leonard Wise."

"Len, this is Tylissa Booker," her warm voice came through the car speakers.

I breathed a sigh of relief. "Officer Booker, I wanted to—"

"Doc, Jyanette Emery is gone."

"How did that happen?" Darren demanded.

"Is that Darren?" Tylissa said suspiciously.

"Yes," I said. "What happened?"

"I just got here for my shift. Turns out Ms. Emery asked the policewoman on duty to get a soda for her. When the officer got back, Jyanette and her clothes were gone."

"Damn," I muttered. "Could you find out if she got a phone call?"

"Already checked on that. One call got put through the switchboard. Some guy claiming he was Homeland Security."

"Our friends have been busy," Darren snapped.

"We're tracing the number now," Tylissa reported. "But I don't think it will do much good."

"I understand," I told her. "Thanks for the heads up, Tylissa. You're a good friend."

Darren spoke up. "Tylissa, I'll be in touch after this is all settled down."

"Please. I want to know what happens."

The call ended, and I looked at Darren. "You have her number?"

He grinned. "I sure do. If I live through this, I want to see her again."

"You're about a foot taller than she is," I noted, my eyes on the road.

"Maybe, but she is an interesting lady." He sat back in the seat.

I turned into the driveway where a state trooper vehicle was waiting. A man stepped out of the car. He wore a light-blue shirt, and I recognized the yellow inverted triangle on his sleeves at the shoulder. His pants had a pair of yellow stripes down each side, the same color as the emblems.

He was a strong Caucasian man, clean-shaven, even his head, and held up his hand to stop the vehicle as I pulled up.

His partner, a red-headed man with a bushy mustache, was out of the car and crouched behind the vehicle, and I had the feeling he drew his weapon.

I opened the window. "I'm Leonard Wise, and this is my bodyguard, Darren Ward."

The trooper nodded. "We were told you'd be coming. Can I see some ID?"

I showed my hands empty and carefully pulled out my "Civilian Consultant" magnetic MPD ID badge and offered it to the man. He gave it a once-over, returned it to me, then signaled his partner. The redhead rose from the car and returned his pistol to the holster on his belt.

I threw the van into park and quickly opened the door and turned my seat out, grabbing my cane as I reached the ground.

"Any idea what happened, officer?"

"We received an emergency call. Someone got on the correct frequency," he explained. "We are up here from South Jersey, so I assumed it was the dispatcher. We only left for ten minutes."

"South Jersey?"

The trooper's nod confirmed the grim reality: the influx of state units wasn't just a routine surge, but a full-scale mobilization.

In New Jersey, there is a Threat Assessment Plan in place that triggers this exact type of regional cooperation, pulling troopers and specialized resources from across the state.

I winced. This situation was indeed like a terrorist attack.

A very well-planned one.

If my inkling that Vanya wanted to blow up my loved ones and a building was close to being correct, it would be the largest homegrown terror attack in New Jersey history.

"I appreciate you being here at all, Officer...?"

"I'm Daley. My partner is Hennessey. How can we help?"

"I need to get into the house. Did you see the men that came here?"

"They were in a truck marked 'Mountainview Windows and Doors.' Two guys, Caucasian, dark hair. In retrospect, they looked like they both might have military training. They showed us paperwork and took two damn windows into the house."

I sighed. "I'm not surprised. They planned this."

"Well, it surprised the hell out of us. After we got back, and found the men and the lady missing, we put an APB on the truck. They located it, abandoned two miles from here. Turns out two gunmen stole it this morning."

Truesdale and Vanya had arranged another attack. I was at a complete disadvantage, as they had moved pawns and plans into action while I played catch-up.

Hennessey came around from the other side of the police car to join the conversation. "They did all of this just to kidnap that nice lady?"

"Possibly," I surmised. "They might have thought I would be here as well."

"Good thing we kept moving," Darren muttered.

"We're on duty here until the next shift. Let us know if you need anything," Daley said.

"Might be a good idea to call a forensics team," I said. "Maybe they can find fingerprints or something."

"We're on that," assured Hennessey.

Daley looked at the ground for a minute. "Sorry they grabbed her, Mister Wise."

"There was little you could do," I sympathized. "We are dealing with some very dangerous and highly organized people."

I headed to the back of the van. I removed two pairs of latex gloves and offered one pair to Darren, and we headed for the front door, which was unlocked.

Inside the house, we looked down the long hall and saw the troopers had indeed been correct. One window that looked to be close to the correct size was leaning against the wall next to the space where our intruder had smashed his way in. Mrs. Higgins had covered the open space with heavy frosted plastic held in place with a significant amount of heavy gray duct tape.

Farther down the hall, a second window complete with a frame rested on the wall next to the window damaged by the high-caliber weapon. Mrs. Higgins also covered this opening with plastic, showing that she had been busy since last night. The "workmen" had not removed the plastic at the point of her abduction.

My phone rang, and I saw Bill's name on the display.

"Bill, what's going on there?" I asked.

"Len," he had his voice very low. "Don't come back here. More Homeland Security is arriving. If you're at home, don't stay long. They are asking for you."

"Crap," I cursed, and looked at Darren. "We have little time."

"I'll get what I need," Darren said and bounded up the nearby stairs.

"Bill, I just got a call from Tylissa. They got Jyanette."

"*What?* How?" he hissed.

"A call came through, and she tricked her protection into getting her a soda and left."

"Damn."

"How about your kids?" I asked.

"They're fine, but my sister said two men claiming to be detectives came to her house looking for them."

"Did she fight them?"

"Ha!" Bill said, and then added, "The kids were never there, Len. I won't say anything more."

I was silent as I thought about this. "Bill, you prepared incredibly well for an attack on your family."

"When I was with the FBI, I brought down a major crime figure. I always thought they might pursue me or my family. Laura and I had plans in place since the kids were born."

It surprised me that one of my closest friends, my sponsor, held secrets I had never imagined.

He went on. "You better get moving, before they come looking for you at your house. I'll be in touch."

He ended the call as Darren came downstairs with his bag over his arm.

I put the phone away. "I need a place to be alone, to do what I can to find Mrs. Higgins."

"In your special way?"

"Yes. Mrs. Higgins and I have a bond. I can use that to help me find her, as well as the others. But we can't stay here."

Darren shook his head. "Okay, so where can you do this?"

"I have a place."

"I'll get us sandwiches."

He moved into the kitchen. I walked past him to my sitting room, through the damaged door, and made my way to the desk. The Taser sat in one drawer where I had left it. I loaded it and grabbed the extra cartridge, which I put in my pocket. The unit had come with three cartridges when I bought it, and I had only fired one.

I looked at the damage around the room, the results of the shotgun and Jyanette's rampage. Now, they had Jyanette, and I didn't know where she was. She had blood loss from her self-induced abortion, done in ways I didn't want to imagine.

The point was, she was weak, but hopefully no longer bleeding from internal injuries. She was in a precarious place, and now that monster, Vanya, had her under her sway.

It was a lot that fell on my shoulders, and if I allowed it, it would crush me. I hadn't even considered the loss I was experiencing: the unborn child, unexpected, but not unwanted. We could have raised him or her as a married couple, but I would have done my part as a father, no matter what. I would have to take time to mourn that life which would never be.

The feelings were like the loss I had with my fiancée, Cathy. Years ago, I swerved off the road because I saw a giant demon in the roadway, and our car toppled down a mountain.

In the last few moments of Cathy's life, as the pair of us hung upside-down in the crushed car, I saw the life we would have shared. I saw us together through the difficulties, ebbs and flows that any marriage must have. I saw her give birth to our children and us together into our old age, in love so much more because we had stood the test of time.

It had taken me years to get over her loss, the life I would never have. And now Vanya had snuffed out another life.

I wanted to scream to the heavens, rage against the cruelty of fate, gods, or demons that did this to me, but I needed to focus as there were people I cared about in danger, and if I allowed myself to be blinded by rage, I could not help them. My abilities work at their best when I am calm, focused, and detached. All of Vanya's attacks had the same basic concept: keep me off balance and unable to cope with the latest loss.

My only chance was to open myself up and let the answers come. Before I did, I needed to check on the less-than-legal side of this operation.

I pulled out the flip phone given to me by Anthony Marconi and turned it on. It took a moment for the little screen to light up, and I then hit the only number on the device.

The phone rang, and the efficient young lady I'd spoken to previously picked up. "International Shipping. How may I direct your call?"

"This is Leonard Wise," I stated. "I am calling to be updated on the situation I had called about the other day."

There was a pause, as if the woman was taking notes.

"We have some information for you. Please keep this phone with you, and someone will be in touch soon."

"Thank you," I said, but she had already hung up.

I walked back down the hall to the living room, passing the walls damaged by bullets, as Darren came out of the kitchen with a small paper bag of food.

"Let's move," he said, and grabbed his luggage as we went out the door.

We got into the van and waved to Daley and Hennessey as we drove off.

"Where are we going?"

"Someplace where the spirit might be willing," I replied.

"Okay, don't tell me."

It only took about ten minutes, as the place wasn't far. We soon pulled into the lot of the Step Back Inn, the hotel from the previous night. I decided only Galland had known we stayed there, and I doubted he would share that with the men who invaded the MPD.

I wanted the place behind the hotel.

We drove through an open gate, and I followed the roadway into Endless Vistas.

"A graveyard?" Darren sputtered.

"Do you think anyone will come looking for us here?" I asked.

"Probably not, but it pushes the creepiness factor all the way to the max."

I pulled the van off the road so any other vehicle could get past me. Darren brought the paper bag with the sandwiches.

"Tell you what, I am going to head to the McDonald's for more coffee and leave you alone. How long do you need?"

"Maybe twenty minutes. I should warn you, sometimes I fall asleep doing this."

Darren changed his voice to a more nasal tone. "Doctor Wise, this is your wake-up call."

"You scoff, but it happens," I pointed out.

"See you in twenty, Doc," Darren said, and walked in the direction of the McDonald's.

I gazed around me. There were few visitors at this time of day, so I would be undisturbed.

I walked the same route I had in the past to reach the familiar stone. The light granite had black lines that decorated the stone set almost nine years earlier. They chiseled it with the words:

CATHERINE CYNTHIA GARBER
BELOVED DAUGHTER

Tears stung my eyes. This had been the loss on the night I'd received my first vision and experienced the car crash that killed her and destroyed my right knee. The event had disabled me more than physically. For years after, I was an emotional cripple. I finally thought I was moving past it with my relationship with Jyanette.

Now that could be gone, too.

I needed to let go of my anger, fear, and guilt to put my attention on what I could do to find my friends.

I walked over to a nearby bench and sat, the cool wooden staves against my legs and back. I focused on my breath, using a mantra to speed up the process. A mantra is a repeated word that clears one's mind faster than merely concentrating on your breath. When I do a mantra meditation, my breath slows down in a much shorter time.

As I centered myself and repeated the word I used in my head, I pictured Mrs. Higgins and put my attention on her. I used a memory of her in better times, smiling and looking at me.

I had such a great success remote-viewing Emma Truesdale the other night; I hoped for similar luck with Mrs. Higgins.

Images shot into my head: a man grabbing her and pulling the phone away; the second man grabbing her and taking her out to the truck as the first man spoke to me.

Then I saw her put into the back of the truck, which was empty, except for another framed piece of glass. The two men got into the front, started the vehicle, and drove off.

It only took a minute or two before they pulled the van over, opened the back, and took her out. They held her between them as they walked toward the familiar long van I had seen on the video with Bill.

Clever lady she was, Mrs. Higgins's eyes moved to the license plate, a standard New Jersey one that had the number: B60-YM7. It also had some kind of diffusing plastic over it, which had blocked the number from the cameras the previous night.

I repeated the number and gently brought myself out of it. This was a memory, nothing more. Mrs. Higgins might have been helping me by allowing me to see it instead of her current location, and I intended to use it.

I pulled out my phone and texted Bill with the license number with an explanation of what it was. He immediately typed back that he received it and that somehow he would get it to Albertson.

That done, I closed my eyes and slipped back into my meditation and tried to connect with those memories again. I got a flash of a dark room. I think that was where they currently held Mrs. Higgins, but I couldn't make anything out. She was blindfolded or had a cloth bag over her head, because I could see nothing.

The flow of memories started again. I saw one man hold out a cloth to blindfold Mrs. Higgins. From the face, I recognized Martin Hodges, the missing auto-parts man who was now one of Vanya's drones. As he moved the cloth toward her eyes, Emma Truesdale came into view.

"Was she any trouble?" she demanded.

The man with the blindfold stopped moving closer and said, "Was she?"

Emma sighed, then said, "Tell me if there was a problem bringing her."

"There was no problem," the man said.

"Good! Cover her eyes, and let's get out of here."

Before the cloth moved into place, Mrs. Higgins glanced at the open side door of the van to see Teddy Santos sitting in a seat, staring straight ahead.

With her eyes covered, they pulled her hands behind her back, and I could feel a pair of restraints slapped on each wrist. They pushed her into a seat, and there was someone next to her, their right arm against her left one.

I then noted that she had cleverly shifted the piece of cloth that was the blindfold just enough, so she could look down her nose and see Teddy's legs, her own lap, and, by tilting her head back, a bit of her surroundings.

That's my Mrs. Higgins.

I thought she might try to talk to Santos, but she rode in silence, just allowing the sounds and the little she could see to inform her of where they were taking her.

Mrs. Higgins was guiding me, focusing on memories that would best help me.

That was when I received the smell. Not too far away, the scent of salt water filled my nostrils. Well, Mrs. Higgins' nostrils anyway.

This was a vital clue, but still far too broad. New Jersey is a coastal state, and we have some of the most beautiful beaches and waterfronts in the country. The scent of salt water could be anywhere from Cape May up to Perth Amboy, as long as it was close to the shoreline.

I could also hear trucks nearby. No, not just trucks, but also some kind of heavy machinery that made an unusual sound. There was the hiss of air brakes and the beep-beep-beep of a large vehicle going in reverse. I also detected a steady rumbling under everything that was much noisier than a shore town would ever be. Even Atlantic City, with its many casinos, did not have the amount of trucks or the machinery rumble I heard.

The vehicle stopped moving, and Mrs. Higgins leaned her head back to glance out one of the side windows. That was where I got a quick glimpse of large metal structures in the distance that appeared like giant goalposts.

They pulled Mrs. Higgins roughly from the van, as they lowered a cloth bag onto her head. I had seen what I needed to and recognized the structures from my trips down the New Jersey Turnpike.

She was near Port Newark in Elizabeth, and those "goalposts" were the giant cranes used to lift cargo containers from ships to be sent throughout the East Coast.

Her abductors had taken her past the shipping terminals, probably into one of the many large buildings in that area. This made me even more concerned. If what I received was correct, they were near Newark Airport, as well as government and state buildings of great importance.

For the life of me, I couldn't understand Vanya picking this location. How would it impact me or Mountainview? Even if she could blow up a structure that now housed my friends, how would it have the personal impact that her revenge seemed to demand?

While still in this deep mental state, I struggled to remain calm and touch Mrs. Higgins' mind.

Mrs. Higgins...

Doctor? Is that ye...

Do you know where you are...

Someplace dark. Do you hear the machines...

I paused for a minute and listened. There was a different rumbling than I heard when she rode in the van. It had more of an electronic sound, and it seemed to be all around her.

The hum of machines, yet muffled, as if the noise was in a different room than Mrs. Higgins.

I hear it...

Doctor, there are others here, but they aren't speaking...

I think they are under control...

Do ye know where I am...

Elizabeth Port...

Aye...

Stay brave. I'll come for you...

I broke off any communications and worked to bring myself up from the meditation. I had a rough location, and I had realized what the sounds were in the building she was in.

Computers. Many, many computers.

She was being held in a building that housed a server farm.

I was going to bring myself back to full awareness, but I heard another familiar voice.

"Len?"

Still in my meditation, I opened my eyes to see the luminous form of Cathy standing in front of me.

In the state of consciousness I was in, it didn't shock or startle me. She just stood over me, her short blonde hair exactly like I remembered. She wore scrubs, like most of our time together, looking beautiful and not having aged a day since her twenties.

"Cathy?" I croaked.

She gave me a smile that lightened my heart. "You are having a rough time now, my darling."

The tears were unbidden. "Yeah, I guess I am. I miss you."

"I'm still with you, watching over you."

That made me chuckle. "As a guardian angel, you could do a better job."

She became serious. "I wish I could help you through this."

I looked at the ground. "In everything I've done, I always believed I would get through it, survive. This is the first time I ever felt I might not get out of this alive, or be able to save the people I love."

"You always take so much on yourself."

"I lost you, and a part of me believes I'll just keep losing."

I felt something against my cheek, like a breeze or the gentle touch of a hand.

I looked up at my glorious Cathy.

She gave me one last worried smile and said, "You are not alone, Len. Remember that." She faded into nothing but the dappled sunlight in the trees that had been behind her.

12. RANCOR

I was fully conscious, my head reeling from the experience. My eyes were wet as I looked over at Cathy's grave a few feet away. Darren was standing next to the van on the nearby roadway, still with the bag in his hands, munching on a sandwich, with a cup of coffee on top of the vehicle. I stumbled to my feet, needing my cane to steady myself.

I pulled out the phone to call McGee.

He answered on the first ring. "Yes."

"Can you talk?" My voice sounded hoarse.

"I'm in my office with the door closed. Did you get anything?"

"Elizabeth Seaport." I cleared my throat. "They are holding Mrs. Higgins and the others there."

McGee spoke quietly. "Port Newark? That's a big place. Anything a little more specific?"

"They're being held in a building that houses a large server farm. I could hear the computers running."

"A server farm?" he replied. "At the seaport? I'm not familiar with anything like that."

"It's near the bay or that general area. I could smell the salt water."

Bill was silent, perhaps taking notes.

"Why is she holding them there?" I babbled. "I mean, an attack on the MPD or even GSU, I could understand. But why would she make her stand in a building with computer servers?"

"Depends on the building," Bill muttered, almost to himself. "No, that would be impossible."

"Bill, we are dealing with the impossible. If you have any insight, please share."

"You were saying she wanted to strike a blow at MPD, at us. Do you know where the servers for the MPD are?"

"I assume at MPD."

"Yes, but the long-term data storage for the entire State of New Jersey is at a server farm near Elizabeth."

"What? Why?"

"According to what little I have been told, they use a water-cooled system and need a source of water that they circulate through the place to keep the machines cool."

"But the entire state government?"

"Yes, as well as every municipal cop shop like MPD. There's more. Because of the location, they also have the records for the major banks and financial institutions based on Wall Street."

"How?"

"It was a decision after September 11 to have the servers for Wall Street financial institutions off-site, in case of another attack.

The State of New Jersey sold the firms on it. That was how they raised the capital to build the facility."

"How big is this place?"

"If it's the one I've heard about, it's the biggest on this coast. Are you thinking that she wants to take out that server farm?"

"That's where my thoughts would go."

"Len, if it is the place and they destroy it, that could do more damage to our financial infrastructure than the attacks on the World Trade Center."

I paused as this sank in. "That's what she wants, a spectacular statement. We go after her, and she destroys everything, including our loved ones. Can you find out the exact location?"

"I'll have to ask Petrie to get the location, as well as alert any security on site. But, I'll be honest, with these Homeland Security guys running things here at MPD, there isn't much we can do."

"Are they still in charge?"

"Yes, Petrie has called Washington, and I have a couple of calls in to people I know in the bureau to see if these guys are legit. But so far we haven't gotten a response, so we have to let them run the show."

"These guys might be under Vanya's control," I said. "Or they could be people she worked with back when she did her tricks under the careful eye of the government."

"Our tax dollars at work," Bill mumbled.

"She's had months to plan this. She will have considered all possibilities, including an FBI raid on her location."

Bill mulled this over. "That's why she wanted hostages. If there is a raid, she can create a stand-off by using them as human shields."

"You were with the bureau. What's the standard situation in that scenario?"

"We negotiate to free the hostages."

"Yes, but she's not interested in negotiations. She's interested in destruction. She can leave a drone to talk to the FBI while she rides off with a detonator in her hand."

"Christ, Len, what can we do?"

"I'll see if I can get the location of that building on my own."

"By yourself, Len?"

"I have Darren with me. I'll see if I get a bead on the place."

"Yes, but what can you do, Len? If Vanya or Truesdale sees you, they'll shoot first."

"Darren and I can assess the situation and get word back to you or Petrie."

I had reached the van, where Darren watched me, listening. He took another thoughtful bite of his sandwich.

Bill was speaking. "You know she'll be watching for you. The entire reason to kidnap these people and send the Homeland guys was to make you do something exactly like this."

I set my jaw. "I am aware of that. Do you have a better plan?"

"Sadly, no."

I ended the call and turned to Darren. "You heard?"

He nodded while chewing. "Pretty much: server farm, hostages, boom! Have I summed it up for you?"

"Pretty much."

He looked at me. "I apologize for ever suggesting you have a boring life, Doc."

"I could go for some boredom about now."

I white-knuckled the steering wheel as I merged onto Route 3, gunning the engine toward the Garden State Parkway. My plan was a straight shot south toward Route 78 and the sprawling industrial maze of Newark Airport.

Once I cleared the toll booths, I banked onto the interstate, following the neon-bright airport signs as they funneled us onto the jagged, asphalt artery of Route 1 and 9.

The afternoon was deceptively beautiful. The few trees lining the highway were bleeding vibrant ochres and deep crimsons, their leaves shivering in the wind. But the sun was already a dying ember on the horizon, pulling long, distorted shadows across the pavement.

The autumn darkness would soon engulf the world.

We were cutting east against the grain of the rush hour; while the westbound lanes were a stagnant river of brake lights and frustrated commuters, our path was eerie and wide open — a runway into the unknown.

I pushed my consciousness outward, trying to catch the specific, sharp frequency of Mrs. Higgins' mind. I searched for anything — a flicker of her sharp wit or her warmth.

Nothing.

I tried to find Jyanette or Teddy, but where their vibrant personalities should have been, there was only emptiness. Vanya's hypnotic shroud had turned their minds into lead-lined vaults. They were there, but they were also gone.

Beside me, Darren had pulled his sidearm from its leather shoulder rig and was methodically inspecting the action. In the dimming light of the cabin, he checked the weight of his spare magazines before tucking them back into his pockets with grim finality.

He didn't need to say a word. We weren't just driving to an airport; we were driving into a kill zone.

Finally, he spoke. "A graveyard. Did you get the ghosts to tell you what you needed?"

"Just one," I said. "My dead fiancée."

"Of course, silly me. You told McGee that we're doing reconnaissance, is that right?"

"That's the plan."

"Why do I have problems believing you? When we were looking for Erica Marconi, you went in alone."

"Antoine Powell had driven me to the location, and as I explained to you afterwards, he attempted to take me prisoner and threw my phone into the woods. So, I couldn't call you."

"Good thing the FBI arrived to save your bacon."

I exhaled deeply. "Good thing. Now will you let me focus on the road and where I'm heading?"

"You mean, you don't know?"

"I... have a rough idea," I admitted.

"Great." He rolled his eyes.

We were cruising down Route 1 and 9, and I saw the exit for the huge Anheuser-Busch Brewery on our right. We continued past the multi-storied red-brick complex as the smell of roasted barley permeated the air, even inside the van. The company had several buildings in New Jersey, where they brewed beer both day and night, and trucks and cars pulled in and out of the facility constantly.

We drove past single-story buildings and then two and three-story edifices. The last building we passed was a huge rectangular tower with a giant version of the company logo on its roof that lit up at night.

We continued past multiple billboards, some so high it looked as if they were advertising to landing planes instead of the drivers of cars. There was a plethora of car parking lots promising "Great Prices" and "Free Shuttles" as we continued. Newark Airport was to my left, the bright buildings of the three terminals, and up ahead the turnoff for the Elizabeth Seaport.

Pulling off on an access road toward the Seaport area, we passed bobtails, the trucker term for a cargo-carrying semi-truck without a trailer. As empty trucks headed into the port to pick up a container, we passed trucks laden with containers on the way out to deliver their goods.

The median soon disappeared, and the six-lane roadway wended its way past warehouses, some quite active, others closed and abandoned. Container storage areas full of huge metal boxes stacked one on top of another appeared on the right side of the van. As we followed the road, it took a turn to the left, but a minor road veered off to the right. I took the turn which led past a large freight building, labelled "InFreight Services."

Looking out to the left of my windshield was a large open field with saplings, shrubs, and a mixture of grasses and weeds.

Beyond the InFreight warehouse was another extensive building. It was simple and white, looking remarkably similar to the warehouse. It stood very close to the water, with huge solar panels on the roof. The unobtrusive design would make the casual onlooker believe it was just another warehouse, or perhaps a second building for the same company.

I knew what it was. I could *feel* it.

The second building bore no sign stating its purpose. It had young trees planted on the highway side of the property. This would eventually hide the facility from the nearby, busy highway. The building was off in a corner where it could remain ignored.

People I loved were in it.

I pulled into the lot of the first warehouse and around to the far side, so anyone keeping watch from the second building wouldn't see my van.

Darren looked up at the large freight company structure with trucks in the loading bays, cars in the lot, and employees moving about. He frowned. "Is this it?"

"No, the building in the back."

He looked over at me. "That one looked abandoned. There were hardly any cars in the lot."

I nodded. "That's what Vanya was after. The whole point is to have a location that won't draw attention to itself."

Darren considered this. "That would be the point of the data center as well. The last thing they want is to attract hackers or terrorists. We should call McGee."

I pulled my phone and hit the memorized number.

"Bill, it's Len. I think we've found the server farm. It's off North Avenue on a side road next to a company called InFreight Services." I described our location as best I could.

Bill whispered. "Amazing! Petrie is still trying to get clearance to reveal the location, and you're already at it."

"Just doing my part."

"Are you sure it's the right place?" Bill pressed.

"Not one hundred percent, but I believe so. Darren and I are going to attempt reconnaissance."

"They'll see us coming a mile away," Darren growled.

Bill went on in my ear. "Okay, we're still buttoned down here at MPD, but I think I can head out there and maybe get a couple of uniforms as well if I can talk to them in person, not on the radio. We'll come in silent with a couple of police cars. I'll let Albertson and Petrie know, but I don't know how much backup we can offer you, Len."

"Make sure they come in silently as well. We parked in the InFreight lot. I'm planning to walk over there."

Bill hesitated. "Do you think that's a good idea?"

"No."

"Good. At least you're not totally out of your mind. Stay in touch."

I ended the call and put my phone away.

Darren was looking at the expanse between the buildings. "Doc, I'm not one to tell you your business with all this psychic stuff, but trust a former cop to tell you, this feels like a trap."

"Think so?"

"Like you said, they had time to plan this out. They have a location with no way to approach it without being seen. I mean, the trees are saplings, and there isn't a lot of ground cover. Probably have lights that come on when night gets here. Bottom line, Doc, you go in there, I would doubt you're coming out alive."

"What if I go in alone, let them capture me? Could you sneak in while they're distracted?"

He stood looking at the building in silence, then he spoke. "You got binoculars in this vehicle of yours?"

"Yeah," I grumbled, and hit the fob to open the back of the van. We stepped out and went to the open tailgate. I reached into the large nylon bag I had in the back and extracted my field glasses, which I handed to Darren.

He scanned the structure. "High windows to let in light with tinted glass and only one window at ground level with the drapes closed," he muttered, "a couple of side doors, but I doubt they're open." He lowered the binoculars. "They seemed to have selected this location carefully." He returned the lenses to his eyes and checked again, adjusting the dial in the center to refocus. "They've got cameras outside."

"Not surprising," I added.

"A lot of cameras," Darren corrected. "They can probably see us right now. This suggests that it is the data center, because a freight company wouldn't have this level of security."

"Still think my idea of going in alone is bad?"

"Getting worse all the time."

"They're going to see us coming, anyway."

"Right! So, the best approach is to wait for McGee and anyone he brings and go in with force."

"Which is why Vanya took the hostages," I pointed out.

"If you go in, they'll have one more."

"But if I go in, I might find a way to stop them."

Darren shook his head. "I don't know why I'm arguing with you. You've decided to do this."

"I was hoping for your advice."

"My advice? Wait for the FBI, the state, and the frigging Marines, because you're going to need them. If your bad guy is in there, then she's in a fortified location with hostages." He hung the binoculars around his neck, then stared at the ground for a moment. "Tell you what. I'll make you a deal."

"What?"

"Take a minute, do that thing of yours, read energy, suck on crystals, whatever. Then, you tell me if it's still the right choice."

I frowned. "We'll lose time."

"You don't want to head over there until it is a little darker, which is a few minutes away. Besides, that's the only way I'll let you go."

I nodded. "That seems fair."

"Yes, and maybe your spirit guide, dead fiancée, or fairies will let you know how stupid your plan is."

"I've never seen a fairy."

"That's not reassuring."

I got back into the van and shut the door. I concentrated on my breath and focused my mind on the question: What should I do?

I wished for a moment that I could be one of those superheroes in movies, who could see through time and pick the one winning solution, but I had no such ability. I had a bit of an edge given to me by my talents. Even with all my practice, I still had limits.

Far too many in this case.

As I sat there with my eyes closed, I considered what I could do. At two haunted houses, I moved out of my body into an astral state, one of pure consciousness. In that manifestation, I'd seen what was going on and was unaffected by walls or physical barriers, but it left my body unprotected and the experience was draining. I was lucky that Darren was here to watch my body if I used that technique.

Then I realized I had done a remote viewing through Emma Truesdale's eyes that one time. If I could do it again, it might provide the information I needed. I opened my eyes and gestured to Darren. He was on his phone, but he put it away before he came over to speak to me through the van window.

"I'm going to try something, but I have to go pretty deep," I explained.

"I've got you covered, Doc."

I closed the window. With summer past and night rapidly approaching, it was cool enough to keep the window closed.

Closing my eyes again, I focused on my breath, the image of Emma Truesdale in my mind. I slowed my breathing, taking large, slow lungfuls of air, and went deeper as I reached out... farther... farther...

"For God's sake, Emma, stop pacing," a female voice croaked.

All around I heard the clicking and whirring of computers, and the sound of small fans blowing air, as well as the gurgling of water through pipes.

I saw the room, a corner of a vast space that contained row after row of large metal cabinets, each one purring with the sounds of hard drives, data transfers, and the necessary cooling.

The room was hot, even though the air seemed to keep moving. All those electronics and heat-dispersing fans spread the warmth throughout the room until overhead fans up near the fifteen-foot ceiling sucked it out.

It limited me to Emma's point of view, but she turned to face Doctor Anika Vanya.

Vanya sat at a round table in the corner that had four sturdy chairs around it. It was next to a vending machine and a coffee maker, and I assumed it was where the small staff who usually worked there would go for breaks.

Vanya had changed since I'd last glimpsed her. Her hair was now jet black instead of the blond she had worn in the past. The left side of her face drooped a bit, and her left arm hung by her side, while she gestured with her right.

As I possessed a medical degree, I surmised that between her body and the change in her voice, she had experienced a stroke during our last conflict. Back then, Aubrey had shot her, resulting in massive blood loss. Clotting and any transfusions she received could easily have led to a stroke. The limitations on her face and left arm seemed to be minor. She pulled a heavy wooden cane with a hook on the end from next to her chair to push herself to her feet and limped over to Emma.

It was an odd experience to see that face so close.

"He'll come," Vanya said, with the rasp in her voice.

"How can you be sure?" I heard her all around me as Emma spoke these words.

"He can't help himself. He longs to be the hero. And you and I both know his abilities. He reached into your mind, as well as mine."

"Yes, but I don't see…" Emma's voice faded away.

"We have the one thing that will draw him. People he cares about and the wife of his friend. He will do anything to save them, even sacrifice himself. Just like we sacrificed little Aubrey."

"I'd love to nail Wise to a billboard. That would be fine!" Emma fumed. "I can't forget what he did to you, to us."

"We will destroy all records of us, along with Wise and his cronies. We just have to wait a little while longer."

"When do you think he will come?"

"After dark, with the illusion that the night is his friend."

"I don't see why we couldn't have more men here," Emma complained. "Those Homeland Security agents would be handy right now."

"A lot of men, even hidden, might keep him from making his move. He wants to be a hero, but a large force would keep even him away. We don't need extra bodies in the way when we make our departure. Our explosives expert stated that everything was ready for when we leave."

I'd been right. They were planning to blow the building. Now I wondered if I could get her to look in on the captives? I could experience her mind, but was I able to direct it?

Need to see the prisoners...

I projected the thought and tried to feel a response. I didn't want to push because if she realized my presence, she could shut me out.

"I want to check on the prisoners." Emma's voice reverberated around me.

It appeared I did better than I was aware I could.

Emma walked past several aisles of computers and opened a door.

It was a conference room with a table in the center and people sitting around it. Emma didn't turn on the overhead lights, but the light streamed in from the doorway.

The first person I noticed was Teddy Santos, who sat in a chair, his head uncovered, his thick glasses on, and his hands unrestrained. He stared into nothingness, his eyes blank.

Next to him was Jyanette, looking about the same, her face also in a blank state, and she also wore no restraints. As Emma looked around the table, her eyes fell on a slim woman with a cloth bag over her head, whom I assumed was Laura McGee. Laura's hands were in two pairs of handcuffs, one pair on each wrist, the other ends locked to the heavy arms of the chair.

The next two people I didn't know. One was an Asian man with long hair and glasses who, like Laura McGee, had his hands in separate manacles that were each locked to the chair arms.

Next to him was a Caucasian man with reddish hair, imprisoned in the same way.

Finally, Emma's eyes rested on a short figure who also had her head covered. I immediately knew it to be Mrs. Higgins. They cuffed her hands in front of her, but just with one pair of handcuffs going from wrist to wrist.

As Emma looked from person to person, I heard Mrs. Higgins say, "Doctor?"

Truesdale slammed the door and headed back toward Vanya, but I sensed that suspicion had entered her mind. I felt a resistance, a concern that maybe something was happening in which she was not in control.

I eased back, just as a ringing in my pocket caught my attention. My consciousness was back in the van, and the shadows had thickened.

The ringing was not my cell phone, but the flip phone given to me by Anthony Marconi.

"H-Hello?"

"Is that you, Doc?"

It was Marconi himself. Not a bodyguard or lieutenant, but the man himself.

"Yes, it is. Thanks for getting back to me."

"I understand you have been working with the FBI and the state. Is that correct?"

"Yes, sir."

"And Homeland Security has taken control at the police station?"

I was glad he couldn't see me, as my mouth fell open in astonishment.

"How—?"

He chuckled at this. "I'm keeping tabs on everything. I believe you have tracked the people down to a facility in the Elizabeth Seaport, is that also correct?"

This stunned me, but then I glanced out the window to see Darren still pacing, and occasionally peering up at the building through the binoculars around his neck.

I exhaled heavily. "Darren called you."

"Doc, you got to remember that Darren works for me, got that? Now, I'm familiar with that site, from my import/export business."

I didn't want to think about what he brought into the country. Drugs? Sex workers? Weapons?

"Mister Marconi, if Darren told you where we are, he probably informed you that Truesdale and Vanya—"

"Wait a minute! I thought the Vanya broad was dead!"

"She's not. And I believe she is in that building, with hostages… people I know…"

"Jeez," he muttered.

"The police are on their way, though limited because of Homeland. To be honest, I don't know if they can handle it. I believe Vanya is going to blow up the entire building."

"How soon until the cops get there?"

"I don't know."

There was a pause, as if the gangster was calculating something in his mind. "Okay. If you go in, I got you covered."

I paused at this. "How do you have me covered?"

The phone went dead. I folded it up, fighting the desire to call him back. I opened the van, turned the seat, and moved down to the ground. The air was growing chilly, but I had my suit jacket, which I pulled tighter around my chest.

Darren stood waiting for me. "Did you get anything?"

I tried to focus on the reality of standing in this parking lot with our enemies a few hundred yards away.

"Yes, a call from Anthony Marconi. You told him where we are."

He shrugged. "We need backup, and the police have their hands tied. Besides, if you end up dead, I wanted him to know it was because you went against my advice."

"What if you go with me?"

"Great, that way we can both end up dead."

"I got a reading on the building. Vanya and Truesdale are both in there. They are planning to blow the building with McGee's wife, my landlady, my teaching assistant, and my girlfriend all inside."

"Won't Vanya and Truesdale get blown up as well?"

"They're planning to leave. We have no choice. We have to hit them now, mess with their plans."

"So, you're still planning on going in there?"

I nodded. "I have to, but you don't. Stay here, call McGee and get him to block this road so they can't drive away. I don't think they'll blow up the place while they're stuck inside."

He stared at me and nodded. "Okay, then."

Too easy...

A buzz flashed through my mind. Darren was giving in almost too easily. Did he know something I didn't?

"Leave me your van keys," Darren said, his hand extended and palm up.

I pulled them from my pocket and dropped them into his grip, the metal cold against my skin. "Why?"

He gave a sharp, unsentimental shrug. "In case you get shot. I'll need to get the hell out of here."

I stared at him for a long beat, my grip tightening on the head of my cane. "Your faith in me is truly reassuring, Darren."

"Let's look at the math, Doc. You're walking into a fortified nest of professionals with nothing but a glorified toothpick and a 'feeling'. You really think you're coming out the other side?"

I didn't answer. I couldn't. Instead, I turned toward the building, my jaw set so tight it ached. "The prisoners are in that conference room," I said, pointing to the floor-to-ceiling glass that slashed up the height of the north wall. "If you find an opening, get in there and get them out."

He looked at the glass, then back at me, his eyes unreadable. "And what about you?"

I took a breath, the weight of the moment settling onto my shoulders like a shroud. "Get me out too," I whispered. "If there's anything left of me to save."

13. REDRESS

Without another word, I turned my back on Darren and moved with purpose toward the other building.

Darren had pointed out one thing to me: I may not be able to go into programmed people's minds, but I possessed a strong precognitive talent. If I could be open to it guiding me, let it lead me to the best area to attack and hide, it might help.

It certainly wouldn't make my odds any worse.

The building was a simple one-story box, though it had high ceilings from what I could tell from my peek through Emma Truesdale's eyes. The only separate room I had seen in the building was the conference room in the back, and there were no doors to get in that way.

On the far side from where I approached, there was probably a secure lobby area, like we have at MPD. The question was whether there was another door that I could use to sneak in.

The windows on the building did not look like they opened, and they were about ten feet off the ground, to allow light in but prevent people from breaking in. The only exception was the conference room, which had a large window that went from the ground to the height of the other windows. I couldn't see into it, and it wasn't because there were curtains in the way. They had turned the lights off in that room, hiding in the darkness.

What was also unusual was that all the other facilities in the area had many bays for trucks to pull into the building. Warehouses were constantly moving product in and out as the need arose. This building had none of the bay doors, and as I drew closer, I wondered what other exits Darren had seen with the binoculars.

As a server farm, authorities wanted to limit access to the building. Since the staff on hand were security or programmers, there weren't many people who needed to move in and out of the building.

I felt myself led to my right, and I followed my instincts without hesitation. I was certain that I was being watched on video, or soon would be.

As I went to the side of the building farthest from the street, I saw several steps that went up to a door. I memorized its location on the internal map I imagined in my head.

I climbed the stairs and pulled the door to confirm it was locked. It was.

So much for sneaky.

I continued up the pavement to the next corner and was about to go around it when I received a quick buzz.

A man is coming, get low...

I immediately stopped without going around the corner. Since crouching is not possible because of my frozen leg, I slid down the wall until my legs were straight out in front of me, and my butt was on the ground with my back to the wall.

A man in some kind of security uniform turned the corner, the barrel of a small machine gun appearing first, and his body second. I guess he had been planning to confront a target that was farther away and standing, not on the ground like I was. He turned the corner in one quick move, caught his foot on my left leg, and lost his balance. As he toppled over me, I took the wood end of my walking stick and cracked the metal cobra-head over his head as he fell.

He landed on top of my legs, unconscious.

That had been a very lucky move, but I would have felt luckier if he hadn't landed with his full weight on my legs. Though he hadn't injured either leg, his steel-tipped boots hit my left thigh. That hurt like hell, and his weight on top of me was rather painful.

I rolled him off me, unsure if a camera watched me. I think he had exited the building before I made it to the corner, which was why I had the element of surprise.

I took the small machine gun out of the man's hands. What to do with him? I had nothing to bind him with; no restraints, no handcuffs, not even duct tape.

Then I looked at his boots.

The steel-toed, ankle-length footwear had long, heavy shoelaces.

It wasn't much, but it would slow this guy down. If he were a hypnotized drone, operating on commands, perhaps he didn't have the wherewithal to release himself. Also, knocking him out might have broken the mesmerized orders, but I couldn't take that risk.

I glanced around the corner to make sure there wasn't another guard on his way, then quickly untied the man's boots, pulled them off, and slid the shoelaces from their eyelets.

I inspected the man and realized I had seen his face before from one of our meetings at MPD. He was none other than Martin Hodges, the owner of the shotgun Jyanette had used, and the man who never returned to his auto parts job.

It appeared Mr. Hodges had been traveling with Emma since her release.

I rolled him over onto his stomach, pulled his hands behind him. Using one lace, I tied his wrists together with multiple knots. I then took the second lace and bound his stockinged feet at the ankles. I left enough slack to fold his legs and tie the laces to each other.

I would have preferred something sturdier, but this would have to do.

I used my cane to push myself up and looked at the machine gun. What the hell was I going to do with this? I wasn't an action hero and certainly had little training with firearms. So, pulling the magazine with the bullets, I gave it a throw. I followed it with the heavy gun, which dropped far closer than I'd managed with the magazine.

I moved to the corner and peeked around it a second time. No one had come out in pursuit of Martin. Why should they? They knew I was coming to them; surely saw me on video. I just hoped that Truesdale and Vanya didn't leave before McGee could blockade them in. Once they left, there was sure to be an explosion, and I didn't want to be in the building when it went off.

This side of the building was the front and faced the bay. There was still some sunlight cresting the horizon from the setting sun, turning the sky fiery red as the world turned to night. The bay was beautiful, filled with many ships that were moving into positions to dock or heading back out to sea. I saw the huge cranes north of me, Bayonne directly across the water, and Staten Island to the south. The sun cast its golden rays upon the clouds of billowing smoke from nearby power generators, turning them bright red as the sun dipped below the western horizon.

In the front parking lot were three cars of different makes and conditions. The handicapped space directly in front of the door held a 2015 Ford 350 XLT van with tinted windows: the vehicle Truesdale and Vanya had been driving and would probably act as their escape vehicle.

"Best get to it then," I muttered to myself. I put my back to the wall and slid toward the front door.

Two towering glass panels that stretched eight feet toward the ceiling flanked the door. They weren't just windows; they were fortified barriers, embedded with a tight, honeycombed wire mesh designed to turn a bullet into a harmless lead pancake.

I was looking at a fortress, and I was on the wrong side of the glass.

Movement caught my eye. Behind the reinforced pane stood a man who looked like he'd stepped straight out of a desert conflict — tall, lean, and draped in camouflage. His dark beard and mustache framed a face as hard as the stone outside.

My heart stopped when I saw what he was holding: a heavy tactical pistol, its muzzle pressed firmly against the temple of Teddy Santos.

Teddy didn't move. He didn't blink. He just stared into the middle distance with glassy, vacant eyes, as if someone had switched off his soul.

I froze, my breath hitching in my chest. The gunman didn't look surprised to see me; he looked expectant. He locked eyes with me, a predatory glint in his stare, and casually gestured with the weapon for me to enter.

A sharp, mechanical *buzz* echoed through the glass as he reached down and triggered the electronic lock.

I pushed inside. The lobby was a sterile, claustrophobic box — ten by sixteen feet of blinding white walls and clinical tile. To the left, a massive reception desk of gleaming white Formica, trimmed in cheap gold plastic, dominated the space. It looked like a command center. Thick metal racks rose from the corners, supporting a vertical stack of monitors angled toward the gunman, their flickering screens likely displaying every inch of the perimeter I'd just crossed.

I limped in, leaning on my cane more than I had to. It never hurts to go for the "helpless cripple" routine when facing a man with a big gun.

The door shut behind me with a heavy clunk.

"The mistress wishes to see you," the man said. I was unsure where he was from, but his accent had a Russian sound to it.

I nodded. "Is it necessary to hold a gun on my friend?"

"Is it?" he replied.

Mental control made normal questions impossible for this man. Since he worked so close to Vanya, the level of mental conditioning exerted on him was probably much higher than that of the usual drones.

I tried again. "Tell me why you are holding a gun at my friend."

"I have been told you can be dangerous. The mistress does not want you shot. I will shoot your friend if you do not cooperate."

Well, that was a pretty straightforward answer.

I raised my hands in surrender. "I will cooperate."

"Then I will not hurt your friend," he responded mechanically. He pointed to a door on the far side of the desk. "Go to that door."

I nodded and moved to where he indicated. He pushed another button, and the door buzzed. I held it open as he walked over with one hand on Santos' arm and one still holding the gun to his head.

I held the door until his elbow supported it, then moved into the hall. The sounds of computers whirring and fans spinning increased in volume, like white noise on steroids.

He pointed with the gun at the hall in front of me, basically an opening between the machines that filled the room. I walked along the long passageway, with huge racks of servers on both sides of me.

We continued the long way down the aisle, and there was an occasional aisle perpendicular to the one we walked on that revealed row after row like the one I was in. These breaks allowed access to other aisles and showed how many hundreds of rows of machines were in this building. The data compilation ability was enormous, far beyond terabytes of storage, but petabytes, exabytes, and possibly zettabytes of information passed through these machines.

The man led me to the back of the building and gestured me to the location of the break area I had glimpsed in my vision.

Standing near the table was Emma Truesdale, who was also holding a gun, though it was smaller than the impressive weapon the bearded man carried. Of course, it could be just as fatal.

Sitting at the table with that twisted smile on her face was Anika Vanya, appearing quite delighted with the situation. As I drew closer, she didn't bother to get up, but held her wooden cane in her good hand.

"Nikos, return the boy to the room with the others," she announced. "Tell me if you understand."

"I understand," Nikos said and guided Teddy Santos to the conference room.

Emma held the gun pointed at the floor, and Vanya just stared at me with that smirk.

"I thought you'd be more surprised to see me," Vanya gloated proudly.

"Sorry, I got a peek at you from some other people's minds," I snapped.

This made her smile widen. "Of course you did, with those rather impressive skills of yours." She looked down at the wooden walking stick in her hand, and the end with the hook. "I must remember not to make eye contact with you."

"If he tries anything, mistress, I'll shoot him," Emma promised, her thumb rubbing the grip of the small pistol.

Vanya nodded. "Yes, but don't kill him. There is so much more we can do. Perhaps shoot his lady friend. Or better yet, have his teaching assistant do it."

My blood ran cold. She meant every word. I needed to throw her off-balance. "You're running out of time. The police are on the way. They're going to block the road out of here."

"All part of the plan," Vanya responded. "Do you know why I chose this place, Doctor?"

"Computer records from all the cop shops and financial records from Wall Street. My guess is that you want to blow it up."

Emma looked surprised and concerned, but Vanya waved a dismissive hand. "Very good, Doctor. You never disappoint. But it's more than that. Once I destroy the records, Emma and I will easily create new identities and move to another coast."

"So you can continue to control and steal from people?" I spat.

Emma took two quick steps forward. She raised the gun and bludgeoned me on the left temple with a surprising amount of force.

I dropped to the ground, my stiff leg sliding out from under me, and I hit the floor with a lot of force. I lay there as minor explosions of light flashed in my head, and I fought to remain cognizant.

"Easy, Emma," I heard Vanya say. "He'll be no fun if he's unconscious."

"I will not allow him to mock you," Emma barked, the anger apparent. "After what he did to you, it takes everything I have not to shoot him down like a dog."

I heard a sound like a kiss, and Emma sighed. Then Vanya spoke, "You are so good to me, but let me have my fun, darling."

"Of course, mistress," Emma responded.

I shifted slowly into a sitting position, still woozy. My head felt like several hammers were beating against each other inside it. Emma loomed over me, the gun at the ready. Vanya sat, looking as if she had not moved a muscle since the moment I'd arrived.

"Still with us, Doctor?" she asked sweetly.

"I guess so," I muttered.

"Get up," Emma hissed.

"Not just yet. Emma, please bring me the doctor's cane."

Emma raised the gun, pointed it at my head, and I didn't move. She grabbed the cobra-head cane and hastened out of reach. I gave her no reason to shoot.

She handed it to Vanya, who hit the catch and slid the twenty-four-inch blade from the stick. She looked at it in the fluorescent light, ran her thumb along the blade, admiring the edge. "I believe I have found my souvenir."

"Not to complain," I declared, trying to sound tougher than I felt, "but I need that to stand up. Unless you want me to stay here on the floor."

Vanya held out her wooden cane with the crook at the end to Emma, who took it and threw it to me. I was fortunate enough to catch it before it hit me.

"Do you want me to stand, or sit in a chair?" I asked, my head clearing. "And did I mention the police are on their way, maybe already have the road blocked by now?"

I saw Emma shift her weight and had the feeling that she wanted to hit me again, but she restrained herself with a look at Vanya.

"Oh, Doctor, how little you understand me," Vanya said. She called out, "Nikos! Go to the front and watch it. Call me if anyone shows up. Tell me if you understand."

Nikos came out of the conference room. "I understand."

"You will negotiate with the FBI. Tell me if you understand."

"I am to negotiate with them for one hour," Nikos replied.

I saw Emma smile at this. "You've done well with this one, mistress."

Vanya smiled. "You always were the one who appreciated me most, Emma. Nikos, you are correct, follow those instructions. Now go."

The big man turned and walked away.

Vanya looked back at me. "And you left our other man outside for the police to find. The perfect prop."

"Prop?" I repeated, confused.

"Yes, stand up, Doctor. I will let you face death with a little more dignity than you left me."

This remark made Emma look at me with such hatred, it surprised me I didn't burst into flames.

I used the cane to push myself up. The cane was solid wood, sturdy, and it helped me get to my feet. "Can I sit? I'm still a little light-headed."

"Emma, pull out the chair for the doctor," Vanya ordered.

Emma grabbed a chair, slid it out from under the table, and pushed it toward me. I took it and sat down, out of reach of both of them.

"Thank you," I said.

"You will die here," Emma whispered.

I drew a breath. "I know you hate me, but there is no reason to hurt the others. Let them go. They've done nothing to you."

This made Emma laugh, and she turned to Vanya, who had her eyes fixed on me.

"I wanted to take everything from you," Vanya said. "Just as you took everything from me."

"You're alive, and can create a new identity," I shot back. "You can go back to using your talents in whatever way you want. I can't stop you."

"You don't deserve to live," Emma ranted. "Just like that bitch, Aubrey."

I hung my head, despair filling my heart. "You didn't have to do that to her. She didn't want to shoot you."

"But she *did* shoot me, Doctor," Vanya said with icy calm. "Just as you took my money and prestige. So, I took your unborn child, and now I will take the love of your life."

The grief that washed over me was overwhelming. "No, please let Jyanette go. None of this was her fault. Please, just let her go."

"Now you beg," Emma scoffed, "when you realize how truly powerless you are."

Vanya gazed at me as I stared at the ground. She murmured. "Emma, take the gun and go shoot Ms. Emery."

I brought my head up and looked directly at Emma, who was lifting the gun with a look of glee on her face. I pushed past any resistance and into her mind as I roared, *"No!"*

I was immediately inside the mess that was Emma's mind.

I felt her hatred for me, her love of Anika, and her desire for power over others. How much she enjoyed using the doctor at Ancora, getting him to help her build the plan. I saw her connect over the computer with Vanya while she was in recovery and felt their mutual desire to destroy me.

I was in her mind and in control of her body. I reached out and pulled the pistol from her grip.

The blade of a sword slashed the back of my hand.

I shouted in pain, which broke my concentration as I yanked my hand away. The gun fell to the ground. Vanya rose to her feet and swung the sharpened blade from my cane at my face.

I fell back as Emma dove for the gun. I used the heavy wooden cane to parry Vanya, and stepped back, the cane held high. Emma grabbed the gun and turned as I swung the heavy hook into Emma's head with all my might.

The wood connected with her face, and the shock knocked the gun from her hand as she collapsed unconscious onto the floor. I took another step back and was now at the door to the conference room.

I raised the wooden cane and shifted my weight, preparing myself as the months of Aikido had trained me to do. I had a way to deflect Vanya's attacks with the blade; I just needed to keep her away from the gun.

Vanya stood at the table, the sword out in front of her. "You continue to be an annoyance."

"I'll stop you. I swear I will."

That crooked smile appeared on her face again. "You never could. I've been playing with a stacked deck."

"You can't control me!" I yelled back. "Kate deprogrammed me."

She still wore that frightening smile. "Yes, while I controlled her. You're right. If I say 'Raymond Shaw,' nothing happens. What if I say 'Knave of Hearts'?"

Her voice rose to a crescendo when she said the words, and I felt my arms drop to my sides and my body relax as I replied, "I'm here."

It was the strangest feeling. I was there, in my body experiencing the sweat trickling down my face, the pain in my temple from being struck, the bleeding cut in my hand, and even the floor underneath my feet, but I had no control over my actions.

I stood in a complete, unmoving trance.

14. DESTRUCTION

Vanya approached my still form, limping as she came. She raised the blade to my throat and murmured, "The Queen of Hearts, she baked some tarts."

My mouth moved against my will. "All on a summer's day."

She stepped back and let loose a laugh that was the most terrifying thing I'd ever heard. She regained control of herself and went on, "The Knave of Hearts, he stole those tarts."

"And took them clean away," I replied. I couldn't feel my arms or my legs. I stood, but did not know what was keeping me upright.

She moved closer to me, but I couldn't move, couldn't flinch.

"Tell me who I am!" she commanded.

"You are the voice," I replied without hesitation. "The voice I must obey."

"You are to remember everything. Tell me if you understand."

"I understand," I repeated without emotion.

The nearby phone rang, and Vanya glared at it. She chuckled. "Don't go anywhere."

She limped to the table and the phone as I stood stock-still, waiting to be told what to do.

"Yes," she said into the receiver, then waited as someone spoke. "Good, bring him here."

She hung up and returned my sword to its sheath. Then, using my cane to stabilize herself, she bent to examine Emma and felt the pulse on her neck.

"She was never good at ducking," Vanya sneered with a glance at me. She sat in a chair and pulled Emma up into her lap, stroking her head. Emma let out a soft groan and seemed to be roused a bit.

"Are you awake?" Vanya asked.

Emma's eyes shot open. "Mistress, that man—"

"Shh," Vanya shushed. "It's all right. There he is. He's under our control."

At that moment, Nikos walked out of the hallway with a gun pointed at Darren Ward, who held his hands aloft. He glanced around at the women and me standing with my arms at my sides.

Vanya laughed. "And here is the good doctor's backup. Where was he, Nikos?"

"Outside the building looking for a way in," Nikos revealed with no emotion. "He was carrying this."

Nikos held out the gun I had seen Darren use over the last few days. Vanya rose while Emma remained sitting on the floor. "Give the gun to Doctor Wise."

Nikos held out the weapon to me, holding it by the barrel and offering me the grip.

"Take it, Wise," she said simply. Emma was now slowly getting up to her feet, and her hand rubbed the spot where I had clocked her with the wooden cane.

I reached out and took the gun from Nikos' hand and felt the weight of it. I also saw that the back of my hand was bleeding profusely from the sword wound, but I didn't care.

It wasn't important.

"Nikos, you will return to the lobby and wait for the police. Tell me if you know what to do."

"I know what to do," Nikos answered, turned, and walked away.

"Doctor Wise," Vanya said, and pointed at Darren. "This man is a threat. He wants to hurt you. If he moves, you must shoot him to save your own life."

I pointed the gun at my associate without hesitation.

Darren looked from Vanya to me. "Len, are you okay?"

"No, he isn't," Vanya cackled, which made Emma laugh as well.

"What shall we make him do, mistress?" Emma purred.

Vanya considered this. "Kill everyone, I think."

Emma smiled with evil in her eyes. "Before we go, I'd like a souvenir."

"Really, Emma? What would suit your fancy?"

"Probably his testicles," Emma gushed, and I could see a malevolent light in her eyes.

"A lovely idea, but not possible with our timetable."

"Too time-consuming?" Emma sighed.

Vanya considered this. "It will undoubtedly distract him when we need him to shoot at the police."

"Pity."

"We'd better get to it," Vanya trilled.

"Wait a minute," Darren interjected, his voice cutting through the suffocating tension like a blade. He raised his hands in a frantic gesture of peace, stepping closer to me.

Vanya and Emma watched him with predatory smirks, their eyes glinting with the dark satisfaction of seeing a man cornered.

Darren shifted his weight with a deceptive, innocent grace. Then, in a sudden, violent explosion of movement, he lunged forward.

The gunshot did not merely ring out; it shattered the silence of the confined room. A flash of orange flame erupted from the muzzle, and the roar was a physical force, a deafening thunderclap that seemed to rattle the very foundations of the building.

The bullet struck Darren full in the chest. The sheer kinetic energy of the impact lifted him off his feet, catapulting him backward until he slammed against the cold, unyielding wall. He crumpled instantly, a broken marionette sliding down to the floor until he lay motionless on his chest.

As the echoes faded, the sharp, metallic scent of gunpowder filled the air. Vanya turned her gaze toward the smoking gun, her crooked smile widening into a jagged mask of triumph.

"You see?" she purred, her voice dripping with malice. "One can never say the good doctor fails to do exactly what he is told."

Emma clapped her hands, overcome with glee. "Is it time?"

Vanya nodded. "We shall give the doctor his orders, and then head out to our boat. We can watch the explosion from the bay."

Emma made an exaggerated sigh and stuck her lower lip out in a pout. "Are you sure there isn't enough time to get my souvenir?"

"I'm afraid not, dear. That gunshot will attract attention," Vanya soothed and caressed Emma's hair. "How's your head?"

"It hurts," Emma sulked, but then brightened. "I want to see him shoot the DA bitch."

Vanya turned to face me. I had lowered the hand with the gun after I shot Darren.

"Tell me who I am!" Vanya demanded.

"You are the voice," I responded.

"Good. Listen carefully. There are people in this room," she said with a gesture at the conference room door.

"People in this room," I repeated.

"They killed your child," Vanya growled.

Suddenly, I saw what she spoke of in my mind's eye. There was a little girl I held in my arms — my little girl. She had just been born and was tiny and helpless, her skin a light brown and the dark hair on her head short and curly.

In a flash, I saw her grow. One moment she was learning to walk, and the next she was taller and running. Her hair grew long and was dark and kinky, framing her face in beautiful curls. I saw her look at me, hug my neck, and say, "Daddy, I love you."

"My child," I repeated, overcome with grief… and anger, and my mind seemed lost in a thick mist.

I turned to the door and knew that in that room were the people who killed her, the ones who took her from me. They had plotted and planned this. Together, they came up with a plan to kill my little girl, and now I would make them pay.

Vanya touched my arm with the pistol in it. I looked down at the gun, and it filled me with the desire for revenge.

"Make them pay for killing your child," she commanded. She opened the door and hit the switch, which made fluorescent lights flicker to life in the room as I raised the gun.

Teddy Santos and Jyanette, two young men I didn't know, and two other people with bags over their heads, were sitting around a table.

One was the same body type as Mrs. Higgins.

For a moment, this confused me.

This is wrong! These people wouldn't kill my child. Some of them were my friends; the others were total strangers.

"They killed your child," the voice rang out. "Make them pay. You'll feel so much better if you do."

That mist filled my mind again and made it hard to think. I raised the gun at the hooded figure. I could just put a bullet into that person who appeared to be a woman. It would be easy, pull the trigger and watch her die.

I would feel so much better if I could watch her die.

Then there was something red in my eye that blinded me, and I flinched and turned away. I held my hand up to see a red dot appear on my palm. It was a beam of light that pierced through the window. The beam was so bright that it pulled all of my attention.

Then it moved off me and across the wall. It was so deep red and beautiful; I had to watch it.

I saw it land on the body of a woman behind me. And through the mist, I tried to recognize her. She looked like Anika Vanya. That was impossible. Vanya was dead. How could she be here?

"Shoot, shoot," this strange woman demanded. She pointed toward the light through the window.

Without hesitation, I turned to the window and fired two shots. The explosion inside the room was so loud that the people at the table jumped in surprise, except the one who looked like Jyanette.

The red light was still shining, and there was a loud thump. With a shriek, the woman I thought was Vanya fell to the floor, a red flower blossoming on her shoulder.

She lay still, and a cane — my cane — fell from her hand to the floor.

I watched her dispassionately as her body fell, still lost in that fog. The only thing I wondered was how she had gotten my cane.

I turned back and looked at the people around the table. The two men I didn't know were crying, and I heard sobs from under the hood of the woman.

It didn't matter, and in that mist, rage filled me with a desire to destroy them. They killed my child; her precious face in my mind so clear that I knew she had to be real.

I raised the gun at one of the sobbing men.

A scream came from my left, and I didn't move as a woman came at me with a chair over her head. She struck me with the chair, knocking me off-balance and driving me down to my one good knee.

Then whoever this other woman was, she clawed at the gun in my hand, but I held it tight. I needed it. I had to shoot the people who killed my child; I had to eliminate them.

The chair was on top of me and in the way of the woman reaching for the gun. I struggled, got my good leg under me, and pushed back. The chair rose, and the woman fell against the wall.

I stared at my assailant. She looked like Emma Truesdale!

My mind tried to get around that idea, but I couldn't think. They locked up Emma Truesdale in a psychiatric facility somewhere. How did she get here? Why was she with the people who killed my child?

She pulled herself up the wall and shrieked, "You killed her!"

Although shrill, she even sounded like Truesdale.

She readied herself to lunge at me again, and just then, a red dot appeared between her eyes.

There was a second thump, and her head exploded in a shower of blood and gore, and a reddish mist of blood hung in the air.

Her body fell to the floor, bereft of life, and I grabbed the conference table to pull myself up to my feet.

I looked down at the woman who looked like Anika Vanya. Her mouth had blood around it, and she coughed as she met my eyes. The red on her shoulder wasn't a flower. It was spreading blood, darkening her outfit.

"Not over... this is not over..." she croaked. "I will destroy your MPD." She coughed. "Now... shoot them..."

She coughed twice more and lay still.

I then looked at the people in the room, the ones I must kill, the ones who destroyed my child. I raised my arm to shoot them and found the gun was no longer in my hand.

This was getting stranger and stranger.

I stared at my empty hand, with a slash along the back that was bleeding profusely. When had that happened? I was aware of the pain, but it didn't seem important. I reached my bloody hand into my pocket, where I found a Taser. What was it doing here? I couldn't think how it could have gotten there or if I'd even seen it before.

I lifted it, slid back the cover, and activated it, then pointed at the first face I saw.

It was Jyanette, who stared unblinking at nothing the entire time.

I stopped and forced myself to think. I needed to pierce the fog in my brain, to make sense of this.

Jyanette didn't kill my child. No, she was the child's mother, wasn't she? Wasn't she going to have a child?

I had to shoot someone, desperately needing to do it. I looked around the table at these people, some I knew and others I did not. Then I could see only one logical conclusion.

I lowered the device until I pointed it at my thigh and hit the activation button.

There was a whoosh of compressed air, and a stabbing pain as the needles sank into my leg with significant force. I cried out in pain as electricity shot through me and the device fell from my hand.

I felt myself fall to the ground as everything around me went black.

I was being shaken awake, and all I wanted was to sleep. My face hurt, my hand throbbed, and my leg stung.

"Lemme 'lone, wanna sleep," I muttered. My eyes opened as Bill McGee's face appeared in my line of vision.

"Bill?" I croaked.

"It's okay, Len," Bill assured me.

"Jyanette — Mrs. Higgins—"

"The hostages are fine."

"But your wife was there, with handcuffs—"

"I know. I've spoken with her. We got all of them out, though Mrs. Higgins almost wouldn't go with you lying there. We've got Jyanette and Teddy out of whatever spell they were in, and all of them are on the way to the hospital. You were unconscious and with that bruise on your face, we had to wait until a doctor checked you out before we tried to rouse you."

"Vanya?" I groaned.

"Dead, for real this time. I'm going to make sure she goes to the county Medical Examiner, Casey Latrell, to make sure."

"This building... wired... explosives," I stammered.

"We've got FBI bomb technicians on site. They're going to go through the building," Bill explained. "We have to get you out first. Come on, get up."

"I-I shot Darren," I muttered, and tried to focus as Bill helped me painfully to my feet.

"I know," came a familiar voice. "And I'm pretty pissed about it."

By now I was standing, and I raised my head to see Darren Ward being helped up by Officer Galland.

"Darren?" I gasped.

"I'm still among the living," Darren whined as he rose, obviously in pain. "It was a damn good thing I put a Kevlar vest under my clothes. And that you aimed for my chest."

He opened his jacket. His shirt had a large hole in it, and I could see the protective vest under the fabric.

My mouth fell open in surprise. "Kevlar? Are you all right?"

"The shot knocked the wind out of me," he moaned, as Galland and Bill assisted us toward the now-open back door I had attempted to open earlier. "I'm going to have one hell of a nasty bruise. I hope it didn't crack a rib."

"I'm just glad you're alive," I responded as Bill grabbed my cane from the floor and escorted me toward the open door. I leaned heavily on McGee as Darren did with Galland.

The parking lot of the building next door was filled with police vehicles of different types and jurisdictions, with flashing blue and red lights.

"Did you have a police sniper take out Vanya and Truesdale?" I asked.

"They were both dead when we got here, Len, and someone shot out that back window." We brought two teams in, one through the front and one through the back, who took out the hostages."

"What about the guard? I think his name was Nikos," I grunted as Bill helped me walk through the lot.

"We had to take him out, but we found Martin Hodges tied up and he's in custody, just in case he's still a threat."

As we crossed onto the macadam of the InFreight lot, Gabe Petrie approached me.

"You never looked better, Doc," Gabe said with a glance at my battered face. "Okay, so fill us in. How did you find this place?"

I was in no mood. "Agent Petrie, you know what I do—"

"I know what you *claim* to do," he said. "But you must have had more to go on than your 'feeling.'"

I attempted to speak, but my mouth felt weird, and my hand was still bleeding.

Petrie took my silence as a reason to go on. "The FBI wants to know how you found a secure location in such a short time."

"They were holding friends of mine," I explained as we kept moving. I now saw that there were ambulances and several EMTs were treating the hostages. "That gave me focus, and I sensed them as I got close."

"So now you're a bloodhound?" Petrie scoffed as he walked along with us.

"Basically," I answered in all seriousness as we reached Bill's car. "How did you guys get here without those so-called Homeland Security people? I thought they had you holed up at MPD."

Bill leaned me against the car and handed me my cane, which I held with my left hand to help me stay upright.

"Weirdest thing," Gabe answered. "Right after Bill snuck out to meet you, the lead guy gets a phone call, and without even a 'thank you,' they all leave."

Bill had opened the passenger door of his unmarked police car, and he eased me into the seat. He pulled a medical kit from the glove compartment and took out gauze to wrap my bleeding hand. Galland guided Darren past us to one of the EMTs.

"Whoever was supporting Vanya must have pulled the plug on the operation," Bill suggested.

I looked at Petrie. "Do you think we can find out who ordered them there?"

Petrie opened his hands in a gesture of helplessness. "I called Washington, but no one knows anything, and Homeland Security has assured me there was no team in our area."

"They will bury any information," Bill said, as he finished with the gauze and taped the bandage in place.

I looked at Bill with concern. "Were any of the hostages injured? Was Laura hurt?"

Bill smiled. "Not harmed in any way."

I frowned at this, as I wondered why Vanya had gone to such elaborate trouble to capture her. But Petrie tapped me on the shoulder and pointed up at the building we'd just left. "The bomb crew is about to go in."

I followed his line of vision and saw two men near the door we had exited. One was tall and seemed much larger since he was wearing an Explosive Ordnance Disposal suit. It looked like something a deep-sea diver or an astronaut might wear. It had a huge protective helmet and a heavily padded body covering that made the man look like a giant. He carried a small briefcase that offered him a private air supply.

Next to him was a technician who helped him dress. He stood next to a four-foot-tall device with mechanical arms and a camera on its head. It sat on top of a pair of miniature tank treads. Once the tall man had donned the heavy gear, the other man hung a board with electronic controls around his neck. He then stepped away and activated the robot to enter the facility, as he watched its progress on a small screen built into the control board.

"Do you have any idea when they were going to blow the building?" Petrie asked me.

"No," I worried. "But there probably isn't a lot of time."

Blow up the building…

"Do you have an idea how Vanya was going to get out?" Bill asked.

"Yes, they had a boat on the bay, and probably a rowboat to get to it."

"I'll get on locating her boat once they clear the bomb," Petrie stated.

I was watching the man in the EOB suit as he stepped inside the server farm. But there was something wrong.

I could think clearly now with that strange fog lifted, and a memory came to me. Vanya lay on the floor, a gaping wound in her chest, and she said, "Not over... this is not over..."

Blow up the building...

I couldn't understand why I was getting a buzz about the building being destroyed. I knew that was the plan. After all, Vanya told it to me.

What was bothering me?

"I will destroy your MPD."

My head snapped up, and I felt my mind clear. Of course, it was so obvious.

"Petrie, Bill," I snapped. Gabe glared at me, and Bill turned his attention to me. "Did you say that the Homeland Security guys got a phone call and left? Just like that?"

"Yeah," Petrie snapped. "I told you that. So we all left to come here."

"Distraction," I snapped.

Bill caught my tone. "What are you saying, Len?"

"Remember how the attack on my house was a distraction so you wouldn't be at yours?"

"Sure."

"What if the plan was to do that again?"

"What are you going on about, Wise?" Petrie argued.

"Those agents," I told him. "They were fake, right?"

Petrie shook his head. "We think so."

I nodded. "Okay, so why go to Mountainview PD?"

"To slow us down," Bill said. "Distract us from getting to you."

"Vanya knew the FBI would raid this place. She even predicted I'd end up in a shootout with them," I said, the realization coiling in my gut like a snake. "And then the 'agents' vanish just as you leave? Why pull them out—"

"Unless they wanted us here," Bill said, his voice dropping an octave as he finished my thought.

"To what end?" Petrie demanded, looking between us.

"To finish what she started a year ago," I whispered. The air in the car suddenly felt thin, charged with the static of an impending explosion. "Bill, we have to go. We have to go *now*."

Bill didn't hesitate. He was up and moving before I could even settle into the passenger seat. I slammed the door shut; the metal thudding with a sound like a coffin lid closing. Bill rounded the front of the car and threw himself behind the wheel.

"What are you talking about?" Petrie yelled, leaning toward the open window, his face a mask of frantic confusion.

I rolled the glass down just enough to lock eyes with him, the stiff wind of the Jersey night biting at my face.

"To stop the last part of her plan," I barked over the roar of the engine. "Someone put a bomb at MPD."

15. COUNTERBLOW

Without another word, Bill tore out of the lot and headed onto North Avenue.

"We should call for a bomb crew," Bill announced as he headed back toward 1 and 9 North toward our exit.

"No time," I said. "If the phony Homeland agents left, that means they had the bomb set, and they needed to clear the site."

Bill handed me his phone. "Call Fire Chief Simmons. Tell him the situation. The fire department is on the second floor, and we need to get anyone on duty out of there."

I was glad he was thinking clearly. I was pretty busted up between what Vanya did to me and watching her die. What I really wanted to do was see Jyanette, make sure she was all right, but this was the more immediate problem.

I put "Fire Chief" into the phone's search option and his number appeared. I hit the call number for his mobile phone.

"Simmons," the voice said.

"Chief Simmons? I am calling for Lieutenant Bill McGee. We think there may be a bomb in the public safety building."

"What? Is this a joke?"

I changed the setting to speakerphone and held it out to Bill as he drove.

"Captain? It's Bill. We think there's a bomb at MPD. You need to clear the building."

"Christ, Bill, how did this happen?" the voice inquired through the tiny speaker.

"Long story, Captain. Just pass the word down the line, get them out right now."

"I'm on it, Bill," the man said and hung up.

By now we were blazing our way with the lights and sirens blaring up Route 78 as fast as traffic allowed. Bill was an expert driver, and he wove his way through and around the other cars as quickly and safely as he could.

I tried to think of something I could do besides sitting there. I pulled out my phone and went to the main number for MPD.

"Mountainview Police," I heard CeeCee say as she picked up.

"CeeCee, it's Len Wise. Get out of the building!"

"Len? What is this about?"

"The Homeland Security guys—"

"They're gone, and boy, were they a pain—"

"They were fake. They planted a bomb! Tell everyone, evacuate the building, get out to the parking lot and a suitable distance from the building."

"I thought everyone headed to where you are," she said.

"CeeCee, there's no time! Get out of there!"

She hung up, and I hoped she would hurry. I put my phone away and grumbled, "Can't we go any faster?"

"Len, I'm doing the best I can!" Bill snarled, his knuckles white against the steering wheel. He threw the cruiser into a hard bank, the tires screaming in protest. "Why the hell would she go this far? Why level the entire building?"

"Because the last time she tried to take us down, her drone failed," I yelled over the wail of the siren. "She doesn't just want us dead, Bill, she wants a monument to her victory."

I slumped against the seat, closing my eyes and trying to force my consciousness to reach out toward the station. I needed to feel the building, to sense the cold, mechanical heartbeat of whatever device was ticking inside.

How complex was it?

The question felt like lead in my stomach. I wasn't a hero; my heart was a frantic bird trapped in my ribs, and my head throbbed with a rhythmic, sickening ache. Every instinct I had screamed at me to find a dark hole and wait for the world to stop burning.

But the streets of Mountainview were already blurring past. Bill didn't slow down, weaving through local traffic like a man possessed. It felt like an eternity lived in minutes until the cruiser fishtailed into the MPD parking lot.

The scene was a jagged tableau of panic. CeeCee stood near the entrance, flanked by several officers who looked like they were holding their breath. Two men from the fire department huddled with them, their faces grim under the strobing blue and red lights.

Before the car had even fully settled on its springs, Bill was out, his door swinging wide.

I followed, my breath hitching as I forced my weight onto my cane, the metal tip clicking against the asphalt in a desperate, limping rhythm toward the center of the storm.

"Everyone cleared from the building?" Bill's voice boomed in the night.

"We think so," CeeCee said.

One of the uniformed men spoke up, a Caucasian man with black hair. "What about Sergeant Tice?"

"What do you mean?" Bill asked.

"He was taking a break in the bunk room, said he needed to get a little shut-eye."

CeeCee looked distraught. "I didn't think to check the bunks. I thought we had to get out fast."

"You did fine," Bill said. "Fire guys, you got a bomb suit up there?"

"No, sir, we call in the feds for that kind of job," a muscled young man answered.

His associate, a strong-looking Asian man with a shaved head, turned to us. "We got a PAN disrupter, though."

McGee looked at him. "Do you know how to set it up and fire it?"

The Asian man considered this for a moment. "I think so. I was there when they did the demo."

McGee nodded. "What's your name, sir?"

The man offered Bill his hand, his powerful forearm speaking of his strength. "I'm Sergeant Wu. This is Jacobs."

Bill shook the offered hand. "Please get it and set it up out here."

"Out here?" Wu repeated.

"Yes, do it over there." Bill pointed to an area on the lot far enough away from the building, but empty of cars. "Once it's set up, we can move it into place wherever we need it."

Jacobs gulped. "Yeah, but we need to go into the building to get it."

Wu shook his head. "I'll get it. I'll use the back stairs. Then you help me get it ready, okay, Jacobs?"

"Yes, sir."

Bill spoke up. "Jacobs, you can assist by keeping anyone else from getting close." He then turned to me. "Len, do we have enough time?"

"I'm not getting a warning to stay away, if that's any help."

"Not much of one," Bill said, his voice tense.

We walked toward the building, Sergeant Wu, Bill, and I. Bill pulled out his cell, quickly dialed a number, set it to speaker, and I heard it ring.

Tice answered groggily. "What is it, LT?"

"Tice, this is serious, I'm not kidding around. We think the Homeland guys were fake and that they planted a bomb in MPD."

"Christ," Tice hissed.

"Len and I are coming in to find it, but I want you out."

There was silence for a long moment. "Wouldn't another pair of eyes help?"

Bill exhaled loudly. "I am not asking you to risk your life, Tice."

"I'm volunteering," Tice asserted. "I'll throw on my pants and open the door for you." He ended the call.

We kept walking, Bill slowing down so I could keep up.

Wu said, "Your officer doesn't lack courage."

"Just common sense," Bill swore. "But he's right. If we are to have a chance, we need more eyes."

We were now about to reach the side door when it opened and Tice stood there in a T-shirt and a pair of dark-brown pants. He gazed at us. "You two look like hell, especially you, Doc."

Wu moved to the nearby stairs. "I'll set up in the parking lot, but I can move the equipment in here when you find anything."

"Thanks, Wu," Bill said as the sergeant went upstairs.

"What's he getting?" Tice worried.

"Turns out MFD has a PAN disrupter."

"I hate to sound foolish, but what is that?" I asked.

Tice turned and headed in as we followed. "Doc, it's a fancy water cannon."

I accepted this and asked, "Tice, you were here when the Homeland team was crawling all over us. Where did they spend most of their time?"

"They practically lived in the conference room," Tice said, gesturing down the hall.

Bill's eyes met mine, sharp and questioning. "Could it really be that obvious?"

I gave a grim shrug. "Why wouldn't it be? They thought we'd be busy in Elizabeth. They didn't think anyone would be looking."

The three of us moved with a sense of haunted urgency, our footsteps echoing against the linoleum. We pushed into the large conference room. At first glance, it was sterile and undisturbed — just a heavy oak table, a cluster of empty chairs, and a projector pointed at a blank screen. But the air felt heavy, charged with a localized, mechanical malice.

"Under the table," I said, the words feeling like ice on my tongue. "If I were them, I'd want it centered. Maximum structural damage."

Bill didn't hesitate. He dropped to his knees and slid onto his back, disappearing into the shadows beneath the massive table.

"Any luck?" Tice asked, his voice tight.

"God dammit," Bill's voice came from the floor, a harsh, jagged whisper. "I'm looking right at it. Tice, get me the toolbox. Now!"

Tice gave me a frantic nod and bolted for the door. I stepped closer to the edge of the table, my heart hammering against my ribs. "What are we dealing with, Bill?"

"It looks like a nightmare, Len."

"Be specific. Is there wiring? A timer?"

"It's a single unit," Bill grunted, his breathing heavy in the cramped space. "Round cylinder, maybe fifteen inches across. Brushed metal cover. There's no countdown clock, just a single, pulsing red light, like a heartbeat."

I felt a cold sweat break out on the back of my neck. "Is there an antenna? Is it possible they can detonate this thing remotely?"

"Sure, or it could be on a timer, or have a motion sensor, or have a photoelectric cell, I don't know. If I could pry it open, see the insides, I would have a better idea. But it looks like a screwdriver will be too thick to get between the cover and the casing."

I got down on my one good knee, hit the hidden catch on my cane, and slid the sword free and offered Bill the hilt. "Try this."

He looked at the blade. "This might work. I hope it doesn't go off if it's opened."

"If it does, that's it for us both."

I closed my eyes and tried to reach out, to see if there was anything I sensed, but I received nothing. I was afraid that since one of Vanya's drones had placed it there, there might be a mental block.

I opened my eyes to see Bill pry the case open. The top fell off and hung by a pair of wires about six inches below where the device attached to the table.

Tice came into the room with a small toolbox. "Any luck?"

"I see nothing lucky here," Bill fretted. "It appears to be on a timer, and I believe we have about ten minutes."

"Can you defuse it?" I asked.

"This?" Bill griped. "I did work with the FBI bomb squad in my day, but this isn't some improvised device. I wouldn't even know how to get started."

"Why don't we just carry the table out of the building?" Tice suggested.

I exchanged a look with Bill on the floor, who raised his eyebrows and answered, "That might work."

He carefully pushed the cover back in place and handed me my sword, which I returned to the cane's sheath.

"You still got that thing?" Tice grinned. "You know it's illegal in New Jersey, right?"

I looked up at Tice. "Are you going to turn me in?"

"Not today," he quipped. "You should get outside, Doc."

I stood as McGee slid out from under the table. "I want to help with the table."

"With your leg?" Tice asked. "You'll only slow us down."

McGee got to his feet. "He's right, Len. Head out."

I exhaled, but nodded. "Can you guys lift this big table?"

"I sure hope so." McGee grimaced as Tice cleared the projector that rested on the surface of the large, oblong piece of furniture.

I hurried across the hall, swiping my magnetic ID through the reader with trembling fingers. The side door hissed open, revealing the asphalt of the parking lot and the cool evening air. We were lucky — the conference room sat on a direct line to the exit, but the geometry of the escape was a nightmare.

"Watch the legs!" I shouted, though my voice was barely a rasp.

I heard the synchronized, guttural grunts of Tice and McGee as they heaved the massive oak table off the floor. It was a lumbering, awkward beast, made a thousand times more lethal by the cylinder clinging to its underbelly.

Tice pivoted his end, the wood scraping against the doorjamb with a sound that made my hair stand on end. It cleared the frame by less than an inch. One sharp jolt, one slip of a sweaty palm, and the hallway would become a wind tunnel of fire.

Out in the lot, I spotted the two firefighters — Jacobs was frantically unfolding a heavy metal stand, while Wu knelt over a rugged plastic case, his hands moving with surgical precision through a nest of tools.

"Jacobs! Wu!" I bellowed, my voice cracking under the strain. "Forget the gear! We need muscle!"

The two men left the equipment where it was and ran up to the door with two uniforms following. CeeCee wisely kept her distance and spoke into a radio she took off her belt.

It proved how paranoid I'd become, because I couldn't help but wonder who CeeCee was talking to. A part of me wanted to go to her and force eye contact to see if Vanya had gotten to her.

Surely this was merely my obsession and not a psychic warning.

With all the men carrying the table, they quickly brought it out to the lot and placed it with as much space away from the cars as possible.

"How much time do we have?" Wu yelled as he put the table on the ground and ran to get his kit.

"Not sure," Bill said, huffing and puffing from exertion. "Only six minutes or so."

Jacobs grabbed the metal stand and hauled it into position near the table, dropping onto his back to adjust the tripod's height with practiced ease. Wu was a blur of motion, pulling a long, stainless steel barrel from the plastic case. He chambered some kind of cartridge and funneled clear liquid into the barrel before mounting it onto the stand.

"What is that thing?" I asked Bill, watching the clinical precision of their work.

"It's a Percussion-Actuated Non-Electric Disruptor," Bill answered.

"A name designed by a bureaucrat, no doubt," I muttered.

"It basically fires a high-velocity water jet," Tice explained, his voice low. "The pressure is so intense that it shatters the internal circuitry and separates the components. If it works, the bomb is dead before the fuse can even think about reacting. If it doesn't..."

I leaned in. "And it uses just plain water?"

Tice nodded. "The idea is to use the kinetic energy of the water to short out the power source without generating the heat or friction that would actually trigger a detonation."

Bill looked over at Tice, impressed. "Joseph, you've done your homework."

Tice shrugged. "I figure I should learn a thing or two about bombs, ever since the last time MPD almost got blown up."

Jacobs unspooled a coil of vivid yellow wire; the plastic line humming as it whipped off the reel. Behind the PAN disruptor, Wu's fingers moved with a surgeon's cold precision, clicking a detonator disk into the rear of the steel barrel. The connection was seamless — a direct nerve line from the firing mechanism to the remote trigger.

With the device primed, the two men didn't walk; they executed a practiced, high-speed retreat.

Jacobs backed away, feeding out a golden trail of wire that snaked across the dark asphalt like a fuse. Wu followed in his shadow, clutching the heavy plastic equipment case to his chest.

They moved with silent, frantic grace, leaving the table — and the ticking cylinder beneath it — alone in the center of the empty lot.

CeeCee drew near to our group. "Those Homeland guys left that?"

"That's what we think," Bill said.

"If they come back, I'll give them something to think about," CeeCee threatened.

"I'm sure you could, CeeCee," Tice replied with affection.

Wu reached us, and using a pair of clippers, cut the yellow wire from the spool. From the case, he withdrew a small control device. "Time?"

Bill checked his watch. "I gotta say, maybe two minutes."

With steady, clinical precision, Wu stripped the insulation from the wire ends, exposing the bright copper beneath. He looped them around the two brass thumbscrews on the remote detonator, tightening them until they were snug.

He flipped a guarded toggle switch. A small green LED on the handheld unit flared to life, casting a sickly emerald glow over his features.

The link was live.

Between the click of that switch and the table across the lot, there was nothing left but a thin yellow line and a heartbeat of time.

"This'll be loud," Wu warned, and hit the red button on the control.

The air didn't just vibrate; it shattered. The roar of the PAN disrupter was a singular, bone-shaking crack that felt like a physical blow to the chest.

A millisecond later, the table didn't just move — it erupted. A violent plume of orange-white fire blossomed from beneath the wood, a volcanic burst of hot gas and smoke, that catapulted the heavy oak into the air as if made of cardboard. It rose eight feet, silhouetted against the night sky.

Then, gravity reclaimed it. The table slammed back to the asphalt with a loud impact that sent a shockwave through the soles of my shoes. Its supporting legs simply disintegrated, buckling like dry twigs under the force of the fall. Then, the massive top struck the ground and splintered into jagged, blackened sections, settling into a smoking heap of scorched electronics.

A thick, pungent cloud of gray smoke drifted over the debris, carrying the sharp, metallic tang of combustion and the acrid scent of ozone.

Car alarms from the few vehicles in the lot wailed in annoyance at the untimely detonation.

"That was something!" CeeCee said as we stood looking at the wreckage.

"Good thing that didn't go off inside the building," Tice grunted.

I nodded, my gaze drifting back toward the station. Then, the world tore open.

A violent wall of orange flame geysered through the windows, shattering the glass into a million diamonds of light. The heavy back door didn't just open; a massive pressure wave punched it off its hinges, tumbling through the air like a scrap of paper. I threw my arm up, bracing for the hammer-blow of the percussion, my muscles tensing for a heat that never came.

I blinked.

The fire retreated into nothingness. I saw the station silent and intact, the door firmly in its frame, the windows dark and unbroken. The asphalt beneath my feet was cold, not scorched.

I slowly lowered my arm, my heart hammering a frantic rhythm against my ribs. The transformation had been so absolute, so visceral, that my skin still prickled with the ghost-heat of the blast.

"What's wrong, Len?" McGee said, watching my face.

I moved toward the building, not knowing how much time we had, if any at all. Damn Vanya, she knew me too well, knew my abilities, and planned backups to take MPD down.

I was moving as fast as I could with my bad leg to the door, used my card, and yanked it open.

In the distance, I heard Tice say, "What's his hurry?"

If I had stopped to think, I'd have stayed paralyzed. Logic couldn't find a second bomb in a building this size, but I wasn't using logic. A cold, magnetic pull tugged at the base of my skull, dragging me down the corridor until I slammed my shoulder into the door of Bunk Room Two.

The room was unnervingly tidy; the bed made with military precision, the heavy wool blanket draped low, brushing the floorboards to hide the hollow darkness beneath the metal frame.

I dropped to one knee, my joints screaming, and yanked the fabric back.

There it was.

The twin to the device we'd just destroyed sat nestled in the shadows. It was a heavy, brushed-metal disk, roughly the size of a dinner plate, looking entirely too much like a landmine. On its crown, a solitary red LED pulsed with a rhythmic, cheerful malice. *Blink. Blink. Blink.*

My breath hitched. I reached out, my fingers hovering over the cold steel. If someone had bolted it down, all would have been lost.

I slid my hand underneath, praying the bastards hadn't rigged it with a mercury tilt-switch or a proximity trigger. If someone were watching from the tree line with a remote, I was already dead.

I stood up, cradling the device in the crook of my left arm like a sleeping child made of high explosives. I staggered back into the hallway, my cane striking the floor in a frantic, uneven beat. Every step felt like a gamble with gravity as I pushed toward the side door, desperate to reach the open asphalt before the "merry" red light decided its work was done.

The others all looked at me as if I had gone insane, and they were probably right.

I was gasping, my lungs burning as if I'd inhaled ground glass, but I managed a ragged scream: "Move back! There's a second one!"

Before I could take another step, the two firefighters were on me, Jacobs and Wu, yanking the cold metal weight from my trembling arms.

"You can't—" I wheezed, the world spinning.

"We can move faster, Doc, and this is our job," Wu snapped.

Together, they sprinted toward the blackened remains of the first blast site, the heavy disk in Wu's arms. My vision blurred, a jagged psychic spike stabbing through my temple.

Going to blow...

"Throw it!" I shrieked, my voice cracking. "It's going to—"

The world didn't just end; it turned inside out. A brilliant, white-hot flash of light bleached the parking lot into a colorless void. Time didn't just slow down; it curdled.

In the periphery of that blinding glare, I saw Bill, Tice, and the others becoming silhouettes, diving for the asphalt and shielding their heads.

Then came the roar — a deafening boom that felt like a mountain collapsing. The shock wave hit me like a wall, lifting me off my feet and slamming me back onto the hard pavement. My skull met the ground with a sickening *thud*, and the world dissolved into a cacophony of wailing car alarms and a ringing in my ears that swallowed the night.

16. GETTING EVEN

I opened my eyes to the familiar, sterile landscape of the Mountainside Medical Center ceiling. It was a view I'd memorized over the years, and frankly, I loathed seeing it again.

I gingerly reached up to touch the left side of my face. It was a landscape of heat and pain — puffy, swollen, and radiating a dull throb that traveled all the way down into my jaw. The back of my skull felt like someone had used it as a doorstop; a localized, agonizing lump marked the spot where the MPD parking lot had greeted me.

Down at my side, my right hand was a heavy club of fresh white gauze. Beneath the wrapping, I could feel the rhythmic bite of stitches where Vanya's blade had found its mark.

The door groaned open, cutting through the hospital hum.

"He's awake," Gabe Petrie announced. He stepped into the room, followed closely by McGee.

I didn't wait for an invitation. Fumbling for the plastic remote, I touched the 'up' button, the bed motor whirring with a mechanical groan as it forced me into a sitting position.

I wanted to meet them eye-to-eye, despite one of my eyes being swollen shut.

"Well, you're a sight," Bill grumbled.

"Always have to play hero, don't you, Doc?" Petrie said, deadpan.

"The firefighters?" I muttered.

"Jacobs is in the hospital," Bill reported solemnly. "We lost Wu."

I shook my head. Once again, I didn't act fast enough, and it cost lives. "They were two brave men," I said.

Petrie and McGee nodded.

Gabe gazed at me. "We got the bomb out of the server farm… and the backup—"

Bill interrupted. "After the explosions at MPD, I called Gabe and advised him it appeared Vanya used two bombs, just in case. The FBI team removed both and deactivated them without incident."

Gabe went on. "The hostages are safe, and we have a trained hypnotherapist coming up from Washington. He's going to deprogram everyone."

I nodded. "That's good."

Bill smiled. "Galland found that database you were theorizing about. The reason he couldn't find it was that your teaching assistant was helping to hide it."

I shook my head. "It's not his fault, Bill. He was being controlled by Vanya."

"The point is, we now have the list of all of Vanya's controlled people, complete with their keys and locks, to put them under. With that, we should be able to get everyone back to normal."

"If the specialist can fix Kate first, she can help with the others," I suggested.

"That was our plan as well," Petrie said. "Turns out Vanya had programmed people in high places in the government as well."

I shivered. "That's a little scary. How's Jyanette?"

Gabe and Bill exchanged a look.

Bill cleared his throat. "Not good, Len. She's in a coma."

I sat forward, and both men held out their arms to stop me from getting out of bed.

"Hold on, Doc," Gabe said. "You just woke up. You're in no condition to do anything."

"The Hell I am. I have to see her," I said, struggling to get loose.

"Damn it, Len, this won't help," Bill snapped at me. "You are in no condition to help anyone right now."

He pushed me back, and I had to admit I was weak as a kitten.

"Besides, we have questions you need to answer," Petrie demanded. "Like who killed Vanya and Truesdale?"

I lay back, too weary to fight. I shuddered to remember the red laser between Emma's eyes and the sight of her head exploding. "What do you mean?"

Petrie sighed. "They were both brought down with a high-caliber weapon, and the guns we found at the location weren't capable of firing such a round. But we figure you knew who did it."

I shook my head. "I thought you did it. An FBI sniper."

"It wasn't us. We weren't even there when Vanya and Truesdale got shot."

I tried to think. "At the time, I was under Vanya's command. She ordered me to kill everyone in that room, but I shot myself with the Taser to keep from doing it."

"What did she use with you?" Bill asked.

"Use?" I repeated.

"You told me that a hypnotized person will only follow commands if it is within his own moral code. What did she make you believe that was strong enough to get you to kill?"

My mind went back to the images I'd seen while under Vanya's sway. That beautiful girl, with caramel-colored skin and long curly hair, and Jyanette's features softened by what could have been my influence. She had seemed so real. I would've killed for her, or died for her.

"It's all pretty hazy," I responded, but felt my eyes grow wet. "Look, I'm exhausted, can I...?"

"Yeah, sure," Petrie said. "But, as soon as you're out of the bed, I'll need a statement."

Bill glanced back at me with concern, and the pair of them left the room.

I attempted to doze, but now that I was conscious, my brain wouldn't shut down. I wanted to see Mrs. Higgins, Teddy Santos, and, most of all, Jyanette.

About an hour later, there was a knock on the door. Darren Ward stepped in, walking gingerly.

"You okay?" he said as a way of greeting.

"Well enough, since the people who tried to kill me are all dead," I said. "More important, how are you?"

He grunted. "My chest has a bruise the size of Manhattan, but I'll live."

I set my jaw. "Who shot Vanya and Truesdale?"

He shrugged innocently. "Don't know what you mean. I was lying on the floor," he surmised. "I heard you shoot out the window. After that, I just lay there."

"You want to know what I think?"

"If it's relevant."

"I think Mister Marconi sent someone, and you waited in the van until he arrived. Then, you went out and let yourself get captured, so you'd have an alibi and could claim you didn't know who did it."

"I let you shoot me to have an alibi? Man, I'm good!"

"I think you know the guy who was the shooter."

Darren shrugged, but a slight grin appeared. "Who said it was a guy?"

I frowned. "A *female* hit man?"

"I'm not saying there was a hit person of any kind. But, yeah, a woman can shoot as well as a man. And maybe leave a scene a lot easier than you or I could. Doc, they're looking into who Vanya had control over, so I'm not in the loop anymore."

"Time to move on?"

"You're alive, so I did my job. I just wanted to tell you I'm leaving and reporting everything to our... mutual friend. It's a good thing I was there."

I held out my bandaged right hand, and he shook it gently.

The grin turned into a smile. "Is it okay if I keep you in mind when I need some help?"

My eyebrows shot up in surprise. "It's the least I can do."

"Hey, I'll even pay you. That's more than MPD does, right?"

"That is true…"

"Bye, Doc, until next time."

"Thanks, Darren," I said as he headed for the door. "Where are you off to?"

He stopped, turned, and his smile turned wolfish. "I have a date with Officer Booker."

"*Tylissa?* But she's a cop and you work for… um… someone involved in… um… things."

He took a step toward me, his face hard. "Look Len, let's get one thing straight. I do work for Marconi, but he knows I won't do anything illegal for him." Ward said, and I could see this bothered him. "And I thought you would know that."

"Darren, I didn't mean—"

"Later, Wise," he said and was out the door.

Great. With my usual charm, I had offended one of the few people I could depend on in an emergency. Good thing I have a bad leg. That way, I can only insert one foot in my mouth.

The mystery of who shot Vanya would remain just that. If the truth came out, one of her programmed minions might go after the shooter, so keeping it a secret was best.

The next morning, the sterile routine of the hospital felt like a cage I was finally ready to break. At around 10:00 a.m., the door swung open, and Bill appeared with a wheelchair.

I'd navigated the cramped stall in my room for a lukewarm shower, the water stinging the stitches on my hand and face, but it was worth it to feel human again. I'd used the meager shaving kit they'd provided — a plastic razor and a packet of translucent gel — to scrape away the stubble. My reflection was a mess: the left side of my face was a mottled map of purple and yellow bruising, and my jaw felt like a freight train had realigned it.

"You look like you went ten rounds with a wood chipper," Bill noted, though his eyes lacked their usual bite. He locked the wheelchair's brakes.

"I've looked better," I admitted, my voice a dry rasp. "What's the word on Jyanette?"

"She's still in a coma." Bill looked at me sympathetically. "I thought you'd want to see her."

"More than anything." I eased myself out of the bed, the world tilting for a second as my head injury made its presence known with a sharp, rhythmic pulse behind my eyes. My cane held tightly in hand, I sank into the chair.

Bill gripped the handles, and as he pushed me down the hall, he said, "The hypnotherapist is up from Washington, guy's name is Bayer, like the aspirin. He worked on Kate last night, completely deprogrammed her."

"That's good," I answered. "Did you get her out of that mental hospital?"

"With Doctor Bayer's blessing, she's free and assisting with the deprogramming of others."

He wheeled me into Jyanette's room.

I murmured. "Bill, I need to be alone with her."

Bill didn't say a word, but left me there.

The gray, waxy cast of Jyanette's skin sent a jolt of pure ice through my chest. It was a mask, a cadaverous distortion of the vibrant woman I knew.

I rolled up to her bedside, the rhythmic, clinical chirping of the monitors marking time in the silent room. Beside her, the blood pressure cuff hissed and squeezed.

I took her hand — cold and unresponsive — and closed my eyes.

I began the descent. I slowed my breathing, letting the hospital sounds fade into a distant hum until I slipped through the floor of my consciousness.

Plunging into the altered state, I felt as if I were drifting into a vast, obsidian void. It was a place of thick, cloying mists and absolute silence — a psychic limbo where time held no meaning.

"Jyanette?" I called out. My voice didn't echo; the fog swallowed it.

Nothing moved. The shadows remained heavy and indifferent. A cold realization hit me — I was looking for a version of her that Vanya had already erased. I needed to go deeper, back to the roots of her soul.

"Ebele," I whispered. I was one of the few people who knew Jyanette's middle name, having been told it when I met her mother.

The mists stirred.

"Len?" came a voice in the distance.

"It's me! Where are you?" I replied.

"I don't know. I'm lost," Jyanette called to me.

"Follow my voice, come to me."

The mists surged with a newfound aggression, thickening into a heavy, suffocating grey as if the void itself was trying to blind Jyanette from my presence.

But I wasn't bound by bone or muscle here. I was pure spirit — a flicker of raw consciousness in the deep.

Turning my focus inward, I stoked the embers of my psyche until my inner energy bled through. I let it shine; the light radiating from my projected form like a sun breaking through a storm.

I thought of a quote from Rumi: "They weave your body from the light of heaven."

In this place, it wasn't just poetry; it was my anatomy.

The brilliance acted like a scythe, shearing through the psychic fog. Suddenly, the mists parted, and Jyanette was there. She didn't walk; she flew into my arms; her form colliding with mine in a desperate, ethereal embrace. I pressed my lips to hers, the kiss that she returned with a fervor that shook the void.

"You must come back with me," I commanded, the words vibrating through our shared spirit.

I anchored my will to hers, reeling us in, fighting the gravitational pull of the limbo that had swallowed her.

The darkness didn't go quietly; it clawed at us, a cold, resisting pressure that tried to anchor her to the shadows. I gritted my teeth and pulled harder, refusing to yield a single inch of her soul.

The void snapped like a rubber band.

Suddenly, the smell of antiseptic rushed back. I was sitting by her bed, my lungs heaving as if I'd just run a marathon. My hand still locked in hers, I gripped it white-knuckled and trembling.

Slowly, her eyelids fluttered. The waxy, dead look was gone, replaced by a spark of life as her eyes finally found mine.

Machines all around her beeped faster, and I heard a small alarm go off.

"Len?" she croaked.

"I'm here," I answered.

"Is that woman dead?" she asked simply.

I exhaled, and the weight of the last few days fell away. "Yes."

She nodded weakly. "Good!" Tears slid down her face. I felt helpless, but I grabbed a napkin off an empty tray and touched it gently to her face.

"Len, they killed our baby," she sobbed.

I took her hand again. "I know."

I held her hand as she wept and said nothing.

By now, nurses and orderlies were coming into the room, surprised and pleased that she was awake, asking her questions, checking machines.

She answered as best she could and asked for something to eat, as an orderly pulled me away from the bed and wheeled me out of the room.

Bill stood in the hall, and next to him were Jyanette's parents, George and Deka Emery.

George's face was a map of etched worry as he looked down at me. "Leonard! How is our girl?"

I tried to force a smile, but it felt like cracking dry leather against my swollen jaw. "She's awake, George."

Deka didn't wait for the rest of the sentence. With a sharp cry of joy that echoed down the sterile hallway, she surged past me, her footsteps a frantic rhythm as she rushed to her daughter's bedside.

George let out a long, shuddering breath, the tension leaving his shoulders all at once. "Thank God. We were so worried."

He followed his wife, but he had to hover near the door because a flurry of nurses descended on the room, and their clinical chatter rose as they checked Jyanette's vitals.

Before I could savor the moment, the world pivoted. McGee appeared behind me, his massive hands gripping the handles of my wheelchair. He spun me around with surprising gentleness and began the roll back toward my own room.

"Did you have something to do with that?" he asked, his voice low and knowing. "Her waking up right when you touched her?"

"Whatever do you mean, McGee?" I replied, keeping my eyes fixed on the linoleum tiles passing beneath us.

But as the hospital sounds faded into the background, I couldn't stop the slow, tired smile from spreading across my face.

For once, the light had won.

17. SETTLED SCORE

Days later, Bill dropped me off at my house. It was a great relief to see my van in the driveway where Darren had parked it when he came to collect his own car. There were also several other cars and a large truck in the driveway, and I approached the house warily.

Mrs. Higgins ran out to meet me and hug me. I was relieved to find out that she had no ill effects from her ordeal. She reacted as if nothing had happened, as if we kidnapped her every other day as entertainment.

I came into the house and stopped as I saw workers moving about.

"Are they...?"

"They're supposed to be here. I hired them to replace the windows and repair the damage," she explained.

We sat down in the kitchen, and over coffee and one of her amazing cinnamon rolls, she caught me up. She had baked the sweets for the working people and not me, but I got one anyway.

We sat and seriously discussed the damage and when we would repaint and touch up around the trim. Fortunately, the outer stone walls were undamaged, so most of the work needed was on the interior, and it comprised repairing plaster, woodwork, and the broken windows.

During our discussion, Mrs. Higgins brought in the man who was in charge of the renovations. He had a chart in his truck that explained his plan to restore the damage to the irreplaceable chestnut woodwork with something that he thought could match. He made clear his techniques and bragged that he had a gift for getting the new pieces to blend in with the old in look and color.

Feeling reassured, I had a relaxing afternoon grading the papers I had neglected, and it felt good to do something normal after the craziness.

I called Teddy Santos and checked up on him.

"Hey, Doc," Teddy said as he answered his phone.

"I'm glad to hear your voice. The last thing I knew, you were still in a trance."

"Galland used a Taser on me. Was that your idea?"

"It worked on me," I explained.

"It snapped me right out of it. Then I spoke to this Bayer guy —"

"Oh yeah, the hypnotherapist," I offered.

"Right, he not only deprogrammed me, he did it so I remembered everything. Man! Did you know I hid that database from Galland and anyone else who tried to find it with an algorithm that pushed the information through a series of servers —"

"Teddy, I am sure it was amazing, but you lost me at 'algorithm'."

"Oh! Yeah, I get it. So once I was in my own head again and knew what I had done, because I could remember it, tracking all the records down was easy."

"That's good. Sorry you had to get shocked by a Taser."

"That's okay," Teddy chuckled. "Galland made it up to me."

"I'm glad you're okay," I said. We chatted a little more to work out classes and plans, thrilled to do something mundane.

After I hung up with Teddy, I had one more call to make. I pulled the flip phone I had kept with me and hit the one number.

"International Shipping. How may I direct your call?" came the clipped female voice over the phone.

"This is Doctor Leonard Wise. I wanted to—"

She interrupted me. "Yes, Doctor, we've been waiting for your call. Stay on the line, please."

The phone went quiet, not even elevator music, just silence. Finally, there were a few clicks, and someone came on.

"Hey, Doc," a voice said. It was Anthony Marconi.

"Hello, sir. I wanted to call you and thank you for your help. Especially the... um... specialist who came out to Elizabeth."

I felt the need not to use names or to go into detail. I had asked for the help of a criminal, and now I was acting like one.

I went on, "I wanted to ask if I owe anything for my bodyguard and his efforts."

"You're covered, Doc," Marconi said. "He'll be well-compensated for his time and trouble."

I pressed my case. "I guess that anything between us, good or bad, is now even?"

"I would say so. I mean, my niece would be dead if not for you. You'd be dead if I hadn't gotten involved. Seems like a fair trade."

"And I'm grateful, sir."

"I would advise you to take out the battery and destroy the phone, just to be safe."

"That's good advice."

"Take care of yourself, Doc."

"You too, sir."

As soon as I hung up, I took the battery out, then put the small phone in a paper bag and smashed it with a hammer.

My boss and friend, Jon Baines, showed up that evening with his wife, Jenny, and brought food, knowing that our kitchen was being repaired. I sat around the kitchen table with the Baines and Mrs. Higgins, telling stories and jokes.

It felt good to laugh with friends.

"Oh, Len, I forgot to tell you, I spoke to the lawyers today—"

I sighed. "We were having a good time, and then you bring up lawyers."

"It's okay, Lenny," Jen corrected. "This is a good thing."

"We could use a wee bit of good news right about now," Mrs. Higgins observed.

"It was about that lawsuit, the wrongful death one by the parents of Amanda Prentiss?"

"Oh yes, the student I never met," I replied.

"How are ye involved in a lawsuit like that?" Mrs. Higgins asked.

"He's not!" Jon declared. "Well, not anymore. They're dropping the suit."

"What?" I wondered. "Why?"

"They decided not to pursue it," Jon clarified. "But they are dismissing it 'without prejudice,' which means they can bring it up in the future."

"Oh, the very devil it is," Mrs. Higgins said.

"As is the whole situation, Mrs. Higgins," I added.

The next day, I went to MPD and met with Doctor Bayer. He was of average height, thin, with large eyes that seemed to bore into one's soul. I avoided eye contact because it concerned me how deeply I might look into his mind. Or how deeply he might look into mine.

Using the updated key and lock Galland supplied, he took me through the process, and he was really quite good at his job. He talked me down and through my locks and codes and then disconnected them so they would never work again.

It was odd, because once finished, I completely remembered all the sessions I had experienced, both with Vanya and Kate. I recalled the night Vanya and Truesdale snuck into my dorm room and drugged me, and the instructions she gave me. I also recalled Kate reprogramming me to obey the new key from our session.

Once done, I felt oddly relieved that I would no longer react to commands, but now, knowing all the commands, there was a certain sense that they had violated me in ways I may never fully understand.

Out of the blue, Bill called me up and invited me to dinner, which I accepted, even though I really didn't feel up to it. But an afternoon class where I lectured, and the fact that I was getting back to my old life, helped my attitude.

By the time I drove over to Bill's house, I was looking forward to the chance to speak with his wife and to ask Bill a few questions of my own.

I arrived to see that they had replaced the front door with a heavy steel one, though painted to look like an average wooden front door. I saw the reinforced panels that would not be obvious to most people.

Bill met me at the door and finally introduced me to Laura.

She had the look of a fashion model, tall and willowy with a slim build and raven hair that was a contrast to her light skin. She was tall, maybe five-ten, and was a slim contrast to her muscular husband.

I had brought a bottle of non-alcoholic cider, which she took as she wrapped one arm around McGee's waist.

"Where are the kids?" I asked.

"At their aunt's," Laura said, her voice strong and feminine. "I wanted one night to just be adults."

"And we know we have some things to talk about that I don't want them to hear," Bill added.

I nodded. Bill had picked up on my suspicions.

They had cleaned up the house since the attack, yet scattered toys belied the recent violence. The living room had a large-screen television, not enormous, but affordable. I noted a ceiling-high white bookcase that I assumed was the entrance to the safe room. It was back in its place, which made it well-hidden from the casual observer.

We sat down to dinner, and Laura brought out champagne flutes, which made the cider bubbles float to the top as I poured. We sat down to a salad of mixed greens with a homemade dressing.

Bill began, "You might wonder about some of the security precautions we have."

"If I had a suspicious mind," I pointed out.

This made Laura smile and Bill chuckle.

"From what I understand, your 'suspicious' mind explains how you found me and the others," Laura offered.

"I got lucky," I said.

Bill shook his head. "It's okay, Len. I've told Laura all about what you do and how. She's just grateful you could get in and save them."

I looked down at my empty salad plate. "Bill, if things had gone a different way, I might have shot everyone in that room."

"But you didn't," Bill assured. "You shot yourself with a Taser instead."

I rubbed my thigh where the needles had struck me. It was still sore.

Laura put in, "Half of your face is still purple, you poor thing. I told Bill we should wait for dinner until you'd healed."

"In that case, we'd never meet," I said with a grin. "Bill, explain to me why you have this high level of security."

Laura and Bill exchanged a telling glance, and she rose to collect our salad plates. He rose to help, but she shook her head and told him, "Talk to your friend."

Bill sighed and returned to his seat. "I may have told you how Laura and I met in a way that was not completely true."

I frowned. "You said you were protecting a rich guy, and that Laura was his daughter."

"Well, most of that is true. Except I wasn't protecting the rich guy. I was working undercover to bust him."

"Oh?"

Bill exhaled. "Len, he was organized crime, out of Chicago. He was the head of the Irish mob."

"This was an assignment, back when you were in the FBI?"

Bill nodded. "Yes, I infiltrated the gang, undercover. We were trying to get enough information to take them down. It took me months to work my way in, get close to the family."

Laura walked into the room on the last sentence. She sat at the table and took her husband's hand. "And that's how we met."

Bill smiled at his wife. "I didn't want to get involved with her. It was far too risky for my assignment and would create conflicts."

Laura looked at me at this point. "But I had other ideas."

"I couldn't resist her," Bill said, a loving smile on his face. "And she wanted to be with me, even though I was older."

"Only ten years," Laura pointed out. "I kept insisting that he drive me places, and being the good lieutenant, he did as he was told. But I kept dropping hints—"

"Some not so subtle," Bill chuckled.

"I recall you were a willing participant once I convinced you it was what I wanted."

Bill looked at me. "I never stood a chance."

Laura went on. "So, we became intimately involved, and then one day, we go out for a picnic in the country, and he admits he loves me."

"You said it first."

"You're getting forgetful. You said it first."

Bill continued. "So out in the country, no one around for miles. I told her the truth, why I was there."

"What?" I gasped.

Laura became very serious. "It was a tremendous risk."

"Could've gotten me killed," Bill confessed, "or blown the entire operation."

Laura looked at the table. "Truth is, I knew what my family was doing, what my father did, and I wanted out."

"She helped me gather the evidence I needed to close him down and put her father away."

"That's amazing," I gushed.

Bill nodded. "Yeah, well, it turns out that a few months later, that 'operation' where I almost got killed? It was retaliation for bringing him down."

Laura spoke up. "That's when I told him he needed to leave the FBI. As long as he stayed, he was a target."

"We moved to NJ, created the cover story of how we met, and have been keeping a low profile ever since," Bill concluded.

I nodded. "Which explains why you have a safe room and have trained the boys how to use it."

"And why we have codes for where any of us are," Laura said.

"Saying the boys were going to Auntie Maire," Bill explained, "doesn't mean they go to their aunt's house. It's a code where they go to a cousin's house. We set it up so that if any of Laura's family found us, we'd be able to defend ourselves."

"This certainly clears up a lot," I reflected. "And it explains why I haven't met you until now, Laura. You have to be careful in case someone recognizes you."

Bill smiled. "I figured since you saved her life, it was only fair."

"We should thank whoever shot Vanya," I pointed out.

"Do you have any idea who that might be?" Bill looked at me with suspicion.

"For once, not a clue," I smiled, all innocence.

Laura stood. "Well, I'd better get dinner."

"Need help?" Bill stood.

"I can handle it," she smiled in reply. "I just have one more thing to do before I serve."

Laura walked over to a nearby sideboard, reached into a drawer, and pulled out a very large pistol, which she handled with ease.

"Umm… Laura?" I gulped.

Bill saw the look on my face and turned to look at his wife. He froze when he saw her chamber a bullet in the weapon. "Laura, what are you doing?"

She raised the weapon and pointed it at me. Her expression was that of a stone-cold killer. "He thought he was clever, coming here to get us to admit everything. Like we didn't know that my father sent him."

Bill turned in the chair. "Laura, this is crazy. I've known Len for a year-and-a-half. He's not a spy from your father."

Her jaw set. "That's what he wants you to think, to lull you in."

She moved closer with the gun pointed right at me, and I met her eyes and felt the blocks in her mind, shut away by a program, no doubt created by Anika Vanya.

"Not over… this is not over…" Vanya croaked at me.

This was part of Vanya's plan. This is why they had captured her. She was the insurance that even if Vanya lost, she had prepared someone to take me out.

It made sense that Laura sent the kids away, and it was only the three of us. She had a pre-programmed mission to eliminate me. Vanya told her a story that I was a threat, that I had connections to her old life.

I used my cane to stand, my eyes still on her. I tried to be aware of my surroundings, where I could duck, and what I could use for a weapon. I shifted my weight to be ready to move. I needed more space, but I was behind the large table with limited places to go.

"Laura," Bill said, his voice a low, steady anchor. "He's not from your father. He's my friend."

"No!" she snapped, her eyes locked on me with a terrifying, singular focus. The muzzle of the pistol trembled slightly, but it never wavered from my chest. "You don't see it. He's fooled you, Bill, but I saw through it. Killing him is the only way we can be safe."

Bill didn't hesitate. He rose from his chair, his broad frame moving to intersect the line of fire, positioning himself between Laura's weapon and my heart. The room suddenly felt claustrophobic — a quiet, suburban dining room turned into a staging ground for tragedy.

Plastic building blocks lay scattered in the corners, and the smell of a home-cooked meal still lingered, a jarring contrast to the steel in Laura's hands.

"Put the gun down, honey," Bill pleaded, his palms spread out.

A flicker of doubt crossed her face, a momentary fracture in her resolve, but it vanished as quickly as it came. Her eyes hardened. "No! I have to do this!"

Time seemed to liquefy. Laura leveled the pistol, and Bill lunged, his body a desperate, mid-air shield. The explosion was a physical blow, a deafening crack that shattered the silence of the neighborhood. My precognition flared — a jagged spark of warning at the base of my skull — and I threw myself to the left.

A large ceramic vase behind where my head had been disintegrated into a spray of white shards, and a dark hole punched through the drywall. Bill fell away from her, blood instantly blooming across the front of his shirt. The realization hit like a second bullet: the round had gone completely through him.

He hit the floor with a heavy thud. Laura stared at the smoking weapon, then at her husband; the reality of the moment finally shattering her focus. The gun clattered onto the hardwood.

"Bill!" Her scream was raw, a sound of absolute ruin. She collapsed to her knees, her mission forgotten as she gathered his limp form into her arms.

The air was thick with the scent of ozone and copper. I scrambled toward the weapon, hands steady despite the adrenaline. I ejected the magazine and cleared the chamber; the warm brass casing clinking as it hit the floor.

After shoving the magazine into my pocket, I reached for my phone and dialed 9-1-1.

"You shot him!" she screamed at me. "You shot my husband!"

A woman answered my call with, "9-1-1, what is your emergency?"

"Someone's been shot! There was an accident."

Laura shouted again, "You shot him!"

I gave the address as quickly as I could, and when I looked up, I saw Bill raise his hand to his wife's face. "Laura."

"Oh my God, he shot you," she sobbed.

"No, Laura, you did," Bill groaned.

She stared at him in disbelief. "No, I saw him shoot you."

"It's not real!" I barked at her, the scent of copper filling my nose. "Vanya fed you a lie. She planted those memories like a virus."

Laura's head snapped toward me, her eyes darting between my face and her husband's pale, sweat-slicked skin. "That's not... that can't be possible..."

"Get bandages!" I commanded, using my best 'ER' voice to cut through her panic. "Now! I have to stop the bleeding."

She hesitated, her mind a frantic mess, then gave a sharp, jerky nod. She eased Bill's head to the floor and bolted from the room. I lunged toward Bill, my fingers slick with his blood as I pried open his jacket and yanked his T-shirt upward.

The entry wound was a jagged, dark mouth on the left side of his torso, just below the rib cage. My medical training did the math in an instant: if the bullet had taken the spleen, we were in a race against the clock. If it hit the descending aorta, he was already a ghost.

A roll of white gauze thudded onto the floor beside me. I reached for it, but stopped when I heard the unmistakable *click* of a slide racking.

I looked up. Laura was back, but the bandages hadn't been her only prize. She leveled a second pistol at my head, her hands shaking so violently the barrel traced small circles in the air.

"You shot him!" she shrieked, her voice cracking into a sob. "You shot my husband!"

I stared directly into her eyes. The psychic walls — those cold, Vanya-made monoliths — were still there, but they were vibrating under the weight of her grief.

"Damn it, Laura! Bill is going to bleed out on your dining room floor if we don't help him!"

She looked down at Bill, then back at me. I felt it — a microscopic hairline fracture in her mental armor. Her mental block slipped just a fraction of an inch.

I didn't wait for permission. I surged forward psychically, throwing the full weight of my consciousness into that crack. The world dissolved.

The dining room vanished, replaced by a strobe-light assault of stolen memories. I saw Vanya's cold, reptilian eyes; I saw Emma Truesdale leaning over a desk, her mouth moving in a silent command. I saw that same sterile conference room in the data center, the shadows dancing on the walls as they systematically dismantled Laura's reality and replaced it with a nightmare.

At the center of that mental storm, I found her — the real Laura, a terrified child huddled in the dark of her own shattered mind. I didn't explain; there was no time for logic. I projected a single, raw command, a psychic flare of absolute truth: Help me, or Bill will die.

The effect was instantaneous. The fog in her eyes cleared, replaced by a sharp, jagged clarity. She sank to her knees; the pistol clattering to the floor, forgotten.

"What can I do?" she whispered, her voice trembling but present.

I grabbed the roll of gauze and guided her hands, forcing them against the slick, warm entry and exit wounds. "Apply pressure," I barked. "Both sides. Hard. Don't let go until I tell you."

She leaned her weight into it; her knuckles white against Bill's skin.

"You will not die, Bill McGee," she hissed through clenched teeth, a fierce, desperate vow. "Do you hear me? You are staying right here."

Bill's face was the color of ash, his breathing shallow and thready, but the bleeding slowed under her hands.

I scrambled across the floor, gathered both weapons, and shoved them deep into a kitchen drawer, burying them under a pile of linens just as the first wail of sirens broke through the night.

The cavalry was coming, but as I looked at the blood on the floral rug, I prayed they'd be here in time.

EPILOGUE

The ambulance took Bill to the hospital with Laura aboard and me following in my van. Once Bill was in the emergency room, I drove Laura to the MPD to give our statements.

I had to admit; I was a little nervous sitting in the van with a woman who had just tried to kill me, but we got there without incident.

I had phoned Kate from the hospital, and she was there to meet us.

We used the conference room so Kate could work on Laura. I stayed to supervise, as I wanted to be sure Kate was indeed her old self. Since the elimination of Vanya and the found database, people were being brought into MPD or the FBI field office for deprogramming at all hours of the day and night.

Kate could not know the key or lock Vanya had used on Laura, because Galland's database did not include them. Her programming was new, and Vanya had done it in a hurry. Even so, Kate moved Laura into a hypnotic state and worked to clear her of the program.

Once out of the trance, Laura told us about her conviction that I posed a threat and that she needed to stop me. She had moved the two guns before I arrived to where she could get them quickly and easily. Usually, they locked away the weapons so the kids couldn't get to them.

Once done, I drove Laura back to the hospital. She was silent for most of the trip, and only when we drew close to Mountainside Medical Center did she finally say, "I have to apologize…"

"Don't. It wasn't your fault. Vanya created a scenario in your mind, and you were protecting your family."

She stared straight ahead as we moved toward the entrance to the emergency room. "I could have killed you."

"But you didn't. You didn't kill me or Bill. Let's just be glad that you're free from the things she put in your head."

I went in with her, and the doctor told us Bill was out of surgery and resting comfortably. Laura stayed in his room, and I drove home to collapse into bed, hoping no more assassins lay in wait for me.

The next day, I returned to the hospital, where I collected a visitor's badge at the front desk.

My first stop was to see Bill. Laura was still there, having arranged for the children to stay another day with Bill's sister. Laura looked tired, but she'd changed clothes and freshened up. I assumed she had caught a ride home and changed this morning. Bill was sitting up in bed as I entered. The two of them had been talking.

"Len!" Bill said. "We were just talking about you."

"Hopefully, you were saying nice things," I attempted. "How are you?"

Laura spoke up. "The doctor said there was surprisingly minor damage."

"Still hurts," Bill said. "I'll be out for a few days."

"Two weeks," Laura insisted. "They want to keep him here for the next few days, to make sure there's no infection."

"That seems like a good idea," I told her.

Laura met my eyes. "I've been trying to understand what you did to me last night at my house. The way you kept me from shooting you."

I sighed. "I did whatever I had to."

She gazed at me thoughtfully. "But I felt you, inside my head."

Bill interjected. "Laura, I was telling you, he can just do that. I've seen him do it to other people."

She frowned. "When Bill told me the things you did, a part of me didn't believe any of it was possible."

"And now?" I questioned.

"Now I have to admit, you're a little scary."

"Relax, Laura, I'm one of the good guys." I smiled. "I'm only here now because I wanted to check on you."

"Don't let him fool you, Laura," Bill said. "He's here to see his girlfriend."

I nodded. "That too. I'm nervous. Kate met with her this morning to deprogram her. I'm about to find out how much of what we've been through the last few months was real and how much was Vanya telling her what to do."

"Fingers crossed for you, Len," Bill said.

I headed down the hall and pushed into the sterile quiet of Jyanette's room. Deka Emery, Jyanette's mother, was a silhouette of grief against the harsh morning light.

When she saw me, her eyes didn't just well up; they seemed to age ten years in a single blink.

"Oh, Len," she whispered.

"Good morning, Deka," I said.

She gave her daughter's hand a final, lingering squeeze before rising to meet me. "We need to talk, Leonard. Out here."

The formality in her voice was a warning bell. I followed her into the hallway, the scent of antiseptic suddenly feeling a lot more suffocating. She reached out, her fingers ghosting over the purple-and-yellow bruising that still mapped the side of my face.

"You're hurting," she said softly. "I can tell."

"It's been a rough few days," I managed, the lie tasting like ash.

"I want you to know," she began, her gaze holding mine with painful sincerity, "that George and I still think the world of you. You saved her. We know that."

"I... thanks, Deka. That means a lot."

She took a breath, and I felt the air leave the room. "Jyanette has made some decisions. They're going to be difficult for you to hear."

I stopped dead. My energy didn't just drop; it plummeted. I'd spent every waking hour since the rescue clinging to a single, desperate hope: that her coldness, her rejection, and the breakup months ago had all been the byproduct of Vanya's hypnotic meddling. I thought that once the fog cleared, the woman I loved would wait there.

But as I looked at the pity in Deka's eyes, the truth hit me harder than the blast at MPD. The programming was gone, but her heart hadn't changed.

I determinedly set my jaw. "I appreciate the warning. Should I just leave?"

She gazed at me with compassion. "No, Leonard. You need to talk to her. I just wanted to soften the blow if I could."

I tried to smile and failed miserably. "I appreciate that, Deka."

"Go, talk to her. I will stay out here until you are done."

I nodded and went into the room.

Jyanette was sitting up, the clinical pallor of the coma replaced by a flush of returning life, but her eyes were already miles away. My heart didn't just ache; it felt like it was being slowly hollowed out. I knew this look. I was losing her again, and this time, there was no hypnotic trance to blame.

"I'm glad you're here," she said, her voice a fragile but steady thread. "I wanted to say this face-to-face."

I forced my features into a mask of professional composure, though my pulse was a frantic drumming in my ears. "I wanted to see you, too."

She looked down at her hands, unable to hold my gaze. "I've caused you so much pain, Len. These last few months..."

"It wasn't you, Jyanette. It was the programming."

"No," she said, shaking her head with weary finality. "That's why I have to do what *I* want now. For myself."

"That's a good choice," I lied, the words tasting like copper.

"When my family leaves, they're taking me back with them. Home. To Virginia."

The room seemed to tilt. "Virginia? But your life is here. Your career—"

"There are plenty of opportunities for a lawyer in Virginia, Len." She reached out, giving my hand a squeeze that felt more like a goodbye than a greeting. "My only reason for staying... it was so my little girl would have her father."

The air left my lungs in a rush. "How did you know? How did you know it was a girl?"

She looked up then, her eyes shining with a haunting, otherworldly clarity. "I saw her. While I was under. In that place."

A chill raced down my spine. She had seen the same child I had — the ghost of a future Vanya had stolen from us.

"I need to get away from the shadows, Len," she whispered. "I need to breathe."

"Away from me, too?"

"Don't you see? Every time we look at each other, we'll just see the loss. We'll see the fire and the blood and the child that isn't there. I can't bear it. I just can't."

I nodded slowly, the hot sting of tears blurring my vision. I didn't fight her. You can't force a bird to stay in a shattered cage. "I love you, Jyanette. I always will."

"And I'll love you," she whispered, her voice breaking. "But I need help... I need to find myself again."

"Your mother will know the way," I said. Deka, with the blood of African healers in her veins, was the only one who could truly stitch Jyanette back together. I leaned down and pressed a final, lingering kiss to her forehead. "Rest now."

"Goodbye, Leonard."

I turned and limped into the hallway where Deka stood like a silent sentinel. She stepped forward and pulled me into a fierce, motherly embrace.

"It's hard now," she whispered into my ear, her voice a warm anchor. "But you will be all right, Leonard Wise. You will survive this, too."

I nodded, unable to speak, and strode away.

As I moved through the automatic doors and into the biting October air, Vanya's crooked, ghastly smile flickered in the back of my mind. I had stopped her. I had burned her empire to the ground and ensured she and Emma would never draw another breath of malice. But as I reached my van and stared at the empty passenger seat, the truth settled over me like a shroud.

Vanya had lost the war, but she had won the final move. She had taken my child and severed the heart of the woman I loved. I climbed into the driver's seat, started the engine, and drove away from the hospital — utterly, devastatingly alone.

AUTHOR'S NOTE

Welcome, reader of the odd.

Vengeance In the Mind might be one of the most frightening Leonard Wise tales. The events make Len feel hopeless against an adversary focused on one thing: his death and the destruction of everything he loves.

I often feel guilty about what happens to my characters, and this book more than most. I actually am quite fond of Len and Jyanette, but they are both put through abject misery in this novel.

I pulled in all the characters in this one; Kate Yearling, Darren Ward and even Anthony Marconi. I also like that Laura McGee appears in the book and that you learn more about her and Bill McGee's past because of it.

The scariest part of this book is that our government and other governments have investigated mind control experiments similar to Anika Vayna's techniques.

In the end, Len walks off into the sunset, all alone once again. It was a high-stakes adventure where Len won, but at the price of his own happiness.

As always, his situation is open to change, which you will see in the next book, *Echoes In The Mind.*

—Arjay Lewis

ECHOES IN THE MIND

DOCTOR WISE BOOK 9

ARJAY LEWIS

MIND
BENDER
PRESS

ECHOES IN THE MIND

Brett Morgan jolted awake, an icy grip of fear tightening around his chest, the instinctual certainty that he was not alone clawing at his mind.

He was a man who cherished solitude, with rigidly maintained sleeping arrangements. He even relegated intimate encounters to his dates' apartments or carefully chosen hotels. His bedroom was his sanctuary, a space where he was the sole occupant of his world.

Yet now, as shadows danced in the corners of the dimly lit room, he was painfully aware of the violation of that sacred space.

Why had he awakened?

He struggled to sift through the remnants of sleep, and the prickling urge to flee.

What had disrupted his night? With a furtive glance around, he slipped from the covers, the fine silk of his scarlet pajamas clinging to his skin, creating an unsettling sensation of being unprotected.

Grabbing a plush robe, he padded barefoot through the darkened expanse of his house, turning on a few lights along the way—a cautious beacon against the encroaching darkness.

He reached the alarm panel and turned off the alarm. The last thing he needed was an embarrassing visit from the authorities on account of a sleepless night.

But something deep inside him urged caution; after disarming the system, he scanned the blank screens of the security feed, unnerved by the reality that something felt deeply wrong.

He adjusted the thermostat—though his home usually held a steady warmth, the chill in the air crawled over him, wrapping him in a shroud of unease.

Brett…

His name, whispered in the shadows, ignited a primal fear. This wasn't a figment of his imagination; he was sure of it. A voice —distinct yet shadowed, layered as if two spoke at once—echoed from the depths of the upper floor.

"Who's there?" His voice trembled, frustration mingling with fear as he called into the silent expanse, tiny and distant against the emptiness.

You know where I am…

The words slithered through the air, taunting, originating from the armory.

With a hesitant determination, he continued to the end of the hallway. There stood the formidable door of his collection—the armory. It wasn't an actual armory, but it held an elaborate collection of ancient and unique weapons from around the world.

He had studied, purchased, and curated the items from locations that would make powerful men squeamish. Ancient civilizations had used the specific knives and swords in ritual sacrifice, but that did not stop him from acquiring each item.

He often found beauty in their craftsmanship, despite their grotesque purposes in history.

He retrieved the emergency flashlight stowed in a hidden nook of the richly paneled wall, his pulse quickening as he navigated the darkness.

The keypad lit as he punched in the code, the soft beeps mocking his growing trepidation. The door clicked open, and for a moment, he expected—the lights to blaze to life with their comforting glow, but when he crossed the threshold, only deafening darkness met him.

Stepping into the room cautiously, he left the heavy door open behind him.

"Hello?" he called again, the word now tinged with a sense of dread. The temperature in the room was freezing, an oppressive cold that gnawed at him. He saw his breath, ghostly tendrils swirling in the flashlight's beam as he tightened his robe.

The glass cases that lined the walls beckoned him deeper into the chamber. Shadows cast by the flashlight flickered over the sleek blades of Japanese katanas and European swords, weapons of lore and bloodshed. The air was heavy with history, and the chill intensified, pressing down upon his chest like a burden he couldn't shake.

You know what I want...

The voices, now clearer, drifted through the room, reverberating off the glass and ricocheting through his bones—a relentless echo that nudged his heart into overdrive.

He glanced at the secondary panel of the alarm system here in the display room. All he had to do was press a button to summon the police, but his eye went to the thermostat connected to the unit instead.

The device showed the temperature in the room had dropped below thirty-two degrees Fahrenheit. He gasped, a frozen cloud of breath, stunned by how cold the room had become.

He gripped the flashlight tightly, warily skimming its beam through the displays, searching for the source of the unseen voice.

His eyes went to the case containing one of his most prized artifacts: an ancient Kris blade. It was bright silver with a handle made of ancient gold. The blade was wavy, which allowed for a quicker, rougher cut. Whoever had forged this devastating weapon did so for only one purpose—human sacrifice.

It lay next to its scabbard, which was also silver with green jade inlaid into the metal. When he purchased it from the Korowai clan in an isolated part of New Guinea, he could not track down its entire bloody history, although he was sure they used this blade for unholy rituals for centuries.

A burglar had stolen it from him the previous year, and he had been lucky that the police had recovered and returned it.

Through a haze of fascination and fear, Brett felt a dark urge compelling him to free the blade from its storage case. His mind screamed to resist, but his fingers tightened around the door, opening the glass. With his free hand, he grasped the Kris. The coolness of its metal sent chills racing up his spine, but its shimmer captivated him.

The whispers echoed louder now, imbued with urgency.

Very good, that is the one…

The voices were right behind him, and Brett spun on his heel, the knife raised.

The flashlight revealed only empty space—nothing tangible, only the oppressive silence of his sanctuary. Yet the fear clawed at him, raw and real, despite his martial arts training.

Panic stirred within him, sweat beading on his forehead despite the frigid temperature.

"Who is it? Who's there?" The tremor in his voice betrayed his bravado as he moved closer to the panic button, the only thread left to grasp at sanity amidst the gathering storm.

A pity we never met, considering you caused my death…

Brett's rage ignited, chasing away some of his fear. "What are you talking about?"

He had harmed no one—this must be the work of an intruder, a burglar orchestrating this twisted scenario in his carefully guarded life.

"Show yourself," he screamed, his voice rising in defiance, desperation clawing at him.

I will…

Suddenly, the knife quivered in his grip, his own hand now betraying him. The knife moved as if on its own. Brett watched his hand, not believing what his eyes showed him and completely unable to stop what was happening. His right arm slowly, deliberately, turned the blade until it pointed at his chest.

"What the—" With a sudden, violent thrust, he felt the blade pierce flesh and sinew, an unbearable agony blossoming through him as excruciating pain unfurled from the wound like a dark flower.

He dropped the flashlight, its beam spiraling wildly across the room, illuminating the display cases as darkness seeped into his vision. Breathing became a desperate struggle as he fought against the blade buried deep within him. His hands clawed at the handle to withdraw the knife, but it only cleaved deeper.

Screams erupted from his lungs, a raw panic as he collapsed against the stark, chill wall, fingers fumbling blindly for the panic button—a final desperate call for help in the void of despair. The alarm blared to life, flooding the house with a cacophony of red lights and sirens.

As the world spun around him, Brett fell to his knees, despair overtaking him, his body crumpling like a discarded afterthought.

I think we took care of you...

His breath was a mere whisper of life left as he gasped, "Who are you?"

I am an echo of what was...

Wracked with agony, he croaked out, "Why?" His vision blurred, and the final pulse of life flickered within him.

Because I can...

The room exploded in a blaze of light, temperature lifting from the freeze.

The lights in the room came on suddenly, and the temperature rose. Police sirens wailed over the beeping of his own alarms as Brett's heart stuttered and with one last sigh, stopped beating.

TO BE CONTINUED IN

ECHOES IN THE MIND

DOCTOR WISE BOOK 9

ALSO BY ARJAY LEWIS

Doctor Wise Series
Fire In The Mind
Seduction In The Mind
Reunion In The Mind
Haunted In The Mind
Devotion In The Mind
Asylum In The Mind
Specter In The Mind
Vengeance In The Mind
Echoes In The Mind
Infection In The Mind
Justice In The Mind
Ritual In The Mind
Vanished In The Mind

Horror
The Muse
Kept In The Dark
The Vanishing
Digger
Ghost Writer

Romantic Mystery
(With Debra Snow)
A Study In Murder

NYPD Wizard Detective
The Wizards Of Central Park West
The Vampires Of Greenwich Village
The Werewolves Of Washington Square

ABOUT THE AUTHOR

Known as the "Wizard Of Odd", Arjay Lewis is an actor, magician, and multi-award-winning author.
I write tales of the strange and the horrifying.

I have spent my life as an entertainer, amusing people as a street-performer in the 1970s; a Broadway and casino artist in the 1980s; a party performer in the 1990s and 2000s; a cruise ship performer in the 2010s.

Stories have always been in my mind, and I have been writing since the 1990s. My reason to write is simple: to entertain. I write the type of books that I like to read: murder mysteries, strange tales of unnatural gifts, odd happenings and horror.

Please visit my web site and sign up for my mailing list to be "in the know" for upcoming books. Visit me on Facebook, Twitter, or my Amazon Author page.

And thank you for reading. You are the reason I write.

www.arjaylewis.com
www.facebook.com/arjaylewis
www.twitter.com/arjaylewiswrite
www.amazon.com/Arjay-Lewis

www.ingramcontent.com/pod-product-compliance
Lightning Source LLC
Chambersburg PA
CBHW031601240626
47153CB00002B/596